FAIRY KEEPER

WORLD OF ALUVIA, BOOK ONE

FAIRY KEEPER

WORLD OF ALUVIA, BOOK ONE

AMY BEARCE

SECOND EDITION

Snowy Wings Publishing

This is a work of fiction. All of the characters, organizations, and events portrayed in this novel are products of the author's imagination or used fictitiously.

FAIRY KEEPER
World of Aluvia, Book 1

Second Edition

Published by Snowy Wings Publishing
www.snowywingspublishing.com

© 2015 **Amy Bearce**
http://www.amybearce.com
Cover Art and interior art by **Amalia Chitulescu**
http://ameliethe.deviantart.com
Map by Ricky Gunawan
Licensed from Whampa LLC
All rights reserved, including the right to reproduce this book or portions thereof in any form whatsoever. For more information, contact Amy Bearce at www.amybearce.com

The Library of Congress has cataloged the 2015 original editions as follows:
ISBN 978-1-62007-710-8 (ebook)
ISBN 978-1-62007-711-5 (paperback)
ISBN 978-1-62007-712-2 (hardcover)

Second (Revised) Edition 2019
ISBN 978-1-948661-14-0 (ebook)
ISBN 978-1-948661-15-7 (paperback)

To Julia and Keira

SAOL SEA
Midnight Realm
Twilight Realm
KEEPER HANNON'S COTTAGE
SIERRA'S JOURNEY
SKYCLAD MOUNTAINS
PORT BELTANE
PORT MABON
THE ABYSS
MORGANCE MERFOLK VILLAGE
Shallow Realm
PORT OSTARA
COVENSTEAD
CAILETTE DESERT
TUATHAIL
LYR ANCIENT CITY OF THE MERFOLK
PORT IONA
LITHA FISHING VILLAGE
OBAN FISHING VILLAGE
THE ICE-LOCKED LANDS
SOUTHERN SEA
ALUVIA

CHAPTER ONE

The last drops of fairy nectar clung to the edge of the jar fourteen-year-old Sierra Quinn held, poised above the vial containing that day's harvest. One measly vial's worth. The fairies were producing less and less these days. Her father, Jack, was not going to be pleased. He insisted nothing stand in the way of his elixir profits, especially not annoying, moody fairies.

Sierra gave the jar a little shake to loosen those stubborn drops, every bit of it precious. Fairy nectar kept Jack happy. When Jack was happy, he left Sierra and, more importantly, her little sister Phoebe, alone.

Setting aside the empty jar, Sierra squinted at the glowing nectar in the vial, estimating the pitiful amount. It seemed like so little to cost so much.

The ground growled beneath her feet, and she froze. She stood like a statue for a long moment, her hand above the vial. Dread swirled inside her like the golden syrup in the glass. The family's ancient unicorn gave a rusty bellow; he always knew when things were about to go pear-shaped. When his cry scraped down Sierra's spine, her paralysis shattered. She reached for the vial but was too late.

The workroom floor roared up to meet her with a human-like shriek, slamming her to her knees. Glass crashed nearby. Sierra's head smacked against the scarred wooden table on her way down. The walls jittered and bounced, sending clods of dirt, thatch, and rocks skittering at her face. During the big earthquake last year, she saw a two-story cabin crush an entire family. She still woke up screaming, sometimes. So did Phoebe.

Phoebe! The thought of her sister sent Sierra scrambling, grabbing for the table leg to pull herself to her knees. Why wasn't Phoebe calling?

The quake settled down to shivers, but Sierra stayed on her hands and knees. She crawled through the dust and debris in the kitchen and small living room until she reached their tiny shared bedroom. Jagged pebbles pressed into her palms, but she didn't stop to brush them off as she staggered to her feet.

"Phoebe? Answer me!" Sierra cried.

Wild shadows danced on the bare wall from the swaying lantern hanging from the ceiling. She scanned the room, heart beating like a rabbit's, barely noticing the rubble littering the pallet on the floor. When carrot-red hair peeked out from the patched covers, her breath rushed out with a loud sigh. Phoebe was okay. Her red head rose up, wild in disarray; wide brown eyes stared at Sierra.

"Is it over?" Phoebe said. In her ten short years, she'd already lived through countless quakes, but that didn't make them any less terrifying.

"Yes, Bug, we're fine." Sierra sank to her knees in relief, even though the floor had stopped its wicked dance.

"Then what's that stuff all down your leg? Are you bleeding?"

Sierra glanced down at her legs and touched the dark wet pants. Her hands came away sticky. A golden and glowing residue stained her fingertips. Cursing under her breath, she ran back to the workroom, Phoebe following like a shadow. The sweet smell of fairy nectar filled the air with the scents of honey and cinnamon.

"Jack's going to kill me," Sierra said, surveying the shattered glass and the spilled nectar across the floor. Their father called fairy nectar his goldmine for more than its color.

"Dad can't blame you for another earthquake," replied Phoebe, reaching up to stroke the long braid down Sierra's back.

Sierra just raised her eyebrow. Phoebe bit her lip and

got out the mop, glancing back with eyes even wider than before.

Sierra sighed. "I'll get more before he gets home. Don't worry, sweetie. He won't even know. It'll be okay."

Hopefully there'd be enough to collect. Another fairy run, this late in the afternoon, with the sun already touching the horizon? Perfect. Just perfect.

They quickly cleaned the mess and managed not to cut their hands on the glass. They couldn't do anything about the remaining honeyed scent of nectar in the air, but it was a common smell in their house. Maybe Jack wouldn't notice. Sierra stuffed her nectar-stained pants in the bottom of the wash bin and pulled on another pair she used when she collected. They were tough and rugged homespun, with pockets to hold whatever tools she needed.

Stepping off the back porch, the girls were slapped hard by the air, even wrapped in their coats and shawls. Spring couldn't arrive soon enough. At least the house seemed to have withstood the quake fairly well. The grey mud and clay packed between the wood logs made it fairly sturdy. The house might not be pretty, but it kept the winter winds out, which was more than most could say about their homes on the far outskirts of Port Ostara. Their village of Tuathail sat along the edge of the busy port, but Tuathail remained small and basic, set off in the forest as it was. Satisfied that their house wouldn't collapse on them in the night, the two girls set off to the fairy meadow.

The empty woven bag and a glass jar hung heavy on Sierra's hip, but she quickly adjusted her stride to their bulk. They crossed the tiny back yard to check on the unicorn, Old Sam, before they set off to the fairy hatch. His ragged neighs had not stopped with the quake. He'd yanked so hard on his rope that the ends hung frayed and mangled. His dark eyes followed Phoebe's every move—they adored each other.

Sierra had a harder time loving the beast. It wasn't that she didn't want to take care of him. She could never leave a magical creature in pain or in need. But her skin crawled at the sight of that empty hole left behind every winter when he dropped his horn. Jack made special arrow tips from it, small, but powerfully strong. Even though Sierra knew it would grow back in the spring, just looking at him hurt. He'd been around since Sierra was four, right before Phoebe's birth ten years ago.

Phoebe gave Sam a sugar plum that lifted his ears and thankfully stopped his fussing. Sierra had to smile at Phoebe whispering loving endearments to the shaggy old beast. Her little sister was the sweetest girl in all of Aluvia.

Sierra's hand brushed against her empty jar, and her smile faded.

"Time to go," she said, eyes tracking the dimming light.

They headed down the icy trail to the fairy hatch. As Phoebe often did on this walk, she sighed and said, "I wish I were a fairy keeper."

"No, you don't," Sierra replied, as always.

The girls were rare in having keepers on both sides of their family tree, so it was a miracle Phoebe wasn't born a keeper too. Sierra was just thankful her sister didn't have to deal with the often-agitated fairies.

Phoebe usually argued at this point. She thought their tiny little glowing wings—about all you could see of most of them—were charming. So did lots of people who didn't actually have to work with the treacherous creatures. But today, perhaps seeing the weariness stamped across her sister's face, Phoebe summoned a smile. "Let's pretend we can do anything, then. What would you rather be?"

"Anything. Anything but this."

Phoebe's smile faded, and Sierra wanted to kick herself. She didn't mean to sound so harsh, but it was true. She hated that her fate had been decided the moment she was born with a keeper mark on the back of her neck. The fairies would never leave her alone. The mark was only the outward evidence of some inner trait or ability the fairies were drawn to. If she knew what it was, she'd change herself and be free.

Phoebe was quiet; only the sounds of the crunching stones beneath their feet filled the frosty air. They passed the old oak that snapped in half in last year's big earthquake.

Phoebe finally said, "At least you know you matter, Sierra. The fairies need you."

Sierra just sighed. Yes, she took care of her fairies. If she didn't, she'd never have a moment's peace. The little worker fairies weren't very clever. Sierra built a special hatch for their home and found the exact mushrooms the queen needed to thrive. The fairies lived on the far edge of the Quinns' land, close to the forest. Sierra made sure no wild creatures encroached on their territory and that other people left them alone. But in return, she took their nectar for Jack, even though she didn't want to.

She'd told Phoebe how the fairies often fought during nectar collections but had glossed over how bad it really was. She didn't allow Phoebe in the fairy meadow during actual collections. Too dangerous. Plus, if she saw what it was like, she'd worry more than she did already. She had seen the bites, scratches, and pinches. Sierra ran her fingers along two large scratches on her forearm, shaking her head. Never a sting, at least, since queens never attacked to kill their keepers. Well, they never had before, though Sierra sometimes wondered if her queen would be the first. Why the fairies stayed with her, she didn't know, since they seemed to hate being stuck with her as much as she hated being stuck with them.

When they turned the corner at the clump of

blackberry bushes where Phoebe would wait, Sierra paused. A haunting silence sat heavily in the meadow. No bass-deep thrumming of the fairies in their hatch rode along the breeze. No tiny lights like sparks flittered within the darkening trees nearby. Her heart galloped. Where were her charges? Thankfully, her sister hadn't noticed yet.

"Phoebe, I need you to go back and start cooking, okay? We don't want dinner late for Jack. This won't take long, but they get irritated at dusk, and I don't want you to get hurt." That last part was not a lie.

Phoebe's shoulders sagged, but she knew a late dinner meant trouble. She headed back, dragging her feet, head tucked down into her chest. If their mother hadn't died birthing Phoebe, maybe things would have been different. Whatever kindness had been in their father must have died right along with her. Before Sierra could ache over how much more she wished she could give her sister, she turned her attention back to the fairy hatch.

There were no cages for Sierra's fairies. No wires, no lids, no glass. Except for the queen, they were so tiny they could fit through most holes, but they didn't need cages with a fairy keeper around anyway. *She* was the reason they kept coming back. They did live in a slatted wooden box that allowed easy access to their nectar, but otherwise they were free to come and go as they pleased. Unlike Sierra. She was trapped by her mark, her father, and by her love for Phoebe.

Sierra tiptoed forward. The sky was darkening, but there were no glowing wings covered in the nectar that dripped off them in their hatches. Her skin prickled as it did in that still moment before an earthquake hit.

Next to the hatch, a pile of tiny rainbow flower petals were spread on the ground. For one moment, she didn't understand. Then her knees gave out when her mind made sense of the sight.

All the fairies were dead. No movement, no noise, no vibration, no light. Sierra searched the pile for her queen, the tiny wings rasping softly as she sifted them through her hands. They were like dry silk as they slid down her palms, which began to shake. She dropped the last dead fairy from her fingers and stood in shock. All dead but the queen, who was missing. Where was the queen?

She spun around but saw nothing in the meadow or surrounding forest. A fairy queen was bigger than the rest, as large as a butterfly, easy to spot. She was definitely not in the pile at Sierra's feet.

Sierra grabbed the wooden hatch and turned it upside down, hoping for clues. The box was empty except for the last remains of nectar dripping down its sides. The heady scent floated in the air since she'd disturbed the hatch, but no angry fairies swarmed around her. The cry of an owl startled her, brought her back to herself. The sun was now only a red glow glaring over the treetops. What could have done this? She had no idea. Fairies were so strong.

Working quickly, Sierra scooped the tiny fairy remains into her jar, looking over her shoulder around the glade again and again. She'd examine them later. She kept moving. The sun was almost below the horizon, and Jack was probably arriving at the house right now. She was really in for it. She cursed as she picked up the last of the fairies.

They lay in the jar, still and silent. Except for the queens, fairies were so tiny you couldn't even see arms and legs except beneath an apothecary's magnifying lens. But all fairies glowed, at least when they were alive. Sierra had never seen more than one dead fairy at a time. In all the history of Aluvia, nothing like this had ever happened that she knew of, anywhere in the world. The pile of dull wings looked terribly wrong in the fading light, but they were beautiful even in death. She slid the jar into her bag. Her heart pounded demanding action.

Sierra's thoughts jumbled together as she ran home, like the fairies sliding around in her jar. Maybe she did this? Did they die because she wasn't a good keeper? No feeling followed these thoughts. She was too stunned.

This was not the first time she had wondered if there was a mix-up at birth. She had never felt a special connection to her charges, not like her best friend

Corbin, a keeper who loved his fairies with all his heart.

Sierra was the first keeper born in her family in two generations, but their bloodline boasted an unusual number of keepers. Her father liked to claim their great-great-great-however-many-great grandmother was the first keeper in Aluvia. Jack liked to make a lot of claims, though. Didn't make them true.

The ground blurred beneath her feet as she ducked under branches and leaped over fallen logs. Maybe her fairies dying meant she wasn't a keeper anymore? She touched the base of her neck where the fairy wings birthmark sat. Warmth swept through her body as it always did when she touched it. Corbin would have ideas of what she should do next, wonderful keeper that he was, but Sierra was fresh out.

"Where are you?" she whispered aloud, as if her queen would answer.

Sierra raced through the darkness, stifling a sob on her fist. It wasn't seeing the mishmash of crumbled wings and glitter on the cracked red dirt that made her want to cry, not really. Fairies didn't talk or communicate like people. Crying over the deaths of the little worker fairies would be like crying over a bunch of dead bugs. The fairies' deaths were sad, even tragic, because they were beautiful and important to the world. Still, it wasn't like losing someone you loved. Even the queen, who was clearly more intelligent than the workers, had never managed to communicate much. She'd shown affection, and she'd shown anger. But even though Sierra hated her calling, she wouldn't wish for them to die. What would a world be without their magic?

No, what was filling her with despair was the question: what would she tell Jack? What would he do when she told him the makers of his precious nectar were gone? If her fairies were all dead, she realized there was a good possibility she was as good as dead, too—her *and* her little sister. It wouldn't take some kind of magical disaster to wipe them out.

Jack was enough all on his own.

CHAPTER TWO

The aroma of grilling onions greeted Sierra as she neared the back door. Through the window's speckled pane, she saw Phoebe cooking at the stove. She was singing, as she often did, her high voice clear and sweet.

The cast iron pan practically overflowed with sizzling onions, mushrooms, and venison. Jack was back already, and he must have invited a guest to join them for dinner. Her mouth went dry. Telling him the news in front of one of his business associates would be like pouring lamp oil on herself and then lighting a match. The critical conversation would have to wait until later.

Two sets of footsteps came down the hall: one lighter, one heavier. Jack was always light on his feet, although he had long since graduated from thievery and assassinations. Now he focused on the more profitable business of selling poisons and unlawful elixirs, including the most powerful in existence, made from fairy nectar. Handy to have a keeper in the family when you had ambitions to be one of the most successful dark alchemists in the country.

Sierra scanned the tiny back yard, looking for a place to hide the fairy jar. Two shadows fell across the wall by Phoebe. Sierra untied her fairy tools from her belt with trembling fingers and made a split-second decision. Sam's pen. She raced over, reached through the wide slats of his pen, and pushed the jar into the corner of his hay.

Jack's voice came through the open window. "Sierra, what are you doing out there?"

She eased through the door. "Hello, Jack."

Her father disliked that she called him by his given name, which was one reason why she did it. It also helped her forget they were related, which was hard given that Jack's dark hair, brown eyes, and pale skin were stamped right on her.

When Sierra's gaze met his, her stomach clenched, but she kept her face neutral. She'd had a lot of practice.

Elder Graham Bentwood stepped up next to her father. Bentwood was a big man with big fists, a big temper, and big ambition in the world of dark alchemists. A thick white scar sliced across his left cheek, compliments of a knife fight years ago, and his head nearly brushed the top of the doorway. His black hair was peppered with white now, but he hadn't slowed down at all. His blue eyes were as cold and hard as ever.

Her heart sank. Naturally, of all the people who could be there now, it had to be her father's most important customer and colleague. Bentwood had been in the business for years, leading the dark alchemy crew two ports over. He bought large, discounted quantities of Jack's popular mind-altering elixir to sell in his own port for an easy profit. Jack called this special elixir Flight.

Its base ingredient was fairy nectar, distilled to its most pure essence, with other secret components added, too. Potent stuff. People loved the carefree way it made them feel, but they sometimes ended up starving to death in a happy stupor, or trading everything they had for another dose. Sometimes they saw strange things that weren't really there, too. Didn't stop people from lining up to buy it, though, which Sierra had never understood.

Bentwood also bought a great deal of her father's specially crafted poisons. Unlike Jack, though, Bentwood was less likely to poison someone than simply beat them to death.

Sierra nodded at him. It did not pay to disrespect one of the biggest tyrants in the area, even if she detested him. Bentwood nodded back respectfully. As a fairy keeper, she was a key ingredient in the world of alchemy with its potions, poisons, and elixirs. But they all knew to whom she belonged and where her loyalties were forced to lie.

Jack was thin and strangely graceful, only a head taller than Sierra. He had cropped brown hair, narrow hands and a short brown beard that effectively hid his lips. His dark eyes rarely showed emotion, and reading his expression could be difficult for most people. Not for Sierra. It had been her business to know when Jack was in a bad mood or when he might be feeling generous. Today, he was pretty happy. She wanted to keep it that way.

The men made small talk as they sat down, obviously already having conducted their business. Sierra noticed Bentwood was scrutinizing Phoebe like a man buying a new horse. He ran his finger along his jaw as she carried the water jug to the table. He looked like he wanted to check her teeth, and a chill ran down Sierra's spine.

The men talked about the quake, pondering the increasing frequency of them. The savory scent of roasted venison wafted by as Phoebe sat the pan in the middle of the table. Sierra's shoulders relaxed slightly. She hadn't even realized how on edge she'd been. She took a deep breath.

Then Sam began to bray, and sweat burst along her palms.

Everyone froze. Was it another quake? The ground wasn't moving yet.

Sierra rubbed a fist across her forehead. *Of* course *a*

unicorn wouldn't take the death of fifty fairies lightly, she thought. All magical creatures shared a connection through the magic they used and created. How stupid of her to leave them where Sam could sense them!

Phoebe's breath caught and she braced her arms against the table. When nothing happened, puzzlement pushed fear from her face.

Bentwood said, "What's wrong with the unicorn?"

Sierra glanced at her father, and she didn't even have to feign the concern in her eyes. Jack jerked his head at the door, giving her silent permission. She ran, door slamming behind her.

Oh, those screams! They sounded practically human. Sierra slapped her hands over her ears even as she bolted the short distance to his pen. Sam stood over in the corner with the fairies, the whites of his eyes showing all the way around the black irises. His breath made small puffs in the air with each shriek.

Sierra vaulted over the fence and plunged her hand in the hay, yanking out the jar of fairies. She stuffed it inside her jacket without tying it to her belt, trying to hide the evidence from Sam. She frantically petted him, wishing she had thought to grab a sugar plum or carrot from the kitchen.

"Shh, Sam, it's going to be okay…" The words tumbled out, as much for her as for him.

Sam kept screaming.

She looked back over her shoulder and saw Jack at

the window, glaring. This was making him look bad in front of his business partner. If only he knew the alternative. The jar of fairies was cold, pressed against the thin cotton of her shirt. She needed to get it away from Sam.

On rubbery knees, Sierra backed up, hands held palm up to Sam as if to say, *There's nothing of interest here.* He advanced toward her, head lowered, the gaping wound on his head aimed right at her. Then he charged. Sam—sweet, skinny Sam—charged right at her, as if his horn were still there.

Sierra did the only thing she could think of. She dove out of the way, under the bottom railing, into the dead grass. The jar rolled beneath her. *Crack!* Glass sliced cold and slick across her belly, followed by the warmth of blood dripping down her skin. When she stood, the glass slid farther down her belly on its way out of her shirt. She kept moving, making it almost to the house. Then the glass cut a half-moon into her skin before falling to the ground at Sierra's feet—and the feet of her father.

Jack stood at the door, staring right at her.

CHAPTER THREE

*D*ead fairies fluttered to the ground around Sierra like gently falling snow, rainbow brilliance gone dark. It was like she was in one of those dreams where she couldn't move, at least not quickly enough, because she saw his hand coming at her and couldn't dodge. She couldn't speak. She couldn't even blink.

Pain exploded as the back of his hand connected solidly with her cheek, sending zigzags of lights swimming in front of her eyes. Sierra crashed to the ground, the metallic taste of blood blooming in her mouth.

She must have lost some time, because the next thing Sierra knew, Jack was standing over her, chest heaving, eyes wild with fury. But his lips were locked tight. She tried to think past the throbbing pain in her head, that moment of shock that always came when her own father hit her. This wasn't the first time, but it was the first time he'd done so in front of anyone else.

"You'd dare steal fairies from the hatch? What's your scheme?" he hissed.

As if she'd risk Phoebe. She attempted to speak, coughed, and then tried again. "Look at them."

Jack looked down, and she saw the moment realization hit him. What little color his face held simply drained away.

"What happened?" he said in a low voice.

Sierra whispered, "They were dead when I got there. I don't know why."

He sucked in a breath, plans processing behind his eyes, recalculating, analyzing cost and risk. Bentwood stepped out of the doorway behind them, and Jack's bubbling rage instantly cooled into a chilly professional smile.

He spun around and said, "Elder Bentwood, it has been a strange night. I apologize for the disruption. Why don't we continue the meal?"

He attempted to steer the bigger man back inside. But Bentwood was too large for steering.

He unexpectedly smiled and turned to Jack. "Looks like we have further business tonight after all, Master Quinn."

The use of her father's official master alchemist title

brought a new level of formality to the discussion. Bentwood was up to something.

Jack's brow furrowed briefly before he waved the other man inside, sending one last seething glance her way. The two men returned to his office at the far end of the house.

Phoebe stood in the doorway, now visible without their hulking bodies to block her. She grasped the doorframe so tightly Sierra was afraid she would cut herself.

"Hey, Phoebe, Bug, it's going to be okay…"

Phoebe met her eyes, and Sierra couldn't lie, not again.

"Are you ready to run?" Sierra asked instead.

Phoebe swallowed but nodded.

"Good. We need to go right away."

Phoebe looked at Sam, eyes shiny with sudden tears. They would have to leave him behind, which certainly didn't bother Sierra at the moment. She knew he'd be fed.

Sierra had long considered what they would need to bring with them if they had to run for it. They'd tried running away before, but Jack found them and made them regret it. Sierra was too profitable for him to lose. The oldest tales said keepers had an inborn talent, a connection that allowed them to live easily among magic. It didn't seem easy to Sierra. The fairies liked to swarm around keepers, sing to them, or attack them, depending on their moods. The fairy antics made Sierra pretty obvious in a crowd. So she had given up hope for herself, but not for Phoebe.

Jack and Bentwood were still in the office, voices low but rising. Jack said, "But we've worked together for years, Graham... you know I'll come through..."

Bentwood raised his gravelly voice. "History isn't something I can count on..."

Sierra didn't want to be around to find out what they were arguing about. She slunk down the hall, leaving Phoebe to eat something in the kitchen, and slipped into their tiny bedroom.

Sierra reached the trunk in the corner, eased open the lid, and then dug in her fingers. She sifted through the pile of socks Phoebe liked to knit for her but hit the bottom of the trunk without finding the leather bag she kept ready in case they had to run. It held only a few items but enough to get them started. She tried again, mixing the socks around like she was stirring a pot of soup, but the bag wasn't there. Cold seeped into her bones. The only person who could have taken it was Jack.

She collapsed on the edge of their straw pallet and put her aching head in her hands. If Jack knew she had an emergency stash for escape, he surely knew her first move after something like today would be to run and take Phoebe.

A hundred pound weight pressed on Sierra's

shoulders, but Phoebe was waiting. It didn't matter if Jack planned to follow. They had to go.

Sierra grabbed another leather bag and stuffed a spare pair of pants and shirt for each of them in there, as well as some underclothing and socks. Lots of socks, with the rain and ice this time of year. At least winter was almost over. No money, but that was okay. They could always wash dishes or care for stable animals. She couldn't grab any of the food in the larder now. She thought of the meat and onions in the pan, and her stomach growled.

Sierra picked up her pace and jogged into the kitchen, wondering if she could swipe one of the towels to use as a bandage. She stopped short, seeing Jack, Phoebe, and Bentwood at the table. Phoebe sat between them, eyes bigger than the moon. Jack gave a booming laugh. That wasn't his real laugh; it was his business laugh. He wasn't happy.

Sierra dropped the bag behind her, hoping no one noticed. Phoebe was taking quick, shallow breaths, and Sierra stepped toward her involuntarily.

She glared at the two men. "What's going on?" The threat in her tone was obvious, judging by the way their eyebrows moved: Bentwood's went up; Jack's went down.

Jack stood and said, "Congratulations are in order. Bentwood has accepted your sister into his alchemy crew to settle payment for a deal agreed upon just today.

Given the unexpected change in our situation, he has been very generous to renegotiate terms."

Jack's eyes flinched for only a second when he met Sierra's.

Whatever she had expected, it wasn't this. A common practice among dark alchemists was to send family members to work for a neighboring alchemist. It was considered a lifelong appointment. Usually, the exchanged workers became elixir runners, sent to secretly deliver unlawful elixirs such as Flight. The next step up was delivering—or administering—poisons, but that required more trust. Mostly, competing dark alchemists kept one another's family members to prevent betrayals. It was a treacherous business, selling poisons and elixirs. Children, no matter how grown, made excellent hostages.

Sierra had expected her sister would be spared. Bentwood was already their priority client, and no one else could do for Jack's business what Sierra could. But no. The taste of bile sat rank in her throat.

Bentwood glowered at her. "What, you want to take her place, little fairy-girl? Jealous? My crew's the top in the country."

They were fast, all right, because they were terrified. His people had twice the death rate as everyone else's.

"She's just a child," was all she could force out before she swallowed a growl.

Along Phoebe's temples, blue swirls of vein stood out

like pale lace against her fair skin, and her arms and legs were like sticks. She couldn't possibly help his profits, but he'd get what he wanted: assurance of Jack's continued cooperation and future supplies. If it wasn't Flight, Jack would find some other elixir to sell. Dead fairies or not, business went on.

"Not 'just a child.' She's a child with keeper heritage, Keeper Quinn," Bentwood replied. "When she grows up, she'll marry someone in my port and have children who will also live in my port. Children who could very well be keepers themselves."

Sierra's stomach turned. Bentwood shrugged. "Besides, there are children younger than her tying nets in the harbor for their fisherman fathers. Elixir running is hard work, but she comes from sturdy stock." He waved his hand at her.

Sierra bared her teeth. Compassion was Phoebe's perfume. If she had to take part in destroying lives by dispensing Flight or poisons, it would kill her. Sierra calculated the heaviness of the skillet, in case she needed to hit Jack and Mr. Bentwood.

Jack said to Sierra, "This would have happened eventually." Surprisingly, he sounded like he regretted that. "But your stupidity sped things up. Tonight, Bentwood had agreed to accept payment of a certain number of future Flight batches in exchange for allowing me to immediately expand our business closer to his territory."

He expelled a harsh breath that flared his nostrils and pointed to a dead fairy all alone in the middle of the table. "Now I had to pay by sending an... employee... that I was not expecting to send any time soon in order to fulfill our agreement."

Phoebe was watching Sierra with horror-filled eyes.

Desperation grabbed at her. Sierra blurted, "I'll go. I'll go work for Elder Bentwood."

Bentwood looked interested, but Jack waved her suggestion away, like she had feared he would.

"Don't be ridiculous. I need you here, especially now. Without fairy nectar, we would have no Flight. Having a wider business area will scarcely be helpful if I have no product to sell. We will discuss the issue about the fairies *later*." He glared at her now.

Sierra cast about for anything that could save Phoebe. Anything, it didn't matter what it was.

"The queen!" The words popped out of her mouth, sure and forceful.

She took a deep breath and tried to sound calm, less like the terrified fourteen-year-old she was. "She's not dead. She's only missing, which means I can find her again."

True, she didn't know that, and really didn't particularly believe that, but she also didn't know for sure if the queen was dead. What mattered was if Jack believed it. Sierra explained how she found them, and Jack's eyes grew dark and thoughtful.

When he didn't interrupt, Sierra continued, remembering something Corbin told her a long time ago. "When a queen leaves her hatch and goes too far away for too long, the little fairies left behind, the servants, they die. They need her magic to live. I've never heard of a queen leaving her hatch on purpose. Someone or something could have stolen her, but the hatch would have attacked a human and left a mess. So this must be a bigger problem than my hatch."

The words were coming faster now, and he was still listening. "I think she's out there, Jack, and I can bring her back. Then she'll start a new hatch and you'll have nectar again. You can make rivers of Flight for hundreds of people. You don't have to trade Phoebe off."

Sierra paused, swallowing the crack in her voice. "Please don't send her away so young."

Mr. Bentwood leaned back in his chair, his face clouded, like a man who believed he'd been cheated out of a great deal.

Jack stroked his beard. After an eternity, he said, "Fine."

Sierra clutched the back of the chair in front of her to stay standing.

Bentwood jerked to his feet, his chair falling backward with a clatter that made both girls jump.

"You can't change our deal!" His voice was like thunder. A flush spread across Bentwood's scarred face, bringing the white line in sharp relief.

Jack, though, looked coolly at the bigger man and remained seated. He raised one finger in the air, which was more effective than a slap.

Without changing his expression, Jack continued, looking right at Sierra, "You go look for your fairy queen. But I cannot change my plans for Phoebe."

Sierra's breath left her body all at once. She might loathe Jack, but she couldn't say she came from stupid stock. He knew a deal was a deal, and if he backed out of his promise, he could lose stature and, most importantly, power. Maybe even his life.

Phoebe's skin was so pale from shock that she looked translucent, lips pressed into a thin line. Coldness descended from Sierra's bones and merged into her heart. It was a quiet, icy place there, a place without fear.

"Then I won't help you start another hatch. I'll die before I stand by and let her get sent to a man like that!" Sierra spat out each word like an arrow, pointing right in the red face of Bentwood.

Father and daughter stared into each other's eyes, and understanding passed between them. They were a lot alike in some ways, which scared Sierra when she considered it. Whatever thin connection he might have felt for her as his daughter severed. This was all about business, but that was more respect than she had ever received from him.

"Very well. I'll make a bargain," he said. "You'll have two fortnights to find your fairy. One month. And if you do not bring back a queen in that time—I really don't care if she's yours or not—then your sister moves to Elder Bentwood's city. There, she will work in his distilleries and run for him, whether you are here or not. If you *do* return with a queen before the deadline, Phoebe will go to Elder Bentwood *next* year. I think this is a fair compromise, don't you?"

Bentwood's face was past scarlet and moving toward purple, but Jack sat without apparent concern.

"Could I have longer?" Sierra had no idea where her queen could be.

"We have only enough nectar stored for one more month's supply for Elder Bentwood to take with him until you either return or do not. I will send that nectar with him now as a sign of good faith. But one month is all I will ask him to wait. When the nectar runs out, so does your time."

Sierra could tell Bentwood wanted to argue. But even if she succeeded, he still had a promise to get Phoebe next year, which was more than he'd been offered before.

They had had a long partnership, Bentwood and Jack. Bentwood wouldn't ruin it for one month's delay.

"How do I know you'll wait?" Sierra asked. No way would she leave without assurance. "I want her to come with me."

Jack laughed. "Nice try, Sierra."

His wry smile acknowledged she'd learned from his

negotiations. At one point he had hoped she would take over his business. A fairy keeper as a dark alchemist. Couldn't beat that combination, but turned out a keeper with a conscience didn't make a good dark alchemist.

Sierra knew fairies weren't intended to be used for that. Nectar could be used for healing, if prepared properly. Corbin's parents were healers who used his fairies' nectar in healing potions for the ill and wounded. Naturally, her father turned it into something addictive, mind-altering, and even deadly.

Jack said, "You'll have to trust me. *I* have never lied to *you*, have I? But you can't say the same to me."

A new slither of fear broke through Sierra's numbness and iced her neck. He was talking about their pre-packed *leave in the middle of the night* bag. She figured she was lucky he didn't beat her for the thought of betrayal alone. And honestly, he was right; he had never lied to her. She had never been important enough. Someone wouldn't think to lie to a dog, either.

Sierra's stomach roiled. Her father kept his word with his business colleagues, though, so she had to believe him now. Of course, even if she were successful, she could still lose Phoebe to Bentwood eventually. No matter. Sierra would figure something out between then and now. One problem at a time.

Jack continued, "So, go ahead, only I can't have you go out alone. You broke my trust."

No, no, no. She didn't see how this night could get worse. If it wasn't Phoebe, Sierra didn't want a partner.

"Therefore," he continued, "I'm going to send Nell with you as my enforcer."

Sierra closed her eyes and tried to keep breathing.

The night just got worse.

CHAPTER FOUR

Sierra carefully packed for her journey while waiting for Nell to arrive. The few items stuffed in the bag earlier wouldn't be enough for the trip. Phoebe sat on the edge of their pallet, mindlessly petting the old toy unicorn Sierra had sewn for her years ago from fabric scraps.

Sierra tried to think ahead to what she'd need: clothing, a cooking pot, medical supplies. But all she could think of was how getting tied up in Bentwood's alchemy crew might as well be a death sentence for Phoebe. He wouldn't likely kill her on purpose, but there were other kinds of death.

"Don't forget to bring the sweater I knitted for you. Winter still has a month to go." Phoebe's voice was soft.

"I wouldn't dare." Sierra smiled sadly, and all at once,

Phoebe was in her arms, her red hair pressed to Sierra's shoulder, face squinched tight.

Sierra rocked her. "Do your best to hang on while I'm gone, okay? Maybe I won't even need the whole month. Maybe I'll be back in a week."

"You don't really think that, though."

No, she didn't. Sierra suspected her queen was quite far away if she was still alive. Maybe even captured. She couldn't think of a reason the queen would leave the little fairies to die otherwise. She'd need every day Jack had allotted to solve the mystery and find her queen.

But what she said was, "Anything's possible. Okay?"

Phoebe nodded, sniffled, and backed away to curl up on the edge of the pallet like a little kitten. Sierra forced out small talk as she packed. "Your sweater will be perfect, and the scarf you made, too."

Phoebe's smile kept Sierra going, even though every step closer to leaving hurt.

She laid out her thickest sweaters, her favorite canvas pants, her knee-length coat, and the fur-lined boots that had recently cost her a day's collection of nectar. She'd slowly siphoned off the top of her daily harvest for several weeks until she could trade for them. Corbin was the one to point out she needed thicker, sturdier boots for the wilderness of the forest.

He would joke with her at the start of each winter: "Your feet will freeze right to the ground, silly ragamuffin!" He laughed, but he truly worried about the inadequacy of the thin leather shoes she usually wore.

She'd chuckle and tell him, "Then I guess you'll get the fairy keeper statue you've always wanted."

"Thanks, Corbin," Sierra muttered now.

Next came her toolkit. Fairy keepers didn't need many tools, but they did need jars to collect nectar and nets to contain aggressive fairies. For a rogue queen, there wasn't a lot she could do except try to win her back through whatever strange attraction she held as a keeper. No box was strong enough to hold a fairy queen, but the net would be useful in case it became necessary to grab some lesser fairies to lure the queen.

Sierra packed a small cooking pot.

"Are you actually going to try to hunt?" Phoebe attempted a joke, but her smile wobbled.

Phoebe couldn't stand to hunt, and Sierra was simply not good at it at all. "I'll manage to eat. Don't worry," Sierra assured her. "Think of the possibilities—field greens with nuts and honey, mushrooms grilled on an open fire…"

Sierra's stomach, which had missed dinner tonight, roared. The gurgling growl was staggeringly loud in the grim silence of their room. Phoebe giggled. Her bubbly noise sounded impossibly inappropriate, given the circumstances. She tried to stop, covering her mouth, but snorted instead, which only made her giggle harder.

Sierra stared at her sister for a long moment, at those

sparkling brown eyes and the mane of shaggy red hair, and giggled, too. Some days, you either laughed or lay down and cried. Sierra laughed and laughed until her sides hurt, until the scrape on her stomach tore open slightly and blood oozed around the edges again.

"Looks like I missed the joke," a girl said in a low, drawling voice from the doorway.

Sierra stiffened, then stood and turned to face the girl standing there.

At fifteen, she was a year older than Sierra and taller than many boys her age. A heavy wool jacket covered arms that Sierra knew were well-toned. Long white blonde hair hung in a single braid, emphasizing pale blue eyes. The girl was actually quite pretty, though her disagreeable expression downplayed that fact. She looked at Sierra with undisguised dislike.

Sierra said, "Hello, Nell. No, you're just in time."

CHAPTER FIVE

When Sierra was six and Nell was seven, they competed in a village race with all the children. Nell was bigger, older, and tougher, but Sierra outran her anyway. During their victory lap, the infuriated Nell hit Sierra right on her keeper mark, hard enough to send her flying. Nell didn't like losing, ever, and even second place was unacceptable. Poor Corbin got a distant fifth, but he didn't care. He spent most of his time reading books, already preparing for the day when his fairy would arrive.

That race proved critical for Nell, though. Even second place showed her potential. Elixir runners had to be quick. She was quick *and* smart—a critical combination in Jack's estimation. Within the next couple of years, Nell's father died and she began working for Jack, adding her small income to what her mother earned taking in people's laundry.

Nell had worked her way up in Jack's business since then, working in the distilleries, then as a spy when stealth was necessary. People rarely saw a young woman as a threat compared to the usual hulking bruisers, but she was just as dangerous as any of them. She'd never liked Sierra, who didn't know why and didn't particularly care.

Sierra refused to run Jack's elixirs and got several lashings, but he was nothing if not practical. He eventually stopped asking her to distribute along even the easiest routes. She earned him more simply by being what she was: a keeper.

Now, her speed would come in handy. Sierra potentially had a lot of ground to cover and not much time. At least Nell would be able to keep up. Her current job as enforcer meant being smart and skilled with weapons, not merely strong. She needed to prove her worth to promote any higher. Jack was undoubtedly using this as a test. Two birds, one stone.

Nell leaned against the door, crossing her arms. She sent a short wave, almost a salute, at Phoebe, who solemnly waved back once and then cuddled deeper into the blankets.

"Nice boots," Nell said, jerking her chin at Sierra's fur-lined pair on the bed.

Nell was clearly running a price estimate in her

mind, a black-market value that had her raising her eyebrows. Sierra shrugged.

"I imagine you get a lot of good deals on things like that, right?" Sierra asked, turning away to keep packing.

People feared Jack. If anyone crossed him or the people he worked for, they might find themselves turning blue while eating dinner at a tavern sometime. His crew members often preyed on scared villagers and paid less for items than they were worth, or didn't bother paying at all. They called such exchanges "good deals." They didn't tell Jack about it, and Jack didn't ask. Sierra had never actually seen Nell do something like that, but wouldn't put it past her.

Nell glared, flushing at the implied insult.

"We may need more supplies before we go. Jack gave me some money." Sierra kept her voice even, unaffected. Nell either went along with the change of topic, or fell for it and let Sierra change the topic. Sierra couldn't tell which.

Nell had already packed. She must have felt weaponry was more important than food or survival gear. She bristled with sharp points: silver knives, an honest-to-goodness full-sized sword worn in a back sheath, and two bows. As if one was not enough. The one she had strung and ready was a black walnut bow, with a quiver of arrows fletched with some kind of golden feathers. Sierra had never seen anything like them.

"What kind of feathers?" she asked, because she hated not knowing details like that.

"Griffin." Nell smirked.

Sierra hid how impressed she was. Arrows made with incredibly rare griffin feathers were top of the line. They weren't as good as Jack's, but then, no other arrows were.

Phoebe stayed curled in the corner of the bed. Nell made her nervous, and she should have.

There finally came a moment when Sierra had packed everything she could possibly need, under Nell's watchful eyes.

"Are you sleeping here?" she asked Nell, striving for a neutral tone.

Nell had been placed in authority over Sierra, and both girls knew it. Nell gnawed her lip for a moment and scanned the room. Looking for possible exits, Sierra was sure, like a good little enforcer. Nell was in luck, though. Their room barely fit their pallet, one knee-high nightstand, and the trunk. There were no windows. Nell compromised by laying a sleeping roll across the entry to the door, but on the other side of the closed door, so Phoebe and Sierra had the room to themselves. That was more consideration than Sierra had expected, but maybe Nell simply wanted to avoid Sierra. The feeling was mutual.

Phoebe scooted across the little pallet until she was

next to the wall, like always, and Sierra blew out the tiny oil lamp Jack afforded them.

As she crawled in next to Phoebe, she shivered in air that was quickly dropping temperature as the night deepened. Sierra wrapped her arms around her little sister, hugging her close, and whispered last minute advice, voice hardly audible.

"Okay, listen carefully. Go to Daniel Lee for vegetables on Mondays, before the sun comes up. He'll sell before he's officially supposed to, and you'll get the best pieces."

"Farmer Lee sells on the black market?" Phoebe's shocked whisper was the barest breath.

Even a rumor of black market vendors would draw Jack's men to the door, weapons in hand. But tired of their abuse, the villagers arranged their trades when Jack's people couldn't find them. The locals knew Sierra wasn't like her father and treated her accordingly. But Jack's increasing notoriety made traveling beyond their local village and port depressing and difficult, given her clear resemblance.

"Just listen. Elizabeth Scryer sells her best leather in the attic of the Lazy Lady tavern. You act like you have a question about how to tie a knot in a harness, or something like that, and she has the stuff in her bag."

Her heart ached. Phoebe shouldn't have to take on this responsibility.

"You remember where my emergency nectar stash is?"

Phoebe nodded against the flat pillow.

"Use it if you have to, for any supplies you need. You can get double or triple value for the money for nectar during winter, especially at the medicine booths."

Sierra shared every last thing she could think of to make this month better for her sister, including running to Corbin's family if things got too bad. Sierra hated to draw Jack's attention to Corbin's family, but for Phoebe, she'd put even Corbin at risk.

Phoebe listened and soaked in all the information like Sierra was a prophet, nodding against her shoulder now and then. So brave, her Phoebe.

Then there were no more words between them, only a deep silence, the kind that seemed to carry words in the thickness of the dark. Sierra squeezed her sister tightly and *knew* Phoebe understood how much Sierra loved her. Nobody knew her like Phoebe did, not even Corbin.

Sierra took a deep breath, sure she'd never fall asleep. Horrific images flooded her mind: Phoebe tortured, dead fairies strewn about like fall leaves, the missing queen trapped somewhere dark. It made her head feel full to bursting, but it had also been a very long day, and her body ached from too much abuse and too little food. Phoebe's ragged breathing slowed. Sierra fell asleep with the sweet scent of her little sister chasing away her nightmares.

The next morning, they stood under Nell's flinty gaze. It was time to say goodbye.

"Give us a minute, would you please?" Sierra asked politely. She'd swallow her pride plenty, if it meant an easier goodbye.

"I'm going to be right by the door," Nell said, a warning clear in her voice. She watched Phoebe for a second longer and shook her head, but then she wiped her expression clean, completely blank. She stepped outside, a sentry on duty.

Sierra's throat ached, and she feared she'd cry if she spoke. Phoebe deserved an image of courage and hope to hold onto. The upcoming weeks would likely be long for Sierra, and hard, but how much harder would they be for Phoebe?

Sierra crossed the room and buried her face in Phoebe's hair. The scent of grilled onions still clung to her, but beneath that was her natural aroma, a sweet smell that conjured images of sunshine and laughter.

Clasping her arms around Sierra's neck, Phoebe sniffled. If she cried, Sierra would melt. She knew she would.

"Kick Jack for me if he gives you any grief," Sierra said, trying to earn a giggle. It worked.

"I'll let you do it when you get back." When Phoebe

pulled away from their hug, her eyes sparkled with wetness but did not drop tears. Sierra's brave little bug.

"We're going to fix this," Sierra told her, cupping her little sister's cheeks in her hands.

Phoebe smiled, the heartbreakingly sweet smile Sierra loved so much. "I know."

Losing her fairies was shocking, getting knocked down was painful, but this... leaving her little sister was torturous. Who would take care of her?

Phoebe waved from the porch. If she was crying, Sierra was too far away to see. Waving back, Sierra walked toward the dirt road. Her pack lay heavy on her shoulders, but not as heavy as the responsibility she felt.

Nell gazed at the grey jagged points of the mountains in the distance. "Don't suppose you've got a plan, Fairy-Girl?"

Her tone stiffened Sierra's back and pushed the last of her tears away.

Luckily, she did have a plan.

CHAPTER SIX

"We're going to ask *Corbin*? *That's* the big plan?" Nell whipped around, lips forming a disbelieving O.

Sierra raised her eyebrows. "And so?" They'd all gone to school together since childhood, at least off-and-on, in the one-room schoolhouse of Port Ostara. Sierra had never noticed Nell and Corbin having a falling out, though they'd had plenty of arguments over the years. Then again, Nell had plenty of arguments with everyone.

Sierra pulled a slice of laurel tree bark and popped it in her mouth with a grimace. The foul taste of the bark was bitter like over-brewed tea, but chewing on it reduced her headache a bit while it made her sore jaw ache.

"Look, you know he loves his fairies. He's studied

fairies more than anyone I've heard of besides the ancient scholars. If anyone could have an idea of what's going on, it's him. What's the problem? You used to play with Corbin when you were little."

Nell grumbled, "Times change. He's more likely to go off daydreaming through the fields than help us find our way. What does he know about danger? He doesn't believe in hurting anything. We'll end up spending all our time rescuing him instead of your ridiculous fairy."

Sierra fought to not roll her eyes. "Okay, he's not a fighter, but he can still help—he really knows his stuff. It's all we've got."

Nell kicked at a rock. "Fine, but none of his little girlfriends can come. All those air-headed twits that follow him around are more annoying than his fairies."

Well, that was a point that they could actually agree on, but Sierra didn't want to admit that out loud. Corbin did have quite a batch of admirers, especially since he turned fifteen, the official age many young men set off on their own in the port villages. His deep bronze skin, black hair, and brown eyes made all the older girls swoon, but he mostly ignored them. He'd courted a few, but he always said it just didn't work out.

Sometimes people got the wrong idea about her and Corbin. He was Sierra's best friend, nothing else. But he meant the world to her, in part because he could always make her laugh.

Once, after a particularly rough afternoon with Jack

when she was eleven, she went over to Corbin's house for more healing poultice. His expression softened with compassion, not pity, as he handed her the pack for her black eye, but then he said, "We could get you a pirate patch, if you'd like, looking like the scallywag you are. You'd better practice saying, 'We be lookin' for buried treasure!'"

He screwed up his face into the worst imitation of a pirate ever, and she couldn't help but laugh.

If ever there was a time when she needed some laughter, it was now.

They kept walking toward Corbin's home in Covenstead, the next tiny village over from theirs, in a silence that stretched like taffy. Covenstead held a tiny collection of homesteaders, slightly farther to the northeast. Healers settled the area years before and developed their own small, unique community. Sierra and Nell's village, Tuathail, was nearly three times that size, but anyone sick or wounded went to Covenstead.

Luckily, the two villages were within a candle-mark's walking distance of each other and of Port Ostara, the biggest port in the whole country. The youth of both villages usually attended the single school located in Port Ostara, at least the ones who got to go at all. Corbin always did great in class, and teachers loved his cheery attitude.

Sierra missed a lot of class time thanks to Jack. That

was how Corbin and Sierra first became real friends. He noticed she was falling behind and offered to tutor her, because that was the kind of boy he was.

They actually had their best conversations while gathering wild mushrooms between their villages. For Sierra, the sharp scent of pine was forever woven together with the rumbling sound of Corbin's voice, so much deeper than expected for his frame. They'd spent hours collecting mushrooms for the fairies and greens for their tables during countless long summer afternoons.

Nell could beat him up with one arm and foot tied behind her back. Sierra wasn't sure why she was acting upset about seeing him. They even used to walk home after school together when they were younger, if Sierra recalled correctly. Nell's mother would sometimes watch Corbin when his parents were traveling to a healing. But Sierra hadn't seen them talking to each other in a long time, now that she thought about it.

As they approached Covenstead, Nell began muttering again. "Idiotic plan," she said, "Letting him lead us will give him ridiculous delusions of grandeur."

Sierra ignored her. It made her smile a little, the very normalness of Nell's grumpy response. It was almost reassuring that the entire world had not turned upside down.

They entered the coolness of the forest, crunching

on a carpet of brown and yellow leaves and pine needles. It rarely snowed so close to the coast, but frost still bit the air. A hawk cried high in the sky, hidden by the crisscrossing branches arching over them like hands cupping around a warm flame. Sierra had spent hours in this place, a place where she'd never been hit or insulted. Her stride slowed as she breathed in the chilly, tangy air.

She stopped when she saw the mushrooms, though. They were always running low on mushrooms this time of year. Even though she wouldn't be able to cook them the way her queen liked best, she figured it made sense to have some of the right food on hand. She was trying to think positive now. Her queen really could be out there, kidnapped or starving, and Sierra needed to be ready.

And if her queen was dead, well, then Sierra was determined to capture a wild fairy. She wasn't above stealing another keeper's fairies if she could get away with it, either. She'd figure out some way to return them after she used them to get Phoebe free. Phoebe's survival came first.

Sierra slipped her herb knife from its sheath at her hip. Shiny pink tops glistened as she gently sliced at the base of their stems, and she wrapped them in a cloth she took from her pack. She looked up sharply to see Nell studying her.

"What?" Sierra asked.

When Jack was eyeing someone he knew must be

permanently removed from the equation, his eyes went cold and hard as steel. Nell's expression looked exactly like that right now.

Sierra stood up slowly, legs tensing. It occurred to her she didn't know what sort of job Jack actually hired Nell to do. Whatever he had directed, Sierra felt sure Nell would have no problems doing.

Sierra's mind rapidly plotted out the best paths to run, which way had trees she could climb. She knew this land, and Nell didn't, not like Sierra did.

The hawk cried again, and Sierra shivered despite her winter coat. Nell's lips lifted as she took note of the response.

Sierra sneered right back.

"Do we have a problem, Nellwyn?"

Nell's face flushed at the use of her full name, like she'd always done since she was a kid. It was too soft a name for a warrior. They knew all the other's tender areas. That was rather the point. Prod the angry lion with a stick to see if it would attack. Sierra would rather find out now than later when she was stuck in the wilderness.

Nell snarled but whirled away. "Get the food, and let's go. If we have to go see Corbin, let's get it over with."

Again, her comment puzzled Sierra, but Nell never made sense to her anyway.

By the time Sierra had stored the mushrooms, Nell

had walked ahead, a strong silhouette as she stood where the forest ended and emptied into the open glade that held Corbin's fairies. Sierra walked alongside her and found her frowning and chewing on her bottom lip.

"Ready to go see Corbin?" Sierra asked, a slight emphasis on *Corbin*.

Glaring, Nell stomped out into the glen. Sierra grabbed her arm without thinking, and Nell jerked away so quickly Sierra stumbled. In less than a second, Nell was standing ready with a knife glinting in the sun, crouched, ready to fight.

Sierra stood perfectly still, trying to radiate calm.

"Relax. I only meant this is a fairy glade and you can't go storming through. You could rile them up, and if they attack, it's dangerous. We could get really hurt."

Nell narrowed her eyes, looking distrustful, which was ironic since Sierra was telling the truth.

"Come on, Nell, you've seen me all bloodied up before. You know what fairies are like. You've seen them swarming."

Nell shuddered ever so slightly, and Sierra tilted her head as awareness flooded in. Nell's father had died years ago when she was a little girl. Sierra was six or seven at the time and remembered hearing talk that he died from a fairy swarm. There were a number of them in the area before Corbin and Sierra bonded to their queens and calmed down the fairies. Sierra couldn't help but push to see if she remembered right.

"What a terrible duty you've got, huh, Nell? Gotta chase down a queen who might call all her crazed little fairies to attack. Or maybe she's been stolen by a murderer who'll try to kill us? Bet you're hoping for the second option, since you can handle a human. A hatch of angry fairies, though, they could make you suffer. They might even kill you."

Red flame seared across Nell's face, and she pointed her knife a little closer. "If where we walk is so important, why don't you lead the way, Fairy-Fanatic?"

The name only stung a little. She'd come up with that name years ago when Corbin first bonded to his queen and began spending so much more time with Sierra. Nell didn't push Sierra around, but she never missed a chance to insult her, either.

As far as the strangeness of the fairies, Nell might have accepted them at Jack's place, but she'd never trust anyone involved with them the way Sierra was. Whatever. She had been called a lot worse names.

Nell slid her knife back into some hidden sheath in her clothing. Sierra's estimation of her skills rose grudgingly, and it was pretty high to start with.

Sierra hitched up her pack, thankful for the heat it kept pressed on her back, and began the trek across the field. The grass was brown and crunchy under their feet this time of year, with only a few determined white-lace vines weaving through the frosty shriveled blades.

Sierra steered them slightly to the left so they could

pass next to Corbin's fairy hatch. They'd have to be around fairies to catch the queen; Nell needed to be able to face them.

But when the girls got closer, Sierra stumbled. Even from this distance, the rainbow pile on the ground by the hatch was obvious. She burst into a sprint, Nell right beside her.

"What is it?" she asked, but Sierra had no breath to respond. She had been so sure Corbin would know what to do.

The girls reached the hatch at the same time.

"The fairies are *dead*," Nell whispered hoarsely. Her face drained of color like cloth left out in the sun as she stared at the lifeless, glowless fairies. Sierra guessed even non-fairy keepers sensed the loss of so much magic. As a keeper, she felt a hollow space in the area, a lack of magic that used to be there. She hesitated, but she needed to know.

Sierra plunged her hand into the pile.

"Sierra!" Nell sounded shocked.

Sierra didn't bother to answer. She pushed the minuscule bodies around, until she was sure. Corbin's queen was gone too.

Sierra knew where she'd find him, and that was where she ran, Nell close on her heels.

Corbin had built a big garden when he was ten, between his house and his fairy hatch. The vivid colors and rich scents attracted butterflies, fireflies and, naturally, fairies. In the middle of his garden, a tiny reflecting pool glittered with a bench-like seat next to it. He said that when he sat there, he felt safe.

When they reached him, he was sitting on his knees, arms braced against the ground. Tears still marked his cheeks; his eyes were bloodshot. Nell shifted on her feet and huffed out a breath. He looked up at the girls, dazed, like someone had knocked him hard on the head.

There were many things Sierra loved about Corbin. He was optimistic and happy, one of those rare souls content to bob along with what life handed him. He loved his family, his fairy and his calling. But she guessed now that life had taken something back unexpectedly, he wasn't sure what to do.

Corbin staggered to his feet. Sierra blinked, not realizing how tall he had gotten in the last few months. He towered over her and was even a bit taller than Nell, both the same age.

Her sweet friend looked so sad. She hugged him—the cinnamon honey scent of his charges still clung to him.

When she let go, she was surprised into stillness by the expression on Nell's face: her teeth were gritted so tightly, Sierra thought they might soon turn into dust.

Corbin looked at the blonde girl in confusion for a moment and then said, "Nell?"

The unspoken question *What are you doing here?*

lingered in the air like the chimney smoke from Corbin's family's cottage.

Nell paled and then flushed under his gaze. Amazed, Sierra examined Corbin to see what Nell might be reacting to. He looked much the same as always: black jacket, oversized button-up shirt, and homespun collecting pants stained with grasses and nectar; wavy, black hair ruffled up from the wind; the same amber brown eyes—though his inky lashes were currently spiky from his tears—and golden brown skin. That was Corbin.

Most of the village girls followed him around with hearts in their eyes. Sierra thought part of why he liked being around her was because she treated him the same as she always had. He was simply Corbin, her best friend, even though he was a year older. Nell's obvious dislike of him made it unlikely she was responding to his handsome appearance. Besides, she looked down her nose at girls whose only goal was to be courted by a cute boy. It left Sierra clueless about the source of the tension she felt flowing between them.

Corbin looked at Sierra for an explanation, and she grimaced.

"Jack sent her with me as his enforcer for this trip. My fairies... they died, too, Corbin," she said, "and my queen is missing, like yours."

He hid his face in his hands and moaned. She had never seen him like this.

"Why?" he asked, voice muffled through his palms.

"Why is Nell with us?" Sierra didn't understand the question.

"Why did they die?" he shouted, sending her back two steps. He threw his hands in a wide circle. "What happened?"

A flame of anger spurted through her. "How should I know? You're the fairy scholar here, not me."

"Don't you care why?"

"No, I don't. The point is we need to get them back. I thought... I thought you might be able to help."

Corbin's face darkened, eyebrows angling down over his narrowed eyes, probably upset with her for not crying or something, so she cut him off. "Jack traded Phoebe to Elder Bentwood. I have to find the queen so I can get her back."

Corbin gazed at her with his mouth hanging open. He'd had one too many shocks in a day. "Wasn't Bentwood the one who had a thirteen-year-old runner die the other month? They said she had the pox, but there were rumors she had been starved and beaten for losing her supply during a run."

Sierra tightened her lips and nodded once.

A long moment of silence filled the air. Even Nell looked shaken, shifting from foot to foot.

He said, "Let's go take a closer look at the hatch. I didn't really take time to look for any hints about what happened."

It was clear none of them wanted to go back to that place of death, but there was little choice. When they reached the pile of dead fairies again, they stood shoulder-to-shoulder for a long moment. Then Nell said, "Let's split up. Sierra, you're with me. Corbin, go that way. See if you find any footsteps or clues."

Sierra wasn't happy to be alone with Nell again, but the older girl was focused now, all traces of sarcasm gone in the face of the mission. The glade was quiet, eerily so, but nothing marred the ground. No footsteps, no claw marks, no magical residue of any kind. Admittedly, Sierra was no tracker, but it was as if the queens simply disappeared. Even Nell thought so, and she *was* an excellent tracker. When the three reconvened, they walked back to Corbin's garden while comparing what they saw, which was a big fat nothing.

After a moment of stilted silence, Corbin kicked the seat by the reflecting pool. "I'll be right back."

He jogged from his garden into his little house.

Nell looked at Sierra.

She shook her head. "No idea."

In less than five minutes, he was back wearing his thickest boots, sturdiest pants, and his heavy winter coat. He had a pack on his back and a keeper toolkit around his waist. "We're going to look for them, right?"

In one question, he managed to ask if he could join them, if she trusted him, if she even wanted him there, if they were still a team.

"Are you sure you're okay with coming? We don't even know where we're going." She might have to do things that weren't quite… legal to get a fairy queen. She didn't want him to see her like that. Only one of them should be as cynical as she was. He was older in age, but she was years older in pain and bitterness.

"I have no choice," he said. "My fairy queen needs me too."

Sierra nearly smacked herself in the forehead. This wasn't only about her. Of *course*, he'd never let his queen go without a fight. And if she were truthful, she'd be thankful to have him with her.

Nell looked him up and down. Her flush was gone, and she was all business. "Do you have any weapons in that bag? You've got a good reach if you can use a sword."

With a sheepish smile, Corbin pulled out an herb knife much like Sierra's. The silver blade was only as long as his hand.

Nell didn't bother to suppress a groan. "That's your weapon?"

Corbin shrugged and returned the knife to his jacket pocket. "We've talked about this before. Not everyone needs violence to win a fight. I know a lot. I think that's pretty valuable, Nell." He stumbled a little on her name, and again a flush crept up her pale neck.

Sierra raised her eyebrows, wondering when they had discussed something like that. Maybe they had seen more of each other than she knew. But sunlight was disappearing every minute and, in the long run, it didn't matter. What mattered was getting to Phoebe.

"Then let's get going," Sierra said, and they left the garden behind.

CHAPTER SEVEN

Corbin knew a man named Keeper Hannon, who was quite possibly the oldest fairy keeper alive. He'd been the closest thing to a mentor for Corbin, as Corbin had been Sierra's. He swore if anyone knew what was going on, Hannon would. He lived two ports away, in the opposite direction of Bentwood's town, so they opted to go there first.

"We're going to get Phoebe, okay, little sister?" Corbin said. She smiled at the old nickname.

Nell was behind them as they hiked, so Sierra could pretend she wasn't there.

"Thanks, Corbin," she replied, voice soft. "We've got to, haven't we?" She let her eyes reflect her fear in front of the one person who would never judge her for it.

He put his hand on her shoulder. "I promise. We'll do

everything we can to save her, no matter what happens with our queens."

Her eyes stung, but she wouldn't give Nell the satisfaction of seeing her tear up.

Sierra cleared her throat and walked a little faster. "So, has anything like this ever happened before?"

He shook his head. "Other than a queen's death from old age when there isn't a new queen to take over, I've never heard of a whole hatch dying at once. The queens would never leave the little ones unless there was no other option."

She jumped at the possible explanation. "So maybe our queens died from old age? I have no idea how old Queen is... was... whatever."

Nell snorted behind her.

Sierra stopped and spun. *"What?"*

"Queen? That's your name for your queen fairy? Original." Nell snickered.

Sierra glared, ready to snap an insult at her. But then someone else laughed, only this laughter didn't sound mean. It was a giggle, not a snicker. And it came from Corbin.

She turned slowly. How could her most trusted friend side with that... that... Nell?

His shoulders shook, despite his obvious attempts to keep them still. His lips kept sliding up in a grin before he managed to yank them back to a straight line. He looked over her head—not hard to do—and must have met Nell's eyes. Then he burst into a shout of laughter and ran up along the path, his guffaws chasing him as he tried to avoid laughing at Sierra to her face.

Sierra sighed. It was impossible to be mad at him. It was like trying to be mad at Phoebe, who, Sierra admitted, also found her choice of name for Queen amusing.

Sierra could be mad at Nell, though, no problem. Sierra didn't even look at her as they fell in step again.

"You've got to admit, it's uninspired," Nell pointed out, with a matter-of-fact tone.

"Maybe, but it's also impersonal, and that's the point," Sierra answered as matter-of-factly back.

"You really hate her that much?"

Sierra paused a moment. She thought of her queen, the way she could fit in Sierra's cupped hands. Queen's body was dainty, with elongated arms and legs and a short little tail with an attached stinger. Almost insect-like, but not quite. Her limbs were incredibly elegant, seeming almost jointless the way they could move so gracefully. Long, silky golden hair draped around her body like a dress and her wings hung down her back. Glowing in a golden shimmer, her fairy queen had defined beauty. There was a pang in Sierra's heart. She ruthlessly shoved the unwelcome emotion into a deep, dark corner.

"I don't hate her. I hate my job. I hate having no choice about it. There's a difference."

The only noise after that came from the crunch of their footsteps. They reached Corbin. His upturned lips showed his continued mirth, but she couldn't hold it against him. That boy could always find something to laugh about.

He tugged on Sierra's braid, offering a silent apology with that long-time habit, and picked up the conversation like there had never been a break. "No, I don't think both of our fairies happened to get old enough to die at the same time. Besides, queens don't disappear when they die. They'd have been there. And old fairy queens' hatches produce significantly less nectar over time. Has your production dropped? Mine has, but not too badly."

"Not enough to worry about. How old is your queen, anyway?" Sierra asked him.

He glanced at her, eyebrows high. She couldn't remember the last time she asked a question about his fairy. Her unhappiness as a keeper was the only source of tension between them, given how much he loved being one.

"I'm not sure, but I don't think very old. It's only a feeling I have, though."

Corbin's queen found him when he was eight and watching clouds in the meadow. He had told Sierra that bonding to his fairy was the most amazing moment of his life. "To know this magical creature wanted to be near me, always, and share her life with me... Oh, Sierra,

I don't know how it doesn't make you so happy to be a keeper!"

Maybe it was because her fairy didn't come for her until she was ten. For years before then, Jack tried to force Sierra to bond with any fairy queen, though it was rare for a queen to fly through the area. He sent her out for days at a time anyway, refusing to let her back in the house until she could show him a queen, tame to her hand. He was ready for her to earn her place, to earn him money. She was even relieved the day the queen arrived.

Sierra had been out feeding Sam some burnt bread pudding. She was supposed to throw it away, but Sam had a special fondness for human treats. Then she saw the glow to her left. Her heart squeezed in her chest, and her breath simply stopped. Heat flowed through her, slowly and gently, like melted chocolate pouring through her body, rising in her like floodwaters overflowing.

She walked toward the glow, out of Sam's paddock. It was a miracle she remembered to shut and lock his gate. A pulse of light fluttered in the air. The light moved into the forest, always a few feet ahead of her, leading her forward. In the darkness of twilight, she couldn't clearly see the fairy's size, but she knew she was a queen. Heavy warmth slid up and down her spine, centering at her keeper's mark. This was *her* queen. She was calling.

Sierra didn't notice the grass at her feet or the branches pulling at her hair as she walked deeper into the forest. The scents of cinnamon and honey filled her senses and gave her such peace. She held out her hand, palm open. The queen landed in Sierra's palm and looked her right in the eyes.

That was the moment a scorching heat blasted through her, searing through her keeper mark and rocking her on her heels. The sound of a thousand wings beating filled her mind for a single second that felt like an eternity. The fairy glowed incandescent, leaving Sierra's eyes burning but unable to close. Then the whole earth seemed to shake its head and return to normal. Thrilled to her toes, she ran home to tell Jack and Phoebe. Sierra thought bonding to her queen would make her life better. Maybe she could be as happy as Corbin always was.

She didn't realize what Jack's plans really were until he started ordering her to take too much of the nectar too often. When she realized he was using a fairy's magic for his own gain, to addict all those people, she tried to refuse, but no one refused Jack for long.

The thought made Sierra's shoulders hunch.

"Hey, what's going on in there?" Corbin tapped the side of her head.

"I was remembering when Queen first came."

He nodded, "You were so excited at first." Sadness

shadowed his eyes. "I wish things were easier for you, Sierra, I really do."

A lump gathered in her throat. She swallowed hard.

Luckily, Corbin always knew how to lift her mood. "Hey, do you remember when our queens first met? When the bottleflowers first started blooming in my garden? They played together all day, like romping puppies playing chase."

"Yeah, and we chased them all the way to the bank. Then we tripped and landed in the river."

Corbin smiled. "Phoebe laughed for days at the river moss still stuck in your hair."

He chuckled and pretended as if he were checking for moss in her hair.

Sierra swatted his hand away, but she couldn't restrain her own smile. "She still teases me about that."

Nell stomped by them and called out, "Wasting daylight."

Corbin gazed after her, his eyes running up and down Nell's figure. Then his gaze flicked back to Sierra, and he flushed. He spent an achingly awkward moment pretending to fix a strap on his pack before racing after their quickly disappearing companion.

Sierra was so shocked she actually couldn't move for a moment. Corbin thought Nell was attractive. Many of the men in her father's alchemy crew looked at Nell like that, as something to be desired. But Corbin? And Nell? They couldn't be more different.

An utterly ridiculous jealousy tore through Sierra. It wasn't that she wanted Corbin to look at her like that, not at all, but she didn't like him liking Nell. She wasn't good enough for him.

Of course, at the age of fifteen, Corbin was certainly old enough to court a girl, but Sierra desperately didn't want him to pick the one girl on Aluvia who hated her. He wouldn't want to be her friend if he became Nell's sweetheart.

Sierra kicked a rock as she went and sidled up beside them without saying a word. A faint thought floated through her head for a moment, like smoke from a distant campfire. Maybe one day, someone, somewhere would look at her and want her like that... one day... if she ever got out of this life... but she shook her head even harder. That wasn't something she would probably ever have.

The smell of ocean surf and dead fish floated on the breeze as they neared Port Mabon, the nearest port after their own. There was no fairy keeper here, so they would pause only long enough to eat.

Nell said, "I know a good place."

She led them to a tavern on the water's edge, a two-story wooden building that leaned over the water as if looking for a fish to catch. Sierra hoped no earthquake hit while they were here. The rickety tavern looked like it might tip straight into the water.

When they entered The Lost Dog, Sierra's eyes took a minute to adjust to the darkness within. Lanterns hung from the ceiling, but they were set to lower levels than were normally found at reputable locations. Nell was murmuring something to the barkeep. A belated thought turned Sierra's stomach. Jack never had only one purpose. She took a careful sniff, and yes, it was there: the sickly sweet fermenting fruit scent of the elixir known as Flight.

This bar was a Flight den, an unofficial safe place for those who wanted to spend their hours dreaming and sleeping in a back room somewhere. Once Jack had a reliable source of nectar through Sierra, he had ramped up his production and began spreading his reach.

Nell exchanged a simple brown-wrapped package for some coins, and Sierra threw down her bag, disgusted.

"That's it. Jack's made me run Flight after all."

Corbin whispered, "Can we get arrested? We didn't do anything."

She shook her head. "It's illegal, but since most village elders enjoy it, too, everyone pretends they don't see a thing when Jack and his crew are in town."

What she didn't say out loud was that frequent use left most people really compliant. For village elders, a nicely numb, complacent village meant little trouble for them. They had many reasons to turn a blind eye.

Sierra got in Nell's face. "We can't stay here. You didn't tell me this was a den."

Nell leaned down a little to meet her nose to nose. The white flecks in Nell's pale blue eyes made them look like winter. "This is business, Sierra. You can hate your father's life all you want, but I'm working a job here and you *will not mess it up*."

With each word, Nell jabbed her in the shoulder

Sierra clenched her fists until crescent marks cut into her palm. She traced the bruise along her jaw. "Is this your idea of a good boss, then?"

Nell retorted with a harsh voice too low for anyone else in the tavern to hear, "You have no idea what you're talking about."

Corbin slid between them. "Ladies, calm down. We need to eat."

He put a hand on each of their shoulders. Sierra took a step back, out of reach. Nell appeared frozen to the ground.

Sierra stalked to a seat as close to the door as possible. The fumes from the elixir were fainter this far away. Nell ordered for them and plopped down on the oak bench across from Sierra, wordless, staring over Sierra's head like she didn't exist. Fine. Two could play at that.

The waitress, tired already with hair half-falling out

of its bun, brought the food to the table with such rapidity it was clear they knew who Sierra and Nell were.

"How can you stand it?" she whispered to Corbin. "You know what my family is, and now it's following us. Your family is a bunch of healers, by all the stars. Now we're helping out Jack in spite of ourselves."

Corbin said with uncharacteristic practicality, "They'd get it anyway, Sierra. You know that better than most, I guess. No one will stop an addict. The same people come to my parents over and over for healings, people who can't stop using elixirs or ale until they're sick. But this isn't about them. This trip is for our queens."

Sierra hung her head. "I know. I just hate it."

"And that's one reason I love you," Corbin said.

He glanced at Nell, who remained silent, back stiff. They ate in silence. The fish was fried golden and so hot it burned Sierra's fingertips. Salty potato fries tingled on her tongue, and fresh water helped wash away the morning's hike. They wiped grease from their chins and left without paying. Nell said it would set a bad precedent for Jack. And whatever Nell handed over was assuredly worth more to the tavern than three plates of fried fish. Sierra tried not to let it bother her. There was nothing she could do, and she had a hard enough job already.

A storm was coming; Sierra could smell it as they left

the fishing village. The green scent of rain rode on the wind that picked up until Nell's braid lifted from her shoulders as it gusted.

Corbin's old keeper lived a short distance beyond the next port, about a two hour hike along the rocky shoreline. Thick clouds were rolling in, their bottoms bulging black. Sierra sighed. The best they could do was hope they were near some shelter when the clouds burst.

CHAPTER EIGHT

Naturally, shelter was too far for Sierra, Nell and Corbin to reach before the rain began. It sprinkled before they could reach even the outskirts of Port Beltane, the drops lightly dotting the ground. Soon, the drizzle became a heavy downpour. Sierra's wonderful fur boots squished as she walked along the red dirt path that became slippery and slick as wet glass. Remaining upright took intense concentration.

Nell scouted ahead for any place to get them out of the downpour. Corbin slipped and slid along the melted path, laughing at the absurdity of the situation. Even in this horrible moment, he could find something to laugh at. Finally, Sierra saw an outline against the rain, waving them forward.

She double-timed it to where Nell stood, pointing to

a little overhang near where the cliffs began by the shoreline. It wasn't quite a cave, more like a giant's thumbprint in the wall. It was way too close to the cliff's edge, where waves crashed against the rocks below.

Then thunder boomed around them and solved any question about trying to find a different hiding spot.

The trio packed in the way fisherman packed their fish in barrels. Corbin was in the middle—Sierra wasn't sure if that was intentional. Sierra had to face a little away from them, standing somewhat sideways; otherwise, the run-off from the top of the overhang would pour down her sleeve. The sheet of rain was five inches in front of her face, even with them backed all the way in. Still, crowding into this tiny spot beat walking on muddy roads in such a deluge. The steam of their breath hung in the chilly air.

Lightning flashed nearby, and a crash of thunder made the ground shiver. Sierra froze. It felt like a quake. A quake under a tiny shelf of dirt and grass, near the edge of a sea cliff. She reached out and grabbed Corbin's hand, right next to hers. He knew her fears, knew how long the loss of that family in the quake had haunted her.

"It's only the thunder, Sierra," he said.

Sierra wasn't so sure. There'd been so many quakes lately. She kept her body poised, ready to dive out of the cave, but as the thunder continued, the ground trembled only slightly. No jarring cracks, no sudden drops.

"Is that your keeper mark then, Corbin? I've never seen one this close." Nell's voice was magnified in the tiny alcove. It sounded like she was whispering right in Sierra's ear instead of Corbin's.

His body stiffened next to Sierra's, and she looked over her shoulder at them. Nell's finger hovered right next to his skin, pulling down the neck of his jacket slightly. Corbin wore his shaggy black hair cropped short enough at the neck that his mark was easily visible. He nodded and tilted his head so she could get a better view. Sierra gritted her teeth.

Nell would never get that response from Sierra. Her long hair kept her mark mostly covered even when braided, and she was glad. Their keeper marks looked pretty much the same though: a pale pink birthmark that looked like a set of fairy wings imprinted right at the base of the neck. Nothing spectacular: solid, pale pink wings, rather plain. His had more orange than Sierra's, but then, his skin was naturally darker than hers, too. If she didn't know better, Sierra would say it was a random birthmark. But when everyone with the same birthmark in the same place ended up with the same kind of magical creature coming calling, it ceased to be a coincidence.

"It must be pretty special, knowing you have that kind of important purpose," Nell whispered, voice less grudging than usual.

She lowered her hand, and Corbin's breath let out

like a sigh. The warmth of his breath brushed Sierra's skin, causing her hair to tickle her cheek. She dropped his hand and faced away, staring out into the rain. When could they get out of there?

This was too small a space for all three of them.

CHAPTER NINE

By the time the rain stopped, night had fallen. When they finally stumbled into Port Beltane, they found the first inn. Only two rooms were available.

Nell interrupted Sierra's own mental planning. "I've got orders to bunk wherever you go, Sierra."

Ah yes. Enforcer was Nell's title for a reason. So she and Sierra retired to a six-by-six room with a smoking fireplace putting out little heat. One thin straw pallet rested on the floor, not even raised off the ground. A small oil lamp hung on the wall of their room, and the door had a bolt lock on the inside. She was glad to see it. At home, she never had to worry about someone breaking in. Jack's reputation was enough to make any thief think twice.

Nell unloaded her bows and arrows, her knives, her

sword, ignoring Sierra entirely. Sierra set her wet clothes on a flat rack next to the fire, hoping for the best. Nell dried and polished her weapons with a professionalism that surprised Sierra, but she realized it shouldn't have. Nell was good at what she set her mind to. It was too bad her mind was set on following Jack's commands. They got ready for bed in silence.

"You might as well fall asleep," Nell said, sitting down next to the door, sword across her lap. "I'll sleep right here."

Tired of feeling like a prisoner, Sierra snapped, "Look, I have to get a queen back to Jack. It doesn't serve me any purpose to run away now. Do you think I'd do that to Phoebe?"

Nell matched Sierra's glare, but nodded once in acknowledgement, "Fine. But I still need to keep guard. If I let anything happen to you, your father will kill me."

She wasn't joking, either. After all, and buying nectar from others was pricey, and there weren't many keepers around who would cooperate. None of Corbin's fairy nectar went to Flight; it went to improving people's lives with the healers. When properly prepared, fairy nectar helped people sleep during surgeries and relax during treatments. Corbin overlooked her role in her father's business because he knew she had no choice.

Still, the girls' conversation seemed to have lessened the weight in the room, and Sierra was able to lie down without too much awkwardness. She didn't have a choice now either. Nell could sit there if she wanted. None of it mattered. Sierra had to save Phoebe, no matter what it took.

And she would.

In the morning, Sierra awoke to total darkness. For a split second, she wondered where she was, before her memories came flooding back. *Phoebe.* Her face flashed behind Sierra's eyes and she was up, out of bed, ready to pound on Corbin's door to wake him.

According to Corbin, the keeper's home was on the far edge of the small village that clung to the edge of the port. He figured they should reach him within an hour. They didn't even stop to eat, but nibbled on bread and dried venison from their packs as they walked.

They followed the trail as it wound up the sea cliff away from the busy wharf activity. A few blossoms of purple sea clover and frilly white water mint dotted the ground, adding their sharp, crisp tang to the salty air.

The land atop the bluff sprawled before them flat and bare, full of sand, tall grasses, and chunky rocks. Fairies lived here? In an open place like this?

"I thought fairies preferred the forest," she said to Corbin.

"Oh, no," he told her, leaning closer, eyes bright.

Sierra felt a fairy lecture on the horizon. Good thing she needed one.

"Fairies can live in any kind of environment, really. As long as there are flowers and some other kind of vegetable matter to eat, they'll be okay. Even deserts have cactuses with flowers. Wild fairies supposedly came from the Skyclad Mountains originally and whole sections of that mountain range are just rocks and grass, not a tree in sight. Snow covers the top for a lot of the year, too."

"Really?" Sierra asked. She had heard about the year-round snow-covered mountaintops, but she hadn't believed the stories. The Skyclad Mountains were where grumpy adults threatened to send misbehaving children, as in, "Go to bed, or I'll take you to the Skyclad Mountains and leave you there in the snow for the dragons to get." "It's true," Corbin assured her. "Keeper Hannon told me."

The keeper's little house sat on top of the cliff, all by itself, a jaunty shade of blue with a roof that looked like a giant dropped it on slightly off-center. Corbin walked to the door and knocked, but no one answered.

He jogged around the side of the house and returned moments later at a full sprint.

Sierra's stomach plummeted. "Are they dead, too?"

"Yeah, all of them, with the queen missing… again." He dropped to his knees, and she waited for his tears, but they didn't come. His dark eyes were wild but dry.

"He's got to know why this is happening! We're going to find him!" And with this declaration, Corbin took off, gravel from the path spraying behind him.

Nell and Sierra exchanged a look and chased after him. They retraced their steps back into the village, their feet slapping the hard dirt path. Corbin didn't stop to rest, so neither did the girls. Sierra developed a stitch in her side, and the cold air burned her throat. Nell didn't look winded at all, and Sierra was about to grumble about that, but then she saw where Corbin had led them.

They were at a tavern at the very edge of town. Specifically, they were about to enter another Flight den. The Spider's Web never closed. Jack had bragged about this one for months, so pleased he was still able to establish a hot spot here though the old keeper refused to work for him.

Before Sierra could protest, Corbin had pushed his way through the doors. The dull roar of conversation and music from the early lunch crowd poured through before the doors swung shut, cutting off the noise as if it had never been there.

Heat rose in her cold cheeks as she thought about going in there, the daughter of the man who supplied them with their illegal elixir. But Corbin needed them with him. These people might not recognize her by sight at least, not two ports over. Nell was already opening the doors.

Sierra stepped through after her, and the heat of the bar wrapped around her like a blanket, making her frozen nose and fingertips throb. The pungent scent of fried onions hung in the air, against the backdrop of the too-sweet smell of Flight she expected. By the time her eyes adjusted to the darkness, Corbin was already speaking to someone at the old wooden bar that sliced across the back of the building, gesturing wildly with his hands. Never a good sign.

Nell pushed through the throngs of bodies without difficulty, Sierra slipping along behind her. Corbin's voice rose before they reached him. "But you've got to have some idea!"

He was practically wailing. It wasn't like Corbin to create a disturbance. The man in question seemed to have placed all his hopes in the bottom of a bottle. He leaned at a sharp angle over the bar, steepling his hands against his forehead. Nell sat next to him. He squinted one eye, then the other, attempting to focus on the blonde girl next to him and failing. Instead, he swiveled his head toward Corbin, eyebrows raised high. Sierra saw a keeper mark on the man's leathery, wrinkled neck.

This had to be Keeper Hannon.

CHAPTER TEN

"This is Nell, and this is Sierra." Corbin introduced them to the drunken keeper without any of the usual formality. "Sierra's a keeper, too."

Keeper Hannon sat up a bit straighter and faced her. He peered into Sierra's face and then leaned back, as if he saw a rattlesnake.

"I told your father I would not help him!" he said as he hauled his arm back and threw his now-empty ale glass at her. "Is this his punishment?"

Sierra hopped back. The glass thudded at her feet. A few people looked their way. Great. So much for slipping through unrecognized.

Corbin's great mentor slid off the seat, boneless, but Corbin caught him on the way down. "Please! We need to know what could have caused this…"

More heads turned their way.

Heat climbed up Sierra's neck as the old man glared at her, as if she'd murdered his only child. She supposed he thought she had, in a manner of speaking.

He pointed a wobbly finger at Sierra. "I won't talk to her, daughter of the man who bleeds fairies dry for his own profit."

Shame and fury bled together in Sierra, but she nodded. "I can't do anything about Jack. If you'll help us, though, we'll get the queens back. But we don't even know where to start looking."

The old man smashed his lips together, saying nothing. Fury won out over shame, and she stepped forward until they were nose to nose. A drunk old fool would not trap her sister in a far away city to live as an elixir runner. The fumes of the alcohol in his breath stung her eyes, but she didn't blink.

Sierra cast about for anything that could get the keeper to talk. The words came out without hesitation, even though they made her want to gag. "If you don't help us, I'll be sure to tell Jack what you think about him."

Nell inhaled sharply, reminding Sierra she had a guard. She grabbed onto another idea. Yes, she would use the enforcer to the best effect.

"See this lovely lady?" Sierra pointed to Nell.

His eyes whirled in their sockets before settling on Nell's grim expression.

"She works for my dear father. She's his enforcer. Any idea what that means?" Sierra's voice had turned as sickly sweet as the fumes floating down the stairs.

Corbin looked at her with eyes wide with shock, but desperation propelled her further. She gestured at her bruise. "Like it? Want one? Nell here can help you out, but it'd be better if you'd tell us on your own."

The old keeper spat in Sierra's face. Nell grabbed her arm, and it was only then she realized she had raised her hand to backhand him. Like Jack did to her.

She was just like Jack.

The heat of the room suffocated her, and her stomach turned at the rank odor of onions and meat. She raced out the door. The cold air should have set steam off her body. She took in great gasping breaths, her ears ringing outside in the relative silence of the port town. The wharfs were too far away to be heard, other than occasionally muffled shouts.

Shame blossomed inside at the memory of what she almost did to a helpless drunk, someone in mourning for his queen, someone who was a proper keeper. She took a deep breath and slowly let it out.

Gazing at the sky, she swore an oath to herself in that moment. She wouldn't travel the world the way Jack would. She wouldn't manipulate others and take from them without considering the consequences. Jack might have control of her life, but she wouldn't give him control of her soul.

Nell and Corbin stepped out of the doors, carrying the man between them. His head was lolling.

Nell shook her head and said, "Just dead drunk."

Could be worse. "Do you have any goldenrod roots?"

The older girl smirked. "In my line of work?"

Twenty minutes later, the poor keeper was vomiting up his past hour's worth of alcohol. The smell made Sierra's throat tight, but Nell kept eyeing her, so she stood there, shoulders back. Corbin held up the keeper's head, despite being a light shade of green himself. Keeper Hannon groaned.

"I bet he has some mint leaves back in his garden, if we carry him home. It might... help," Corbin suggested.

"Good idea," Sierra said. She'd just as soon not watch—or smell—the keeper get sick again, but going to his house would also allow them to question him privately.

Nearly two hours later, they were all tucked inside his little cottage, holding mint tea. Sierra sat on the other side of the room—it seemed best—but Corbin spoke plenty loud, and the room wasn't too big in the first place.

"So you are saying the wild fairies, if there are still some around, would be in the Skyclad Mountains?"

"As in, the place people go to die?" Nell looked disbelieving.

The old keeper laughed softly. That laugh raised the hair on the back of Sierra's neck.

He said, "I found my queen there. I went seeking her and nearly died for my trouble. Wild fairies are quite different than the ones bred in captivity, but they were still drawn to me. There aren't enough domesticated queens born anymore, and fewer every year. I tried to warn people about it years ago, but—"

"So you're saying there aren't enough fairies for all the keepers?" Nell looked over at Sierra, as if to make sure she was catching this.

Shock tied Sierra to her seat. Fewer and fewer fairies... so... some born with keeper marks might be unable to even find a fairy queen to bond with? She'd never heard of such a thing. Did that have anything to do with their missing queens?

Sierra felt torn. One part of her wanted so desperately to be free. She'd volunteer in a second to be an unbound keeper, even if it meant always feeling incomplete. The other half of her knew if she got her wish right now, Phoebe was doomed. That was no choice at all.

"What's the best way to get up the mountains?" Sierra called across the room. Her voice cut through the lower voices of Keeper Hannon and Corbin.

Everyone looked at her like she had suggested they chop off their own heads.

Nell said, "It's about a week's journey to get to the base. I have no idea how long it'd take to actually hike up that thing. That's cutting it real close to your deadline, don't you think? Not to mention manticores, griffins, and any other weird and magical creature out there likely to hunt us."

Sierra leaned forward in her chair. "Who says we've got to go all the way to the top? As soon as we find a queen, we'll be out of there. Besides, no one's seen any of those wild magical creatures in years, except the occasional griffin. Everyone knows that merfolk, unicorns, and fairies are only still around because we care for them."

Keeper Hannon scoffed at this answer, obviously in disagreement. "Caring for merfolk? By keeping them in chains? Treating unicorns like beasts of burden? Using fairies to cultivate nectar for elixirs and healing droughts, all for us humans? That's caring for them?"

Sierra wished she had a witty response or a clear-cut answer, but she didn't. Everything Keeper Hannon said was true. Those things squelched in her belly like a meal gone sour. Confusion swirled through her, but one thought remained clear: Phoebe needed Sierra to bring home a queen. That was all that mattered.

She risked walking closer to the keeper because she needed to look in his eyes when he answered her next question. "Why do you think the queens are gone?"

The old man sighed. "I think they left because there wasn't enough magic for them here."

He was wasting her time with that nursery rhyme

business. "Fairies make magic. How could they not have enough?"

Keeper Hannon sat back to explain, as though settling in for a long tale. Sierra decided she had come this far. She might as well hear him out.

He said, "Listen carefully. The world needs magic to sustain it, correct?"

They all stared back at him with blank expressions. He spoke as if they should know this. Sierra sure didn't.

Keeper Hannon growled and burst out, "What are they teaching you in school these days? Corbin, I know I told you this. Bah! Yes, the world needs magic. It's what holds the fabric of the world together. Fairies exude magic simply by living, as do other magical creatures. But fairies are special in that they make more magic than they need. They then spread it throughout the world through the nectar that drips from them wherever they go."

Sierra scowled. This was news to her. How could she not know such a thing if it were true? It was literally her job to understand her fairies in order to keep them healthy.

He continued, "They only consume their own nectar to replenish their magic when they are overworking, usually. In winter, when the magic of the earth is deep and quiet, they will use their nectar then, too. But in the other three seasons, they spread magic all the time. Or should be. We keep taking their nectar all the time, so they keep producing. And producing. They never have enough for themselves, much less enough to spread to others. What if there's not enough magic left for them here or left for them to give to the world? What if instead of keeping them safe, we've worked them to death as a species and the queens have abandoned us? What do you think will happen to the world then?"

Sierra felt an unexpected pang at the word *abandoned*, but she shook her head. "That's ridiculous. We don't all *need* magic. I certainly don't. And my hatch was still producing nectar, even if it was slightly less. We all have bad days. Wasn't yours still producing?"

Keeper Hannon replied, "Yes, but consider how many keepers are taking too much of the fairies' nectar. Not only alchemists of all kinds, but the healers use buckets of it. That nectar is supposed to replenish the magic in the world, but we keep stealing it without giving anything back. Why not return to where they came from? The Skyclad Mountains supposedly are where magic first began. Maybe there's more magic there. If I were a fairy, I'd get out of a life of slavery before it killed me, wouldn't you?"

Slavery. It was a word Sierra had thought applied to her life. But how did you enslave a bunch of insect-like creatures? How was that slavery? It wasn't... was it? Sierra cared for her fairies, fed Queen, cleaned the hatch, guarded their nectar from other humans, and watched out for predators.

Then images flashed through her mind faster than a fairy's flight: her little fairies glowing an angry red as she took more and more nectar, Queen batting at her like a fish beating against a net, Queen gazing through the forest as if looking for something she'd lost. Sierra remembered the pulling pain she could feel during those times, pain she could have sworn actually came from Queen herself somehow. The haunting memories made Sierra shudder. The tiniest part of her wondered if the old keeper was onto something, but she had a mission.

Keeper Hannon knew nothing about the why, nothing but his own wild opinions, but he knew how to get to the mountains. That was what she needed to know. Her pulse picked up, and she smiled.

For the first time, Sierra admitted to herself she hadn't been so sure, deep down, she was going to be able to succeed in her mission. Now she had a real shot. Keeper Hannon didn't want to talk to her. Everyone, though, talked to Corbin. Not because he threatened or threw a fit. They talked because he listened, and he listened because he cared. It was one of his greatest gifts.

Sierra didn't have the emotional energy to care about the man or his queen or the world getting drained of magic. She didn't even care that she didn't care. She cared about her sister and getting the job done. The old keeper would know that, and he might not share everything. She slid out of the room, leaving Corbin to be his usual charming self. Nell stayed with him.

Sierra stepped outside again and walked around to where the back of his house sat, close to the edge of the cliff.

Her shoulders dropped. They'd been hovering near her ears a lot. Her head only ached a little today, though her bruise was still yellow and green. Her lungs expanded all the way. She took another deep breath, and even the cold was refreshing instead of biting. Then a low rumble shivered the air.

CHAPTER ELEVEN

Sierra snapped her head up to scan the clouds. As close to the water as they were, lightning was a real risk.

The sound rolled through the air again, and this time the ground shuddered against her feet. Her heart hurt like someone was squeezing it in their too-tight fist. The lungs that had been breathing without effort suddenly cramped. She scuttled backward off the rock, away from the edge of the cliff. The image of the family's house collapsing like a deck of cards flashed behind her eyes, and she squeezed her eyes shut for a second before running for the others.

"Corbin! Nell!" She sprinted flat out and slid as she reached the doorway, grabbing hold of the frame. She slammed open the door but couldn't take another step.

The ground trembled again, longer this time, and

Nell raced around the corner of the hallway of the house, face pale. "Stay there!"

Sierra had no choice. The ground was shaking now, cracks running along the jittering dirt, and she dropped to her knees and put her arms over her head and neck. Another quake this soon...

Sierra moaned into her hands. She wasn't afraid of much, but earthquakes were it. Sweat slicked her palms. When Corbin touched her shoulder, she realized the ground had already stopped moving. Dirt clung to her face as she sat up, and she flushed at Nell's expression. In response, Sierra glared at the bigger girl, anger and shame fighting inside.

The tension between the girls grew, but as much as Sierra would have liked to be the toughest one, she couldn't stand without help. Corbin squatted beside her and hugged her for a minute. She inhaled his scent, the honey-cinnamon she also often smelled like. Job hazard. It wasn't the same too-sweet smell of the elixir, though. In its natural state, nectar was the perfect blend of sweet and tangy.

"Did you find out what we needed?" she asked, close to Corbin's face as he leaned down to help her stand.

He turned his face to answer her, accidentally brushing their lips together. A jolt rushed through Sierra, unexpected. She didn't know boys had soft lips. So soft and warm, but she wasn't interested in Corbin's lips. She really didn't think he was interested in hers, either. She froze, as did he. So did Nell, who stood behind Corbin. His eyes were huge, the clear amber of a forest floor.

"S-s-sorry," he stuttered and nearly dropped Sierra as if she were scalding. He nodded quickly, striving to act like all was normal as he stepped back.

An insane urge to burst into laughter gripped Sierra, but she didn't want to offend her sweet friend.

He cleared his throat. "Yes, we know where to go." He paused. "Right, Nell?"

Nell's lips were tight. Two bright red spots stained her cheeks. A new understanding swept over Sierra as she looked between the two of them. All of Nell's antagonism toward Corbin was a cover-up. Tough enforcer Nell liked Corbin, too. Sierra wondered how long Nell had harbored secret affection for him.

"Right," Nell said in a gruff voice. She pushed past them and walked up the path.

Corbin offered their goodbyes to the keeper, jogged up the trail, and began speaking to Nell. She didn't look at him, only stared straight ahead. Sierra's mind whirled like she had realized west was actually east.

She didn't know how she'd get along in life without Corbin, but if Nell and Corbin became a couple, it wasn't likely he'd be hanging around much anymore. The thought was almost as frightening as considering the journey ahead of them, in the cold mountains full of dangerous creatures. She threw herself into the preparations.

In what was left of the day, they used up all of their coins buying provisions for their trip down in the port. After a quick supper, they returned to set up a simple camp at the far edge of the keeper's land before the sun set.

Wrapped tightly in her bedroll, Sierra felt like a wooden puppet, unable to relax. The word *slavery* whispered through her mind again, turning her stomach. Slavery. *Ugh.* The ocean waves crashed against the cliff wall louder here than at home, but the familiar melody was enough to soothe her to sleep.

The next morning, they set off early. By midmorning, they were far enough for the salty tang of the ocean to have faded from the air. When the sun sat high overhead, they left the road, trekking away from civilization. All but a few towns and villages in Aluvia followed the coastline.

The rocks of the cliffs smoothed to flat grass plains, with a few trees spearing up into the sky here and there. The brown, tall grasses reached their hips at times.

The first night in the true wilderness was the hardest. There was no nearby house to run to if they needed it. They cleared a small area of the meadow to lie down in, tearing up handfuls of the dried and brittle stems.

Nell's campfire offered only a sullen red glow by the

time they turned in for the night. Like the night before, they lay down like the points of a triangle, each of them as far as they could get from the others while still being near the fire. Sierra had camped out in their meadows many times, but that wasn't the same as sleeping unprotected outdoors on the cold ground far from home. Every snapping twig made her jump.

Sierra hoped Phoebe would sleep better than this tonight at home, wondering if their pallet felt too big with only one person in it. A few rocks dug into Sierra's back, and she wished for her old lumpy pallet. She closed her eyes even though she'd probably never sleep. An owl hooted nearby, and she smiled. That owl would eat most critters that might dare enter their sleeping area. Her muscles bellowed at her, but nothing could stop sleep from claiming her.

She woke up disoriented. She couldn't remember where she was for a long moment, or why she was lying on her back in a grassy field. Then everything rushed back, and it was like ten bags of flour falling onto her chest. The fire had died, and frost lined the ground. A need to go to the bathroom, though, forced her from her warm cocoon. She didn't change clothes at night anymore, so all she had to do was slide on her boots, safely inside the foot of her bedroll, and tromp out to a private distance from the camp. Each step Sierra took made her legs scream.

When Sierra returned to camp, she found Corbin

stretching and wiping his eyes. He grimaced as he stood, and dark satisfaction shot through her. Nell, though, seemed comfortable as she slid out of her bag and didn't twinge or stretch.

As they continued on their journey though, her muscles warmed up, and the pain faded some. There wasn't a lot of talk: strained silences between Corbin and Sierra, glares between Sierra and Nell, awkward silence between Corbin and Nell. Even the land around them was quiet, save for the wind.

There were no villages this far away from the ocean ports, and even wildlife seemed sparse. Sierra wondered if the animals knew something they didn't about the forest ahead of them. She shivered. She wished there were some other place to look for the fairies.

As the sun traveled across the sky, it reminded Sierra of what she'd be doing at home. She wondered how Phoebe was doing without her.

When the sun began to sink, an unexpected twinge of panic grabbed Sierra. She hadn't collected nectar at all in three days. The last two days had been so busy, she hadn't really noticed the missing part of her routine, but walking all day in nature forced her to face reality. Her heart thumped heavily. It was an irrational response, since of course there was no nectar to collect. But she'd spent the last four years of her life collecting nectar daily, making sure she finished her afternoon collection by twilight to minimize damage to herself when fairies returned to the hatch for the night. It felt strange to hike along for days without caring for them. Her fingers began to itch to go collecting.

Despite the awkwardness, she had to ask.

"Uh, Corbin?"

He waited for her to catch up to his side, looking at her only out of the corner of his eyes.

"Do you feel... strange... not having collected nectar? I keep thinking I'm forgetting something important..."

He looked relieved and faced her, stopping in his tracks. He smacked his forehead. "Yes! That's *it*! All afternoon, it's been like in school when you sort of remember an assignment but can't remember when it's due!"

"At least it's not just me. I was feeling a bit crazy," she admitted.

"See, you think you don't like your fairy, but you care more than you think." Corbin never missed a chance to drive home his frequent point. Then he reached to tug Sierra's braid, but his hand faltered partway through. He dropped his arm awkwardly as he glanced at Nell tapping her foot impatiently.

"Uh, thanks for figuring out what was bothering me, Sierra," he said. He stared at the ground for a moment before moving on.

A compulsion to collect nectar didn't mean she adored her fairy, but she'd already told him that a thousand times. He obviously didn't want to keep talking, much less about something they'd always disagreed on.

She noticed he didn't call her little sister, or squirt, and any of his many nicknames, either. Could he have forgotten all their times together? Not all were fun and games, either.

Once, Corbin's mother caught the sea trade pox two years ago, a very serious illness. By the time she caught it, she had already used up their own supplies of medicine treating others with the disease. Sierra worked with Corbin all day and night to gather enough of the right herbs to help his mother survive, and then helped during her recuperation.

Corbin's distant behavior now stung worse than a fairy bite.

Nell and Corbin walked a little ahead of Sierra, who turned her mind to solving the problem of the missing fairies. The fact that no fairies had harassed or flirted with two keepers traveling together suggested, more than anything she'd heard, that all fairies had been affected. Maybe Keeper Hannon was on to something.

Then a new realization blew through her—she and Phoebe could run away! No fairies would give their whereabouts away with their flittering, squealing, pinching presence. Sierra nearly froze at the magnitude of the realization, shocked that it was just now occurring to her, but she kept moving, not wanting to attract Nell's attention. It wasn't an ideal solution, because Jack would search hard for them. His pride would demand it. Phoebe didn't deserve a life on the run if they could figure out something better. Still, she tucked the thought into her heart and used it to keep warm when the dark thoughts inevitably came of what would happen if she didn't find a fairy to trade for her sister's life.

CHAPTER TWELVE

*E*ach day blurred into the next as the mountains filled more of the horizon. The trio made good time. Sierra missed Corbin's upbeat chatty nature, though he finally loosened up enough to describe what kind of creatures they could expect along the way. After all, he'd read every scroll and book in his village on magical creatures and the natural world.

The scent of dry meadow grass blended with the sweet zing of pine needles from the sporadic trees that began to appear. In the distance, the Skyclad Mountains looked like hands reaching out to grab the clouds. Sierra's anxiety ratcheted higher each time the sun set on another day without her sister.

She woke up less and less sore as time went on, but her sleep became less and less restful the closer they got to the jagged peaks ahead. Every night when Sierra slept now, she dreamed wild, vivid dreams about her fairies. Sometimes Phoebe was there, too, and Corbin and even Nell, but Queen was always there, calling to her.

Her dreams were full of blazing reds and oranges, zipping lights of color that made her dizzy. She woke groggy and disoriented.

Corbin still acted strangely around Sierra, leaving her uncertain how to bring up such a bizarre topic as her dreams. She certainly had no intentions of confiding in Nell, either. Nell and Corbin's stilted silence with each other had been replaced with soft chatting about all manner of things. Turned out they both enjoyed hearing the fiddle players down at The Sweet and Sour, an old tavern on the wharfs of Port Ostara. They both loved fried pickles. And hey, what did they know, they both loved a good thunderstorm. Their slowly growing interest in each other would have been sweet to see, had it been anyone but those two. As it was, it was downright depressing. But as long as Phoebe wasn't sent to Bentwood's, Sierra could survive anything.

Six days after leaving Keeper Hannon's, the mountains loomed close. Food had to stretch thinner already, though. Every day, Corbin ate like a mountain giant—which, thankfully, they hadn't actually seen any of.

"Did you eat the last of the dove?" Nell asked in disbelief.

Corbin froze mid-chew and smiled like a little boy

with his hand caught in the cookie jar. Nell couldn't stay mad at him, either. Normally, Sierra would have teased him for his bottomless pit of a stomach, but with his odd behavior, she swallowed the words. She'd been doing that a lot, but all those swallowed words and jokes couldn't fill up her stomach.

Sierra did her best to ignore the rumbling and not take seconds. The food had to last. She thought of Phoebe until it hurt too much, then debated when would be best to run away with her. Now that Sierra had met Keeper Hannon, she wondered if he would be open to helping them escape Jack, given how much the older man loathed her father.

The days passed slowly; they hadn't sighted any fairies. No other magical creatures, for that matter. But surely the fairies would be in the mountains, like Keeper Hannon had said.

Two or three more days remained to reach the base. This morning, when Sierra awoke, she swore she tasted cinnamon honey nectar, but she must have imagined it. Sweat clung to her hairline despite the chilly air, and a kaleidoscope of rainbow fairies danced in her mind from her dreams. The memories of brilliant fairy lights seemed almost more real than the scraggy, cold-frosted bushes along the ground. She staggered as she walked, and Nell paused to take a closer look. Sierra lifted her chin and pressed on. She could keep up with Nell, despite being smaller.

Phoebe would love these strange dreams, but Sierra would go crazy if she thought about her too often now. Sierra missed her little sister, a constant ache pressing her chest, a weight that never left her.

The day passed with glacial slowness. Finally, Nell permitted them to break for the night a bit early because Corbin twisted his ankle earlier in the day. If Sierra had fallen, she knew Nell would have made everyone keep walking until sunset. Nell went to scout the area around camp for any potential dangers, leaving Corbin and Sierra alone for the first time all day.

He still acted awkward and unnatural around her, like he was afraid she would start fawning over him now. Sierra rolled her eyes. She loved him, but he had never made her face flush like he did Nell's. Nor had Sierra been bothered when he'd courted a couple of the village girls, but then, she knew they weren't good enough for him. The thing was, neither was Nell. No one was. She wondered if he knew that.

Before they got fully set up for camp, Nell returned. Corbin grinned at her arrival, and his obvious delight tripped Sierra's heart a little.

A small part of Sierra wished for someone like that, too, but she was quick to silence the thought. She didn't have room for that kind of liability. Jack would use anyone against her. Jack didn't even know how much Sierra relied on Corbin. Since they were just friends, not courting, it was easier to hide. But someone she loved one day? He'd be a pawn for her father to manipulate. No thanks. She wasn't ready for that kind of relationship yet anyway.

Sierra gathered wood for the evening fire and found a few sticks green enough to use as a spit if Nell could get a rabbit. Sierra was a decent cook, but she needed to learn how to hunt, which meant really learning how to shoot a bow. And there was only one person who could help right now. Time to swallow her pride.

"Why do you want to learn to use a bow and arrow?" Nell's suspicious look spoke volumes.

Sierra rolled her eyes. "Relax, I'm not going to shoot you in the back."

Nell laughed, confidence radiating from her. The mere thought of Sierra being a danger was apparently amusing.

Sierra clenched her teeth. "If I decide to shoot you, I'll do it to your face, and you'll see the arrow coming."

The words dropped like the opening spatters of a hailstorm, each hitting with a resounding crack.

Nell narrowed her eyes, and a flush rose on her face.

Sierra cursed her own temper. She couldn't afford to alienate Nell. Maybe logic would work better and would smooth over that last stupid comment.

"If both of us hunt, we'll get more food. Aren't you tired of being hungry?"

Nell caught something nearly every day, but between three of them, there still wasn't enough to eat. Walking all day used a lot of energy. Sierra's knowledge of edible wild plants and grasses was nearly useless this time of year. The purchased grain and way bread needed to last through the whole journey, so all three of them had been stingy with it.

Nell grimaced. She must have really been hungry, because she agreed to teach Sierra how to hunt.

They left Corbin to tend the fire. Sierra followed Nell over a small rise as she looked for a good target in the flat area. They wouldn't reach the forest, which marked the true start of the mountain, until tomorrow or the day after. A sparse cluster of trees up ahead looked like a bunch of old ladies standing around at the market, gossiping. The grass beneath them was thin and short.

"Show me what you can do," Nell said. She marched over to a tall maple about twenty feet away and pointed to a knot on the bark. "Hit that."

She held out her second bow, a redwood, smooth and deceptively simple, and an arrow. Not one of her griffin arrows, Sierra noted, but she couldn't blame her. These were simple stone arrowheads and goose feather fletching. The draw of the bow was hard, as it was built for Nell's height, not Sierra's, but it was all she had to work with.

Sierra ran her fingers along the bow, tracing whorls of deeper red in the grain of the wood. Her stomach felt like it was full of fairies about to swarm. Nell's eyes were cold, measuring, the pale blue irises looking almost silver in the low light.

Sierra widened her stance for a proper position to aim. That part had never been difficult. It was the rest she usually messed up. She wiped the sweat off her palms onto her pants and held the bow up with her left arm, elbow slightly bent, locked into place to avoid ripping the skin off the inside of her arm. She'd done that before and had no desire to repeat it. She softly curled her right pointer and middle finger around the string while holding the arrow against it and began a smooth draw back. Her arms strained a bit as she held the bow in place, the tension fighting her to release the arrow. Sighting down the arrow, she tried to imagine nothing existed except that knothole.

The arrow will go where I'm aiming, she told herself.

Taking a deep breath and holding it, Sierra let go. The arrow flew with a soft twang. Her breath rushed from her lungs, and her fingers tingled from the slide of the bowstring. She watched the knothole, but no arrow appeared. A *thawking* noise to the right drew their attention, and there was the arrow, buried in the tree beside her target. The breath whuffed out of Nell's nose, but it wasn't clear if she was irritated or amused. At least it hit something, which wasn't always the case. Sierra shook out her hand. The jitters in her stomach shifted to excitement. Okay, she'd missed, but the power in the bow was like a song in her hands. It was safety, it was freedom, it was—

"Okay, hand it back." Nell was clearly unimpressed. "We'll work on shooting again later when we have more time. Now, look at these tracks and tell me what made them. You can't hunt what you can't find."

Tracking. Sierra's stomach sank. Containing her wince of frustration, she handed the bow back and leaned down where Nell pointed. After scrutinizing the ground, Sierra did see some tracks. Made by a small creature with padded feet, not hooves, and tiny claws on the end of each toe. Nell nodded as Sierra stated her observation.

"Great, so what are we having for dinner?" Nell waited, arms crossed, toned muscles visible.

Sierra swallowed, feeling as if she were back in school with the teacher about to rap her knuckles for not knowing the answer. She shrugged, pretending indifference.

"Name something. Take a guess."

Sierra hated to guess. She'd probably be wrong. She stared at the ground, as if the answer might float up from the dirt, but she was still clueless. Forget it. Nothing was worth feeling dumb around Nell. She started to stomp away, but Nell's voice stopped her.

"Squirrel," she called, "but not like our squirrels at home. Plains squirrels are bigger. If I can get one, we'll be full tonight."

Sierra didn't turn around, but she didn't walk away, either.

"You can watch me hunt and track this one—or not. Suit yourself. I don't care."

Sierra's pride warred with her stomach, but the stomach won because in the long-run learning this skill would help her pride, too. She walked back to Nell, eyes downcast, hands clenched, not wanting to see her smirk.

"Let's go," Sierra said.

CHAPTER THIRTEEN

Sierra studied Nell's feet as she tracked the prints, the careful way she placed each step. She barely made a stick crackle or a leaf sigh as she moved, which was unnerving to watch. Someone so tall should make more noise.

When Nell froze, Sierra did the same.

Silently, Nell whipped the bow off her back. She nocked an arrow, drew, and shot, all in the blink of an eye. She strode forward, her intense expression indicating she was on high alert, trusting her senses to warn of danger. She reached down and then held up a fat animal by its legs, her arrow protruding from its back. Sierra saluted her, and the older girl made a tiny sardonic bow. Sierra's lips quirked. Nell had a sense of humor. Who knew?

"Next time I hunt, you're coming with me, and every time after that," Nell called as she walked away. Clearly, the lesson was done. But when they got back to camp, she handed Sierra a spare bow.

"Keep it on your back, strung and ready. Practice. A lot." Nell rolled her eyes.

Sierra didn't even roll her eyes back. She was too excited.

The next day, as they walked along, she practiced sighting on distant pine trees sprinkled here and there before the forest began in earnest.

Corbin watched Sierra practice that night, before the sun sank. He stayed curled up on his bedroll on the opposite side of camp while Sierra aimed at a tree fifty feet away. She released the arrow... and missed. Again.

"Gee, Sierra, I thought you'd be pretty good at shooting things. You're quick to shoot people down who argue with you, after all. Your tongue's sharper than a razor," Corbin joked.

It was the first time he had teased her since they accidentally bumped lips. Relieved, she stuck her tongue out at him, and some hurt place in her heart that had felt like an icicle finally began to thaw.

She brought out another arrow and aimed again at the tree. This time, she imagined her feet sinking deep in the earth as she stood there, eyes half closed. Relief at Corbin's normal behavior loosened something tight in her chest, and her breath came easier. Her fingertips protested as she pulled on the string—no calluses yet, so the skin was raw and sore from repeated practice. The string twanged as she released the arrow, her breath whooshing out with it. There was a solid smack, like the sound of a ripe melon hitting the ground.

She looked at Corbin, startled, who sat up in astonishment. She ran to the tree, not believing her eyes in the dim twilight. But there it was, her arrow, finally where she'd aimed. A huge grin split her face.

Before Sierra could think, she ran to Corbin, who swung her around in celebration, her feet not even touching the ground. She was just as happy to have her best friend back as she was to have hit the tree. He set her down with an exaggerated plop and offered a salute. Sierra laughed and saluted back.

He looked over her shoulder and quickly took a step back. Sierra knew who she'd see causing him to back away from her.

Slow clapping came behind her, and she reluctantly turned. Nell walked toward them, clap, clap, clapping her hands, but her face was not shiny with excitement. It was guarded.

"Nice work, Sierra," Nell stated.

Sierra bit the inside of her cheek at the chilly tone.

Nell continued, "Next I'll have to teach our friend Corbin to hunt, too."

Corbin cleared his throat. "I've thought about asking, actually. Maybe sometime you could show me, too..."

He pawed the ground with his foot like a lovesick unicorn. Sierra rolled her eyes but turned her back on them before they saw. The idea of Corbin hunting with a bow and arrow was ridiculous. He ate meat, true, but he loved animals too much to bring them down himself. Anyone who knew him understood how gentle he was.

When he was younger, he was the child who always brought home hurt animals for his parents to heal, or returned little sea crabs washed up on shore back to the water. Even as he grew older, his tender nature remained. During a collection run when he was twelve, Corbin and Sierra found a blue jay fluttering in circles on the forest floor, wings spread out, clearly hurt. He carefully checked its blue feathers, singing softly to the bird all the while. He brought the bird home, binding its wing until the strain had healed. When he set it free, the jay shot through the trees like a blue arrow. She'd never forget his proud smile. He was obviously just trying to impress Nell with this half-offer to learn to hunt.

Nell said, "Let's start now."

Guess this showed who knew the boy better, after all. Sierra smirked.

Corbin looked surprised. "Isn't it a bit dark? Shouldn't we stick close to our camp?"

Nell smiled slowly, eyes twinkling in a way Sierra

didn't know was possible. Corbin blushed. She smiled wider, and Sierra's smirk melted away.

"We can begin right here. We'll use Sierra's tree. I'll show you how to stand."

Nell stepped behind Corbin and moved him into proper position by wrapping her arms around him. If she tilted her head, she could lay it against the back of his neck. His neck appeared too tense to be a comfortable pillow, though.

Sierra chewed on the inside of her cheek and tasted the salty metal flavor of blood. She didn't have to stand right here and watch this nonsense. She went to the far edge of camp, pretending to keep watch but found herself straining to catch every stupid word they said.

She'd just get ready for bed, even if the sun wasn't all the way down. The scent of smoke curled against the sharp clean scent of pine trees. They could bank the fire... later. Sierra fought not to glance at the two bodies silhouetted against the dying light, merged so close as to look like one.

She crawled in her bedroll. She didn't care if Nell saw it as defeat. Sierra didn't begrudge Corbin happiness, but Nell carried death with her wherever she went, and shouldn't be in Corbin's life. But if she was, would Sierra lose him in hers forever?

She might have hit her target tonight, but Nell had gotten the bulls-eye. A sweetheart would always end up being more important than a best friend. At that moment, a laugh floated by that practically held little hearts and roses. *Ugh*. Sierra didn't want to hear that. She fell asleep to the murmur of their voices and told herself it didn't matter.

It didn't. Really.

CHAPTER FOURTEEN

Sierra awoke, once again, tired from chasing fairies all night in her dreams. The flavor of nectar was so strong in her mouth, she almost wondered if someone was dosing her with Flight. She'd never taken Flight itself, but all keepers occasionally got nectar on their hands and then in their mouths. She heard they tasted much the same, and there were definitely no fairies around to make nectar. The weird dreams, the tastes… but she would have hallucinations if she were being slipped the elixir. So far, the only weird things she saw during the day involved her best friend cozying up to Nell. Sierra might wish those images were hallucinations, but, too bad for her, they were reality.

The good news was Nell and Corbin didn't act particularly besotted, despite their cozy scene last night. Things could be worse. He did touch Nell's arm when he asked a question about hunting—*as if he cared about hunting, the liar, the sneak*! And he watched her so closely it was like a puppy watching its master. Nell played her feelings closer to the vest, but sometimes after he brushed by her, she blushed a delicate pink.

But even Corbin and Nell's joking and flirting dissipated as they moved toward the deeper shadow of the forest. They had been in and out of trees the whole day, the tall grasses slowly disappearing, but now they were entering the territory people feared. The Skyclad Mountains truly began here.

The trees crowded tightly together, fifty feet tall and wide as houses, as if to keep people out. An eerie silence hung in the air. The very lack of chittering wildlife made Sierra's skin crawl with goose bumps. An unnatural forest.

The three exchanged glances, survival uniting them even in the face of their tangled relationships. Ten feet into the trees, the darkness was so thick it was hard to see beyond them. As the wind wove through the branches, shifting shadows slid in and among the tree trunks. To Sierra's fevered imagination, the darkness took the form of giant bears, skeletal arms, ghostly screaming banshees. Her feet felt like boulders dragging through mud, but she thought of Phoebe. Picturing her face, Sierra forced her limbs to move.

When they crossed into the shadows of the crowded trees, Sierra's keeper mark flared to life for a split second, burning like someone had touched her with a hot poker. She gasped.

"My mark," she choked out, looking to Corbin, fearing for him as well.

His eyes were dark with concern, but he didn't seem to be in any pain.

Nell held her sword ready. Sierra planted her feet and took a deep breath. Whirls of colors flashed in front of her like streaming ribbons, and she squeezed her eyes tight as the world lurched around her. She wasn't sure what was happening to her, but it was too much like her kaleidoscopic dreams, dreams of queens. What a terrible time to go crazy. Or maybe someone really was messing with her, dosing her to make her more compliant on the journey.

Keepers had a natural immunity to the effects of raw nectar. Flight, though—that was nectar distilled to its strongest essence and mixed with other chemicals to strengthen the effects. No one stood against it, not even keepers.

But who? If Jack wanted Sierra to fail, no doubt he only had to say the word to his enforcer.

But no, as much as she wanted to blame Nell, that didn't make sense. Jack wanted to find a queen, so subterfuge from her didn't make sense. And Corbin would never betray Sierra that way. He wanted to find the queens as much as she did. Was someone else out there with them? Surely Nell would have heard some evidence of other humans out here, but they'd seen no one.

Sierra shook her head, trying to clear her mind. Who else but Nell could it be, if no one else was out here? Who said Jack had to tell her to do it? Maybe she got tired of Sierra's interference and decided to suppress her natural attitude problems, soften her up a bit.

It was so hard to think, the world shivering like a big wet dog, sending colors flying through the air.

Corbin held his hand under her elbow and guided her to sit on a fallen tree trunk.

Sierra ran her hand over her mark, and again heat shot through her skin, bowing back her head.

Touching her mark usually sent a warm glow down her spine, but this was like a flash fire, an explosion of pain along her spine and down her legs. She shrieked and clapped her hands over the back of her neck, as if she could hold in the pain and keep it from spreading.

Her knees shook and she knelt onto the ground, needing to find balance. The clean scent of pine surrounded her, and she breathed in. The smell reminded her of Queen, of Corbin, of time safe from Jack. She dropped her hands and bent her head lower down to get a good whiff of the clearing scent. Her hair fell around her face, past her shoulders, off her neck, sliding cool against her warm cheeks.

Corbin gasped. Sierra whipped her head around to stare at them, both leaning over her. Nell's face paled.

"What?" Sierra asked, staggering to her feet. She saw evergreens shooting up so high they hid most of the sky, but no danger approaching, no wild animals, no magical creatures. They were only staring at her.

"Your mark—Sierra, it looks... darker." Corbin swallowed. "Turn around."

Shaken, she did as he asked. She wanted to touch the mark, but she willed her hands to stay still. Touching it might send shocking pain through her again. Corbin lifted up her hair, and the heat of his hand hovered near her mark. Nell approached and sucked in a deep breath.

Sierra gritted her teeth. She felt exposed, standing there with her neck bared. "*Well?*"

"The mark's as dark as if made by your father's branding iron, Sierra," Nell confirmed.

Fear pitched in Sierra's stomach.

Nell leaned in closer. "Hmm. And the wings are lacy-looking inside now, pretty fancy."

"Have you ever heard of this happening?" Sierra asked.

"Never," Corbin said.

Nell looked at his mark. "They were the same color before," she said to Sierra. "But only yours is different now. Not Corbin's. Why?"

Sierra shrugged. "Why did this happen to me at all?"

Corbin looked stricken, his big brown eyes wide. "Maybe your blood makes you a stronger keeper, all those keepers in your family line."

He spoke so softly Sierra could barely hear him. She recoiled when she pieced together his words.

"Don't be a lunatic, Corbin. No one's a better keeper than you! The fact that you're the first in your family makes you even more special. You've taught me everything I know."

He muttered something incomprehensible and then shook his head. "We'd better keep going, if you're okay to walk, Sierra."

This would have been a good time to tell them about the dreams, the weird taste of nectar, the dizziness. They were probably useful clues, but she looked at Nell, at those cold blue eyes, and couldn't get the words out. Sierra couldn't trust her father's enforcer. Not yet.

While they hiked, Sierra devised a plan. Close to their regular time to stop for the night, she said, "Hey, Nell, can you and I go hunting? I'm more hungry than usual."

That part was true as far as it went.

Corbin smiled. "I could use more food too. Hey! Maybe I can try to hunt!"

"No!" Both Nell and Sierra spoke at the same time. They met eyes, and Sierra had to smother a grin. Corbin had proved to be a much worse shot than anyone anticipated. The girls exchanged a look of amused understanding.

Nell told him, "We need you to guard camp. Get the fire going, and we'll be back soon."

Sierra almost expected to hear, *We'll be home soon, honey*, but wasn't forced to gag when Nell simply strode off into the forest, weaving easily between trees like a wolf. Or a snake. Sierra jogged to catch up.

They walked in silence to get far enough from the sounds of Corbin making camp, sounds that would scare the animals away. Hopefully they wouldn't find anything hunting *them*. Even if the myths of dragons and manticores turned out to be unfounded, there were still deadly bears and mountain lions.

Sierra ran her fingers lightly down her bow. If she accused Nell wrongly, this would go badly. Another flicker of lights behind Sierra's eyes made her stumble. Nell froze, then turned back. In that moment, in Sierra's eyes, Nell looked like a ghost, a ghost on fire. Orange and yellow light streamed all around her like flames, but her skin was snow-white. Her eyes were solid black, like coal.

The vision lasted only a moment, long enough to steal her breath, but short enough to make her wonder if she had imagined it. She shook her head, which sent the world reeling. Nell reached to catch her, but in a panic Sierra grabbed a tree limb that scratched red welts down her arms. She panted as the nausea vanished, and the chilly wind dried sweat from her brow.

"Are you okay?" Nell asked cautiously.

Sierra didn't answer, not trusting her voice. The bow had slipped through her fingers at some point, and she slowly leaned down and curled her fingers around the smooth wood. She kept her head steady, afraid of falling off the small ledge that dropped thirty feet on their right.

She knelt and splayed her palms on the ground, letting the pine needles prick her skin. The forest floor was one point of reality in a world that had blurred with her recent nightmares.

"It's Flight, isn't it?" she whispered. "Or some new elixir from nectar Jack is testing?"

Nell took a step back, eyebrows high. *"What?"*

"I've been hallucinating, seeing crazy colors, flashing images of fairies. I taste nectar, Nell. Are you going to stand there and tell me you don't have something to do with it? That Jack didn't tell you to dose me?"

Nell's eyes were wide, showing the whites around her blue irises. "I have no idea what you're talking about, but you're sounding a little crazy."

It had to be a lie. *Something* was happening. Nausea, fury, and mistrust reared their heads, and Sierra sat up on her knees. She ignored the upheaval in her stomach and drew her bow, arrow ready. Nell reached for her own bow, but Sierra said, "Stop, or I'll shoot."

Nell continued to reach.

"Try me." Sierra's words were cold and flat.

Nell froze, hand in midair. Smart girl.

Sierra's head started to throb. More zig-zigs flashed

across her vision. She tightened her grip on the bow, the sweat on her palms making the weapon hard to hold.

Corbin will hate me. The thought whispered through her mind. *Corbin will hate me if I even threaten to shoot her.* She paused, the string loosening some. Maybe there was another way to get the answers she needed.

But as Sierra began to stand, the world dipped again, and a crash ripped through the air. The trees thrashed, danced, waved their arms, and she couldn't keep the moan from escaping as the world exploded all around them.

But this time Sierra wasn't hallucinating, because Nell shouted and tried to leap away from the edge. Tried and failed.

The forest floor split with a shriek that sent goose bumps racing across Sierra's skin. She scrabbled through the dirt to wrap her scratched arms around the root of a giant tree. The ground rolled and tilted toward the ledge, and she cried out.

A giant wedge of land rose up from the earth like the dead coming to life. It shattered the soil, sending dirt spraying. The ledge crumbled in the space of a heartbeat. And then, before Sierra could move, Nell fell and disappeared.

CHAPTER FIFTEEN

A scream ripped through the air, and Sierra wasn't sure whose it was. After what felt like years, but lasted only a few heartbeats, the ground stopped heaving, and she crawled to the edge to see what had happened. Nell lay sprawled fifteen feet down, a line of scarlet cut across her head. Her arm twisted at an unnatural angle. The ground looked like it had been cut in a circle and dropped halfway down the ledge. She was trapped unless someone helped her.

"Nell!" Sierra shouted, before thinking maybe she should feign unconsciousness and leave Nell to her fate. But she couldn't really bring herself to ignore Nell and leave her stranded.

Nell groaned, stirring.

Sierra leaned as far over the cliff as she dared. "Nell! Can you hear me?"

Nell struggled up, and her scream cut through the silent air, startling Sierra so badly she nearly fell over the cliff. She'd never heard Nell scream. Nell had her left hand clasped tightly around her other shoulder. The right shoulder looked broken to Sierra, angled up strangely where the arm connected, but maybe it was only out of joint. Nell would know. Any good enforcer knew the difference between an out-of-place joint and a break, and they knew how to make both happen.

Sierra's knees shook so much she sank back to the ground. She couldn't believe another quake had already struck, and all the way out here, in the middle of nowhere where no one could help them if they were hurt.

Nell looked around and saw Sierra standing above her. Surprise flashed over her face, followed by hope, before mistrust chased them both away. She cursed under her breath for a long moment, then squinted up at Sierra.

"Are you okay?" Nell called up, trying to sound calm, but the pain was too thick in her voice to carry it off.

"Fine," Sierra replied. "Maybe I can climb down and lift you up, unless your arm's broken."

Nell closed her eyes and touched along her hurt shoulder. She blanched the color of a corpse, but this time her voice remained strong when she spoke, "I think it's just dislocated. You can push it back into place, and then I can manage the climb if you help."

She had to put Nell's arm back into place? Then push her tall frame, and herself, up a crumbly cliff? "Uh... Nell..."

"You may be small, but you're pretty strong for your size," Nell said, as if she could read minds. Her lips curled like she'd admitted something distasteful.

Sierra realized she had the best leverage she'd ever have. She smiled. "Yeah, I can do that. But first you have to answer my question. You remember, before we were interrupted."

Nell froze, eyes trained on Sierra. "Don't be stupid."

"Come on, Nell. You dosing me? You can tell me the truth."

"I told you the truth," she said, scowling, chin lifted.

Sierra's small amount of patience went up in smoke. She whipped out the bow again, and Nell's eyes widened. "You've got nowhere to go. I can shoot all day... arrow after arrow... No matter how bad a marksman I am, eventually I won't miss."

"You're not that cold-blooded."

Sierra thought about Phoebe being sent to a murdering dark alchemist two ports away, for years, because Nell ruined their chance to find a queen. Cold-blooded didn't even begin to describe how Sierra felt.

She let the ruthlessness show in her eyes while carefully drawing back the bowstring. She aimed for Nell's right thigh. Not to kill her, merely wound her, though... if she missed, she could blame it on the quake.

The cold thought made her catch her breath. Flight didn't make people violent, which meant the thought was hers alone. Images of Corbin and Nell in the twilight flickered through her mind. He was so happy with Nell. Her hands shook, but she couldn't quite drop the bow.

Sierra cursed softly. She had to know the truth—no matter what Corbin or Phoebe might think of her later. She tightened her grip on the bowstring again.

"Last chance," she called. Sierra recognized that her voice contained the dead quality of Jack's when he was about to hurt someone. For once, she didn't care.

Nell licked her lips and answered. "I sold all the Flight Jack sent with me. I've been out since the second day. Why would I dose you?"

She must have recognized the tone. She had one like it, too.

"You've always had a problem with me, Nell, and we both know it."

A small snort escaped through Nell's grimace. "I might want to shoot you, but I want a job more. Come on, this is my life we're talking about."

"Yeah, your life. Your life working for a dark alchemist, one that dispenses poisons and illegal elixirs that destroy peoples' lives. What kind of person wants to do that job, anyway? I'm stuck, but you're not. I think you're the kind of person who *likes* to hurt other people."

Nell paled for a moment before her lips mashed into a thin line and a red flush stained her cheeks. If eyes could shoot arrows, Sierra would be riddled with them.

"Yes, poor little you," Nell snapped. "You've never known what it is to go without protection."

Sierra shook her head in disbelief. "Give me a break, Nell. You know Jack. You think living with him is some sort of festival? My home is a cage that I'm stuck in forever."

"Give *me* a break, Sierra," Nell mocked. "All you *know* is Jack. You've never lived outside the protection of an alchemist's circle. You've never seen what happens to families who don't have a master's protection or a father, either. You may live in a cage, but at least a cage keeps out other dangers." Her eyes looked haunted.

Maybe an elixir was at work after all, because none of this made sense. "What are you saying?"

Nell stomped one foot, then winced. "Look. You know how you say you resent being forced into life as a keeper?"

Sierra nodded hesitantly.

"Yet here you are, seeking your fairy. For your sister. I've got three sisters. You've seen them. Three Phoebe's. No father. A mother who can't work except small jobs like doing other people's laundry. That doesn't pay enough for food, Sierra. Now tell me you wouldn't be an enforcer if you were strong enough to do it." Nell's face twisted into an expression of disgust, revulsion rank in her voice.

Sierra couldn't get words out of her mouth. She didn't want to know these things, not about Nell.

All those years of Nell picking on her. Those years of her scathing remarks, Nell working up the ladder of Jack's enterprise. Maybe she'd just been desperate to protect her sisters. Maybe she'd been jealous of what she saw as Sierra's security, not to mention her close friendship with Corbin.

Sierra took a deep breath. She knew what it was to wish your life was different, to want to *be* different, to hate what you had to do. Maybe Nell knew that feeling, too.

A finch twittered its tune somewhere in the trees, uncaring about the tension simmering below, startling both girls as it broke the silence.

Nell closed her eyes and hung her head for a long moment, breathing heavily. In that moment, pity swam up through Sierra's familiar anger, wiping the scowl from her face.

Nell glanced up and her face darkened, eyebrows drawing to a sharp V, making those blue eyes like frost.

"I don't need you to *feel* for me, Fairy Fanatic. I'm doing fine for myself and my family." She stood on the broken bit of earth, leaning to one side, arm cradled against her body. She flushed red like Sierra had seen her naked. It felt that way.

Sierra realized she still had the arrow aimed at her, a girl without a father, a girl with more people to worry about than Sierra. She dropped her arms, holding the bow and arrow to the side like a snake that might bite her. Shame welled up, fighting its way through the confusing combination of dislike, pity, understanding, and mistrust.

"So... no elixirs? I thought maybe..."

Nell met her eyes at last. "I promise. My word. No elixirs. No poisons."

Sierra's breath whistled out of her lungs in relief, her shoulders slumping. She still had no explanation for the weird psychedelic flashes, but at least she felt a truce of sorts had been reached with Nell. But she had one last thing to say.

"If you hurt him, I'll hurt you," Sierra said keeping her tone casual, looking around for anything she could use as rope.

"I could tell you the same."

"I'd never hurt Corbin—"

Corbin. Sierra's breath hitched. Had he been hurt in the quake, too? "We need to get to him!"

Without hesitation, Nell said, "Check on him. I can wait."

Her response finally broke something in Sierra. She laid down her bow and started to climb over the cliff.

"What are you doing?" Nell braced herself against the

rock wall with her good arm as she glared up at her. "Go find Corbin!"

"I'm not going to leave you behind."

"He could be hurt. He could be dying." Nell's words came out in a gasp.

"So he'll need both of us."

Sierra clutched at the roots sneaking through the crumbling black dirt. Her knees sank into the torn earth around the edge of the cliff, and she pushed her fingers through the dirt until she found a secure grip on tree roots and plant stems. The rich scent of decaying leaves filled her nose.

One foot after another, she lowered herself, the dirt digging under her nails. The packed soil crumbled into her eyes, into her mouth, leaving a taste of mold and minerals, grit crunching under her teeth. When her toes touched the rocky solid ground, she gave a sigh of relief, ignoring Nell's increasingly loud curses. Then Sierra craned her neck to look up at the path she had taken and rubbed her hand across her forehead, forgetting about the dirt until its dry crumbs mixed with her sweat to smear across her skin. Nice. Mud on the face now. She had bigger problems, though.

"You may as well shut up and help me fix your arm now," Sierra said, crossing her arms.

Bile rose up the back of her throat at the sight of Nell's right shoulder up close. Sierra wished even more, now, that Corbin was with them. He'd know what to do.

Nell's jacket had fallen halfway down her arm, but even through her thick woolen shirt, the lump of her bone visibly pushed forward at the wrong angle. Sierra pushed the jacket out of the way. Her stomach twisted, but she fought to keep her emotions off her face.

Nell panted and gritted out, "I can fix it myself."

Sierra rolled her eyes. "Sure you could, but why would you if you don't have to suffer like that?"

"Ironic coming from you, don't you think?"

She had a point. Sierra held her hands up in a gesture of peace-keeping. "How about we say I don't want to have to climb down another cliff if you pass out from the pain, all right? We'll pretend you fixed it yourself."

Nell clenched and unclenched the hand on her good arm, shaking her head. "You'll vomit."

"I won't. Nell. Please."

There was a long pause. Sierra waited. Nell's white blonde hair looked dirty blonde now, drenched with sweat around her brow despite the cold air.

"Bend my hurt arm ninety degrees at my waist."

Sierra always figured she'd be more likely to pitch Nell over the cliff rather than help her get back up one. But Sierra leaned close and lifted Nell's arm more gently than if it were a newborn babe. She smelled of forest, that tangy resin of pine, but also of sweat and dirt.

Nell continued, "Now bend my hand over toward my belly, keeping the angle of my arm exactly the same."

She sucked in breath as Sierra followed the

directions, until Nell's wrist was touching her own waist. Sierra swallowed loudly.

"Now"—Nell's voice was breathy—"keep the arm steady and slowly take my fist and move it away from me, toward the outside of my body."

"Like this?" Sierra asked, biting her lip, sweat beading her forehead. What if she hurt Nell worse?

Nell nodded, but froze and hissed at the pain caused by the movement.

Sierra steadily moved Nell's arm until it reached ninety degrees from her body and began to move in an outward arc. Sierra squeezed her eyes shut as she continued the movement until there was a sudden ricocheting *pop*. Nell shrieked, swaying Sierra with its sheer volume and sending a jolt of terror through her. Something must have finally gone right, though, because Nell sagged in her arms, groaning in relief. The bone had snapped back into joint. Sierra dragged gulps of air into her tight lungs.

Nell slumped to the ground, leaning against the cliff wall. "Keep my arm bent, but move it in front of my stomach. I'll need a sling."

Sierra gingerly placed the sore arm in position, but had nothing for a sling. They each had on their only jacket, and there was no way they were going to rip those up. They still had farther to go up the mountains. They had their woolen shirts on and pants but no extra cloth at all.

Sierra had an idea. "Tuck your good arm inside your jacket, and I'll tie your sleeve over onto your other arm to try to keep it in place. Corbin can help us make a sling back at camp."

Alarm flashed on Nell's face at the mention of Corbin's name. She hurriedly stuffed her arm in her jacket. The brown material flapped in the breeze, because she couldn't button one-handed.

Sierra buttoned Nell's coat without saying a word, because now that the moment of pain had passed, Nell was pink, not pale. Nell probably hated that Sierra was the one there, the one who helped. Thinking over their conversation and her memories of their childhood, Sierra wasn't too happy about it either.

Understanding Nell made hating her much harder.

CHAPTER SIXTEEN

The thought of getting up the cliff made Sierra break out in a sweat, but she gulped and moved forward. The girls strapped on Nell's weapons so they could use their remaining hands freely.

"Hurry," Nell said.

"I'm doing the best I can," Sierra snapped. "I want to find him too."

Sierra made a stirrup out of her hands to hoist Nell a few feet up the cliff wall. Once Nell found handholds in the dirt, Sierra knelt and leveraged her hands under Nell's feet and heaved, giving her the strength to pull herself up a few feet, one-handed. Nell clung to the side of the cliff with her one arm and legs while Sierra used the freshly exposed roots and rocks to haul herself alongside.

It was slow work, and Sierra couldn't quite keep the

momentum going. They hung halfway up the craggy wall.

"It's too hard," Sierra said, pulling on Nell's coat to help lift her. Sierra's foot broke through her foothold, and she slid down three feet.

Nell cursed. "Keep going," was all she said.

Sierra pulled herself back up and tried again. They moved ever-so-slowly up, with Sierra scurrying all around. She acted as Nell's right arm, held Nell's leg against the wall, dug small footholds in the crumbly dirt for her feet. When Nell's aching right shoulder swung away from the cliff without the right hand to hold her steady, Sierra pushed her back. They were fortunate that the fall hadn't been a farther drop.

Even so, they were running out of strength, and the top was still out of reach.

Sweat burned in Sierra's eyes, and her arm muscles were on fire. Her legs trembled. She wanted to scream.

"I'm sorry," Sierra panted. "I can't. I can't. I'll have to go on without you. Let's get you back down. I promise we'll come back to you. Do you hear me, Nell? We won't leave you."

The two girls met each other's gaze, faces close in their climbing positions.

Nell nodded and began to lower herself.

"Wait!" a voice said from above. The girls gasped and nearly slid down the cliff wall.

"Corbin?" Sierra cried out.

He leaned over the cliff and waved down at them. "I heard you, thank all the trees! I've been looking for you since the quake! Are you okay?"

Tears stung Sierra's eyes. He was alive. Corbin was okay, and Nell would be okay now, too.

"Nell's hurt! We need to hurry and get her out of here!"

"Hang on," he replied. "I brought some rope, just in case."

Sierra sighed with relief. "Hold tight, Nell. I can help you hold on, as long as I don't have to lift you."

Nell snorted. Despite their shaking arms, the girls clung tightly. A couple minutes later, after many curses from above, Corbin dropped a thick rope beside them.

He swung out on the rope and lowered himself hand-over-hand until he was alongside them.

"What are you, part-squirrel?" Sierra gasped as he managed to pull Nell so she was holding the rope but also leaning on him.

"Hush up and help me," Corbin grunted.

By the time the three of them hauled themselves over the edge of the cliff, the sun was setting.

They brushed off the dirt and mud as best they could. Sierra grabbed her bow from the ground, and they worked their way back to the camp, explaining what had happened as they went. Corbin had thankfully remembered to notch the trees as he came, so they found their way back even with Nell unable to pay much attention.

Sierra and Corbin each walked on one side of Nell. She seemed too quiet and stumbled a lot. Sierra wondered if shoulder dislocations could cause shock, not to mention the fall itself. Sierra's mind seemed fuzzy. Maybe she was in shock, too.

Nell nearly fell while stepping over a fallen log, so Sierra and Corbin both wrapped one arm around her back for support. When no protest was made, Sierra quickened their steps.

The orange glow of the hastily banked fire sent soft light through the darkening trees, the truest beacon Sierra had ever seen. Relief made her giddy and warm.

They'd all survived an earthquake in the mountains, and they had time yet to find a fairy and rescue Phoebe. She smelled wood smoke and, even better, cooked grains. Her mouth watered. The fact they would have no meat in them meant nothing tonight.

"I know I should have put the fire out completely," Corbin earnestly explained, though Sierra really didn't care about fire safety details at the moment, "but I just took off to find you guys after the quake."

Sierra had never been so thankful for Corbin's impulsive, passionate nature. So sweet—so very Corbin! She was glad the forest didn't catch fire, but no harm had been done, and he'd saved them.

They set Nell on a fallen log he'd dragged over by the

fire and he quickly built it back up. "Nell? How're you doing, sweetie? Are you in shock?" His voice sounded calm and strong. Hearing him use the endearment for Nell didn't seem as odd—or as upsetting—as it might have that morning.

"Not in shock, you guys are the ones losing your minds," Nell grumbled. The very mildness of her response alarmed both Sierra and Corbin.

He sat beside Nell, laying his hand on her forehead like his parents did for Sierra so many times.

"No fever," he murmured to himself, and then placed two fingers on the pulse in Nell's neck.

She jerked away, saying, "I told you, I'm fine."

Corbin dropped his hand limply to his side.

Sierra smiled at him from across the fire. "We're glad you're okay, Corbin. We were worried."

She paused, seeing him glance over at the tired girl next to him. "Both of us were," she added, feeling generous.

They helped Nell into her bedroll, then Sierra quickly fell into her own and dropped into deep sleep, thankful to be alive.

The next morning, she was slightly less thankful. Her entire body protested when she stretched. A rosy pink blushed across the pale dawn sky. Corbin was asleep sitting up, propped against a boulder. She guessed he had been keeping watch, bless his heart, or trying to. Nell was fast asleep in her bedroll, but her head was pillowed on his legs, face tilted up to the sky. His hand curled against her cheek. In sleep, their tenderness was bared for anyone to see.

Sierra looked away and took a deep breath. No matter how Nell loved him—and it seemed she really might—it didn't change the fact that she was an enforcer and he was so gentle. Wanting him and wanting to keep him were two different things. Surely she understood the problem. Corbin was crazy to even consider it, but he'd never listen to Sierra's warning.

Well, Seirra couldn't do anything about her teammates' future troubles, but she could do something about an empty stomach. It looked like they'd need to take a day to let Nell recuperate, and they might as well have fresh meat while they waited.

Grabbing her bow and quiver of arrows that they greedily recycled after each use if possible, Sierra slipped out of camp. Treading lightly was one skill she'd honed.

Long shadows reached through the trees like fingers, creating deep blue stripes across the forest floor. The air still smelled fresh with dew, and Sierra expanded her lungs to their fullest. Then she froze as a sudden realization swamped her. Her sleep had been restful last night. No pinwheels of glowing colorful fairies chased her, at least none she could remember. Her hand flew to her keeper mark, fingers reaching toward the skin, but common sense forced it back down. If she had the same reaction, she couldn't afford to collapse screaming in the middle of the forest.

She pressed onward, but not too far. All her life, she'd heard stories about things in this forest, stories meant to frighten and even terrorize. But right now, only the black wings of a crow flashed through the dizzying trees.

She reached a nice clearing deeper in the woods. A bush with berries the color of a bruise grew on the other side. They looked ripe, but one bite of the wrong berry and she'd never see Phoebe again. Their sweetness might bring game here, though.

Sierra climbed three branches high into the gnarled pine overlooking the clearing. Her bow and arrow lay within reach as she sat on the thick wood, back against the scratchy bark, and she waited in the early stillness. The morning sky grew brighter as the sun touched the tops of the trees, the sky deepening to a robin's egg blue. Neck muscles she didn't realize were tense relaxed one by one. It was so serene here.

Sierra closed her eyes and dropped her head to her knees, the rough fabric of her sturdy homespun pants scraping against her cheek. Being alone soothed her... but her fears bubbled up in the silence, too, demanding to be heard.

The truth was, watching Nell and Corbin fall in love both panicked her and made her yearn, an uncomfortable feeling like she was on a tipping boat.

The girls her age in the village were experiencing first kisses behind the mill, and some were even being promised in marriage. But Sierra was not an ordinary fourteen-year-old, and she didn't care about kisses anyway. She wasn't curious about them at all. She scowled at the empty tree branches around her. Nope. Didn't care one bit about a stupid kiss.

She chewed on her bottom lip and gazed at the empty field.

The idea of spending life with someone she could love and trust sounded great in theory, but she had never really thought it would work for her. Corbin and Phoebe were all she needed. Most people were pains in the neck anyway. But watching Nell and Corbin with hearts circling around their heads had made Sierra wonder, a bit, what it would be like to feel that way, too. Not now. But maybe someday.

Corbin might have found his someone special already. A real friend would be happy for him, even if they had challenges ahead. Or at least not fuss about it. So that's what Sierra would do.

The decision gave her some peace. She settled more comfortably into her hunter's stance. Her mind emptied of anything, and she could finally focus only on this moment, attention soft but ready for game.

After an hour, her bottom had gone numb, and her hands were clumsy with the cold. No deer, no squirrels, not even a mouse had wandered through the clearing.

She slid and half-fell on her way out of the tree. Then the clatter of hooves echoed through the trees.

Sierra spun, readying her arrow. The white fluffy tail of a deer flew over the berry bush at the end of the meadow. She zeroed in on the whiteness, the small target that glowed compared to the deep green berry bush. Her arrow soared and connected with a thud on the other side of the bush. Nell would be reluctantly impressed. Sierra drew her knife as she ran, ready to put the animal out of its misery. It looked really big. One arrow wouldn't have killed it.

Then a scream filled the air, and Sierra staggered to a halt in the empty clearing. It sounded like Sam. She frantically looked around for the unicorn. The scream came again, and she took a step back, slamming the knife back in her belt and bringing her bow up and scanning the perimeter. The sound was coming from behind the bush. It must be the deer she had shot, but no deer had ever sounded like this. Its screams were nearly human. With trembling knees, Sierra snuck closer to the bush, arrow nocked and ready. She didn't want to get close to anything that sounded like that.

She drew back the bowstring, pressing her hand against her cheek as she prepared to shoot, dragging in a slow breath through lungs wheezing with fear. The bush was too thick to see through, so she sidestepped around it, keeping a wide berth from whatever was behind there. When she reached the other side, her eyes widened in both horror and amazement, and she dropped her hands uselessly to her sides.

She'd shot a creature she'd only heard stories about. The bottom half was a deer, with the tail she saw flash over the bush. Brown fur, spotted with tiny white dots on the flank, ending in hooves. But the top half of the creature wasn't a deer at all. It was human, with dark brown skin, all uncovered. And its big, brown eyes stared right into hers.

CHAPTER SEVENTEEN

Sierra immediately corrected herself; this creature was not an *it* but a *he*. This was a faun, a creature of legend, and a young faun at that. Wavy brown hair brushed his shoulders, but there was no mistaking that square jaw line and strong brow for anything but a boy, one with one foot—hoof?—into adulthood. His chest was bare and thin, ribs showing, heaving as he lay panting in pain. His torso disappeared into fur, as if tucked into a tight-fitting pair of pants. The long winter coat of the deerskin covered anything private, but Sierra, mortified, kept her eyes on his face just in case.

Oh, *no*. Horror flooded her. She had shot a magical creature, truly wounded him, one that had done no harm. None. Guilt crashed over her so heavily her breath caught. She held out her hands in the age-old gesture of peace and took one tentative, tiny step forward. He didn't move. Good sign.

"I'm so sorry. I'm so, so sorry," she babbled, stricken.

His intense gaze held her paralyzed for a moment; she couldn't look away. It felt like some important message was hidden in the dark depths of his brown eyes.

Sierra offered a hand, unsure of what else to do. Old songs and stories said fauns could cause trouble for travelers, but they also were equally likely to help. Magical in nature, they supposedly knew all of the forest creatures and plants. Sounded like someone to make friends with. Too bad she had shot him already.

Still, the arrow was her mistake—such a stupid one, too—and she'd make it right somehow. Surely that wouldn't be impossible. Thank the heavens she never used Jack's unicorn horn arrow tips—one of those would have killed the faun for sure.

Sierra stepped closer, and he scooted back in the leaves, shrieking. The sound of shocked fear and pain screeched up and down her spine, like it did with Old Sam. The arrow shaft protruded from the fuan's back, with the arrowhead buried near the bottom of the ribcage. She balled her hands into fists. She'd wounded him badly, in winter.

"Who are you?" she asked.

He gazed steadily at her but did not answer. Then he touched his throat once and shook his head. Her heart pounded at this proof of intelligence. Okay, no speech, but he clearly understood her.

"Let me help you, please."

No response.

The sun was now high enough that Corbin and Nell would be wondering where she was. It was time she got moving. She surely couldn't carry him, but she couldn't leave him, either. The faun's eyes were the color of melted chocolate, darker than Corbin's, and they would haunt her. The poor thing looked ill, even without the arrow wound. She could count his ribs; dark circles under his eyes spoke of exhaustion. He looked no older than Corbin, too, though far less healthy.

Slinging the bow over her shoulder, Sierra backed away from the creature, and he tried to stand. Tried but failed. She froze, breath stopped for a long moment, unsure of his plans. The faun waited, staring at her with eyes too calm, before he finally reached out a hand.

Her stomach felt like it had floated into her throat, but she stepped closer. The fur of his deer legs curled a little, sort of like alpaca fur. Was it as soft as it looked? Blood seeped around the arrow, but it must have hit a rib instead of an organ, or there'd be a river of red instead of a trickle.

Sierra breathed a sigh of thanks. Grabbing his hand,

she began to pull him up, but he couldn't lift himself fast enough. She hadn't braced her feet well, and she tumbled into him as he pulled on her arms, causing a low grunt of obvious pain from him and a shocked gasp from her.

The whirls of brown fur were as soft as they looked. He smelled… like Old Sam. She'd always thought the smell of Sam was his unique scent, sort of like rosemary mixed with summer rain. Maybe this was the scent of magical creatures. There were so few of them left. Untangling herself from the poor faun, she blushed a hot red but managed to stand and stammer again, "I'm so sorry!"

Wearing a small smile, he shook his head and held out his hand once more.

Why couldn't the faun speak? The tales said nothing about that. Grabbing him much more firmly than last time, Sierra bypassed his hand and lifted under both his shoulders, using all her strength. His breathing was ragged as he staggered to his feet—hooves—but not a word came out between those delicate human lips. He finally straightened his back, and his gaze locked onto hers for a long moment, those eyes dark with secret knowledge she couldn't reach.

Her chest tightened, but she didn't understand why. He was clearly not a threat to her, so why did she feel like prey that had been sighted by a predator? What else had the tales left out of the stories?

After they took a few steps, it became clear he needed to lean on her. He was a solid weight against her left side, and Sierra hoped he couldn't feel the racing of her pulse. Fear, exertion, and something else she couldn't place made her a walking heart attack. His arm was slung across her shoulders, and she gingerly wrapped her arm around his waist, avoiding the arrow protruding a little higher up. They staggered as they went but eventually made it to the clearing.

For all Sierra's worry and guilt, the looks on Corbin's and Nell's faces were hilarious. Twin sets of eyes bigger than dinner plates stared wildly at Sierra and the faun as they reached the glade. The faun was making a hoarse growling noise over and over. Walking with an arrow sticking out of your back had to hurt, even if you were a creature of legend and magic.

Nell was the first to regain the power of speech. "What in the great green woods have you done, Sierra?"

Corbin's jaw still hung loose, making him look a bit dim-witted. Sierra smothered a smile, turning into the faun's shoulder until she could control her face.

Then he moaned, a clear sound of pain. Her mirth at her friends' shock and her own ridiculous predicament faded like morning mist in the blazing sun.

"He's shot," Sierra explained, in case they had missed the arrow.

Nell, obviously alarmed by the faun's noises, said,

"We need to get the arrow out of him, and we'll need something for the wound."

She reached for her bags but groaned as she stood.

Corbin made her sit back down, saying, "I'll help."

He eased the faun from Sierra's side onto a log. The relief of having his weight off her was amazing, but Sierra sat down next to the creature to ensure he wouldn't tip over into the fire.

"I'll grab the poultice if you can keep him from falling," Sierra said to Corbin. Digging quickly through Corbin's bag, she found a wide bandage and his jar of healing cream, heavy with the rich scent of valderium, the spicy tang of corindan, the sweetness of winter moss.

She spread the poultice across the bandage and tried to hand it to Corbin. "Here."

Nell said, "Corbin has to hold him steady so one of us can pull out the arrow first. With only one arm, I don't think I can do it, Sierra. You'll have to."

Sierra blanched. That would hurt him even more.

Nell seemed to read her expression. "Don't be a baby."

"Come on, Nell, you know how Sierra is about blood," Corbin murmured. He began wiping as much blood off the arrow as he could.

Sierra mashed her lips together. They'd never let her forget that, would they? They'd all been in class the day Nell came to school two years ago with a bad gash over one eye. She'd been working for Jack by then, and learning how to fight. It wasn't easy going in the beginning. The stitches she'd put in herself came loose in the middle of their lesson on the requirements for eldership. It certainly livened up the lesson. Blood gushed down Nell's cheek, pooling all over the desk. Sierra got one look and had to close her eyes and put her head between her knees. Blood was not her friend, no indeed. Luckily, as a keeper, that wasn't usually an issue.

"You'll be fine," Corbin added, holding the faun steady. "You can handle anything, Sierra. You can do this."

At least Corbin believed in her. She nodded, wiped her sweaty palms on her pants, and got into place, taking one more deep breath to steady her nerves.

Nell directed them. "Okay, Corbin, keep doing what you're doing. He may faint when it's done, so be ready. Sierra, it's in a good place, as far as arrow wounds go, and not too deep. You have to grab the end of the arrow and yank. This is going to hurt him. A lot. And it's going to bleed. A lot. But the alternatives are worse."

Great. With trembling hands, Sierra grabbed hold of the arrow. Her lips felt numb. He was shivering, the poor thing.

"I'm sorry," she whispered, before yanking the arrow out with a solid, forceful pull.

His shriek echoed through the clearing, and goose

bumps marched up and down her arms. Blood poured from the gaping wound. Her stomach twisted, and she turned her face away. Nell's voice was low and soothing, and when Sierra looked back over, Corbin had already placed the bandage around the faun's waist. He had passed out. Probably for the best.

Weak-kneed and clammy, she plopped down next to him.

"He'll be okay," Nell told her.

"I thought he was a deer," Sierra explained, gesturing to the obvious reason she made the mistake.

Nell stared at Sierra for a long moment. Then a laugh sputtered through Nell's teeth. She clamped her lips, clearly trying to hold it together, but Corbin chortled and her laughter spewed out.

"Only you, Sierra!" She leaned over her knees, laughing until she cried.

Sierra sat there stiffly, the wounded faun passed out beside her on Corbin's legs, unsure what to do.

Nell continued, "First, you attract a fairy and now a mythological creature no one's seen in years. And you don't want anything to do with magic!"

The laughter must have awoken the faun, because he stirred and sat up. Sierra ignored her still-giggling friends and told him, "It's out now. You'll be okay."

She frowned over at Nell and Corbin.

Nell said, "Seriously, how on earth could you miss the whole human torso and head thing?"

Sierra shrugged. It was a good question, but she didn't appreciate having Nell of all people point out her own foolishness. Not so soon.

The faun ran his hand down Sierra's arm softly. He offered a gentle smile this time, and patted her arm again, soothingly. It was a friendly touch, not scary at all, and there was something of home there in the scent of rosemary and rain. Her shoulders relaxed, and she squeezed his hand to show her thanks for his offer of support. His collarbone was like a strange necklace around his neck, all points and angles, and his skin hung loosely on his boney arms like a too-large coat.

"We'll take care of you," she promised him. She'd take him along with them until he was better healed. The compulsion to do so was too strong to ignore. But none of them could go any farther today.

"We need to take a day to heal," Sierra announced.

Nell tried to argue, but Corbin sided with Sierra. Between the arrow wound and Nell's shoulder, one day seemed reasonable. Nell must have been hurting pretty badly because her arguments were weak, and soon she was dozing.

The faun closed his eyes and leaned his head against Sierra, right on her shoulder, his weight pressing against her. A strange flutter in her chest reminded her of her fairy queen. As if the thought of her called forth her image, the flickering lights from yesterday roared into her vision. The taste of nectar swelled in her mouth, nearly drowning her. The world turned orange, black, and red. Sierra gasped.

The faun's head snapped up, concern clear in his eyes. Nell awoke with a start at Sierra's strangled intake of breath, and Corbin immediately began scoping the clearing.

"Did you see something?" he asked.

Nell narrowed her eyes at Sierra. "What's going on?"

"The colors are back," she whispered.

Jagged edges of lightning shot across the clearing, lightning only she saw.

Nell gave Corbin a quick summary of what Sierra shared right before the earthquake, about the strange dreams and hallucinations. Nell didn't mention the accusation made or the threats exchanged at all. Sierra smiled ruefully and nodded her thanks. Who knew Nell could be so tactful and smooth?

Corbin stared at Sierra, stared at the faun, then stared back at Sierra. Of the two of them, she was the strangest. Great.

She said, "I may pass out again, but the faun still needs help. I'm not able to hold him anymore."

When Corbin shifted the faun off her shoulder, Sierra shivered when the cold air hit where he had been. The streams of colors receded to ripples, and she caught her breath.

Sierra snorted a tired laugh and rubbed her hand across her forehead. She never washed her face last night, and dirt was still smeared on it. Manic hilarity tickled her throat again, and she dropped her head onto her knees. She concentrated on her breathing and hoped her vision would return to normal by the next day so they could go. They had to find a fairy queen soon, or they'd be out of time.

CHAPTER EIGHTEEN

For dinner, Corbin made a nourishing broth, and the taste of nectar eventually faded from Sierra's mouth. As the sun set, she felt cold all the way to her bones, and her fingernails were a light shade of blue. The faun seemed utterly unconcerned by the wind whipping by, freezing their noses, but Sierra appreciated the warmth of the soup cup in her hands. The faun drank some, holding Corbin's cup between wide hands that shook only a little. The faun didn't try to communicate, not with signs or with writing or speech, but his eyes followed Sierra wherever she went. Maybe he was drawn to her the same way she was drawn to him. *Magic.*

She sighed.

They only had three bedrolls, so Corbin, being Corbin, offered his bedroll to the faun before Sierra could even wonder what to do. The faun refused, though, and lay down in the grass at the edge of the clearing. Sierra shrugged. It was probably how he normally slept.

As the campfire died out, Nell squatted on her heels beside Sierra. "You know you can't take him with us, right?"

"How can we not?" Sierra protested.

"Easy. We say, 'Got the arrow out of you, sorry about that, good luck now' and off he goes to frolic in the woods. Sierra, if you want to get back to your sister, you can't adopt a stray pet!"

"He's not some wild animal, Nell. Look at him! Could you really send him into a winter forest with a bad wound, with human eyes staring back at you as you walk off?" *Actually, Nell could*, Sierra thought. But *she* couldn't.

When Nell didn't respond, Sierra pressed her point, voice harsh but still a whisper. "It's not an option. He can't hunt or gather with that kind of pain. It was my fault. He's a magical creature, like our fairies. And what if he gets infected?"

The faun tilted his head toward them, and Sierra wondered exactly how good a faun's hearing was. He was obviously not really asleep.

She continued, "I won't leave him. We'll figure out a way to keep him from slowing us down. Deal with it."

She'd figure out a way to find a queen to save her sister and keep her honor, too. She had to.

The next morning, Sierra's vision was completely normal again, and she could move without falling. She started to call over to the faun to check on him but realized she didn't have a name for him. Calling him Faun seemed too impersonal in the face of his pain and clear intelligence. But with him unable to tell them his name, assuming he had one, she saw no choice but to give him one herself. Suddenly, she had a memory of playing with an imaginary friend when Phoebe was still a baby. Sierra had called him Micah, and in her mind, he had brown eyes, brown hair and lived in her forest where she already spent so many hours. The name suited the faun. She smiled.

Nell asked, "What?"

"I have a name for him, if he likes it."

"Let me guess," Nell said. "Faun?"

She chuckled, and so did Corbin.

Sierra considered sticking out her tongue but opted for the high road. "I was thinking Micah, actually."

They looked at her like *she* had turned into a faun.

"Micah? A faun named Micah?"

Laughter broke loose from them both, though Corbin obviously tried to restrain himself.

Sierra shrugged. Their opinions were irrelevant. She paced over to the faun, sitting on the boulder Corbin used last night. The bandage already showed red, making her wince. She knelt beside him. "Is it okay if I call you Micah?"

She held her breath.

Sierra's reflection was clear in his wide, nearly black eyes, and long lashes curled up from them. The girls in town would have killed for eyes like his. He nodded slowly.

"Micah, then. Nice to meet you." A smile bloomed unexpectedly across Sierra's face, followed by one on his.

The team picked up their journey where they left off, moving slower than they had been. Nell grumbled at Sierra, irritated that she'd brought a wounded faun, but since Nell still couldn't move quickly anyway, she had no room to complain. By mid-afternoon, they reached an area of trees so dense it was hard to tell which direction actually went up the mountain.

"So, which way?" Sierra asked. They could have flipped a coin if they had one left.

Corbin thought for a moment. "I don't think it matters, as long as it feels like we're heading higher. If fairies are still around, seems like maybe they'd be as far as possible from humanity."

Micah snapped around to meet Sierra's gaze. His mouth didn't move, but he vibrated with energy. He tilted his head and lifted his eyebrows, like he was asking a question. Sierra almost slapped her hand on her forehead. Of course, the faun was the one to ask! This was his home, if he'd help.

The others weren't looking at him as they discussed which direction they'd take. Sierra stepped close to him, though, close enough for his scent to slide around her. Her fingers itched to touch the soft fur again, but she forced them to her side instead.

"We need help. Have you seen fairies around?"

He nodded, and she shouted in excitement. The others gathered around them.

"Will you lead us?" Sierra asked.

Micah spread his hands wide and shook his head.

She hazarded a guess. "You don't know where they are now?"

He shook his head.

"Can you at least tell us which way goes higher up the mountain?" she asked him.

Micah nodded and pointed toward their left, beyond two particularly tall trees. Given that no one else had any better ideas, they decided they might as well go in the direction he suggested.

They settled into a rhythm over the next few days. They wore all their winter layers as they climbed higher and higher: coats, hats, scarves. There were few words, as everyone needed their breath to keep up the hike. Micah helped with meals. He was so gentle that even Nell stopped complaining about him. Corbin assisted

Nell when she couldn't do something one-armed. Sierra helped Micah when he needed to lean on someone. But he was getting stronger quickly, healing faster than Nell.

Finally, they reached a section of the mountains that dead-ended in front of them. They would have to go around the sheer rock face by turning left or right, in one of two different ways up the mountain, but no one knew which one would be best, not even Micah. The trees reached so high into the sky that they crowded out even the sun.

Frustration ate at Sierra—they didn't have time to wander. She stepped away from the others for a moment. She closed her eyes and tried to think which would be the best choice. She remembered Queen, her golden glow, and wished more than anything to see her at that moment.

Which way? This way or that?

As Sierra turned to her right, the sound of dry rustling, like a thousand wings in flight, crashed over her. The taste of nectar filled her mouth, sweet honey and cinnamon. Stunned, she paused for a long moment. Was this the next step in her hallucinations? Was she getting worse?

When nothing else happened, she examined the other way around the rock. The sounds and tastes faded to nothing. Intrigued, she faced right again, and once more the fluttering of wings filled her awareness, and sweetness flooded across her tongue. Was she losing her mind?

Then the world flickered in a rainbow of colors; an image floated superimposed over the mountain before her. It was a cave entrance, with gilded lilies blooming on either side of its black mouth. Green grass grew around the cave like an island, surrounded by thick snow on the ground. Impossible. An urgent need pressed against her heart. She *needed* to be at that place. The snow crunched under her boots in her mind as she approached the cave...

Her vision stopped flashing, leaving her in the here and now, aching with a strange sadness. Her lips still tasted of nectar. She realized she was sitting with her head between her knees, her braid hanging over one shoulder, the end of her hair brushing the ground. Her skin felt fevered. Her scarf and hat lay on the forest floor, and Corbin knelt beside her, fanning her rapidly with his hat, brow creased with concern. She didn't even remember sitting down. Micah was next to her, eyes wider than ever. When Sierra looked up at him, he pointed to the back of his neck and then at her, the question plain on his face.

"Yeah, I'm a fairy keeper."

His brow furrowed, and he took two steps back, limping from his injury. His wide-eyed expression was hard to decipher, but it could have been horror, or perhaps disgust. Shock was a certainty.

An inexplicable sadness rose in her at his rejection. She'd tried to help him, and now, well, she guessed if she were a magical creature, she'd be afraid of anyone who somehow harnessed magic too. He couldn't know about the elixirs, though, could he? Exhaustion tugged at her, not only the kind that needed a good eight hours of sleep, either.

She was tired of worrying about her sister, tired of seeking a fairy she didn't want, tired of Corbin and Nell. The one thing Sierra wasn't tired of yet was this new, interesting person-creature, but he acted horrified by her. Maybe she *was* a monster for what she did, stealing from her own fairies. Jack certainly was, and she was his daughter, after all.

She laid her head on her knees, too tired to move. She needed to go to that cave, but she didn't know where it was, and right then, her heart was so heavy it tied her feet to the ground.

A long moment passed in silence. Corbin clamored to his feet and handed Sierra her scarf and hat, squeezing her hand in silent support as he did so. Micah unexpectedly sat beside her, breathing softly, but she couldn't bring herself to look at him.

A lark sang somewhere in the trees far above them. The wind blew against Sierra's naked neck, colder than ever against her skin, except on her mark, which simmered like it was bathed in summer sun.

Tentative fingers touched the top of Sierra's hair, a

caress. Micah slid his hand down her hair, stopping before the keeper mark. When he lightly touched her mark, warmth flowed along her spine. Sierra squeezed her eyes shut, and colors flickered against the backs of her eyelids. What could all those strange visions and sounds mean?

A thought drifted quietly through Sierra's mind: Maybe her queen really was alive and was calling her.

The thought felt so right it almost hurt, like Nell's shoulder snapping into place. Sierra surged up; Micah nearly fell on his fluffy tail. But he stood next to her, almost like a bodyguard ready to protect her.

Nell waved her hand back and forth in front of Sierra's eyes. "Are you seeing weird things again?"

The colors had already faded, but as she faced her right, the taste of honey and cinnamon burst on her tongue. She tilted her head, tasting the potent flavor, so real, so pleasant.

"What would you say if I told you I think we're supposed to go that way? That maybe... maybe somehow I can sense my queen?" Sierra asked, pointing the direction she was facing. "It sounds crazy, but maybe it takes something crazy to solve the situation we're in?"

Nell shrugged. "You're the fairy keeper around here."

She quickly looked at Corbin, realizing her mistake. His face looked stretched too tight, with dark lines furrowed between his eyebrows. He slowly touched his keeper's mark. Nothing happened.

"Why?" His voice was hoarse.

Nell looked perplexed.

Sierra forced herself to meet his anguished gaze. "I don't know. You don't taste anything right now? You didn't hear anything earlier?"

He shook his head, his face crumpling.

Nell stepped closer to him, glaring at Sierra, apparently sure she'd caused his grief. If Corbin wanted Nell to know he had been left out by the fairies, he could share.

If weird lights and taste of nectar were guiding her to the fairies, she would rather pass on the experience than be this out of control. Corbin would have loved to be consumed this way. His face darkened like a raincloud crossing the sun, on the fine line between anger and grief. It was an expression Sierra was used to on her face, not his. It didn't suit him.

"This way," Sierra said, unsure what words of comfort to offer. *Sorry the fairies aren't talking to you? Maybe your fairy is really dead after all?* Nothing worked.

They plunged through the trees, directed by Sierra. Each time she paused to choose a possible path, she waited to see if the taste of honey and cinnamon covered her tongue, or the world went psychedelic as if she were on Flight. Her head felt full of static, a storm looming. Micah followed her like a shadow as they dodged trees, roots, and scrabbly fingers of bushes. The leaves crunched beneath their feet, and soon fresh snow dusted the ground like sugar.

A sense of urgency filled her, rising like rushing water filling an empty well. Her hands clenched, opened, clenched again. She walked faster, her feet flashing under her, uncaring of the many times she skidded on the ice and fell to one knee. The place in her vision was close; she sensed it.

The next time her head started to bow back when the lights descended, a strong arm slid around her waist. Micah's eyes were dark pools, glowing as the lights danced across Sierra's vision. Her heart jumped in her chest. She blamed the lights.

They didn't pause for lunch but continued up the mountain. It was like a hatch of fairies were pinching at her skin, prickling as if lightning was about to strike. Her breathing grew too labored for speech. Micah's arm around her was a permanent fixture. It must have hurt him to help her, but he never made a sound. He was stronger than he looked, like Sierra's fairies.

Two hours into their hike, the landscape changed. Giant boulders jutted from the ground. The trees thinned and then died out. Glaring light bounced off the pale rocks cluttering the mountain and snow blanketed the ground like in her vision. They had reached the top, but there was no cave. She glanced around wildly, as if the answer might be written on the rocks. They'd gone as far as they could. Where did they go from there?

Vertigo swamped her. Blackness wavered at the edges of her vision, a new sensation that had nothing to do with the flickering rainbows and pulsing colors she'd been chasing.

"Down! I need down!" Sierra yelled. The darkness spread, a heavy shadow, and then all was black.

CHAPTER NINETEEN

When Sierra awoke, she was lying on a fur blanket. The sun hung lower in the sky. She tried to roll sideways, but an arm restrained her, and her eyes flew open. She screamed. A startled Micah screamed, too. She wasn't on a fur blanket; she was lying on his legs, warm and soft. Her head buzzed, but she sat up. Cheeks burning, she nodded at him in thanks.

His smile was so sweet and unexpected that it took Sierra's breath away. She had never met anyone—anything?—who made her feel this... safe? Is that what this solid sensation was in her gut? Someone protecting *her* for a change? And she didn't even deserve it.

He pointed behind her, toward a cave. White lilies with gold edges were blooming at the entrance. A small but vibrant circle of green grass spread from the opening, surrounded by snow.

Sierra's stomach jolted like she had fallen from a tree and landed flat on her back. Seeing the place from her vision appear in reality made her skin crawl with goose bumps. Corbin paced and Nell leaned forward, both wearing anxious expressions.

"You were screaming about a cave with golden lilies and 'a circle of spring hidden within winter' when you were..." Nell trailed off, apparently unsure what to say for once.

"You were having some kind of fit. We didn't know what to do to help you. Micah carried you here." Corbin turned a haunted gaze toward Sierra, as though his memories of the event, whatever they were, horrified him still. Questions filled his eyes.

Nell laced her fingers through his in support.

Sierra had no memory of any kind of screaming or fit. At the moment, that seemed far less important that the reality of that impossible cave before her. It really existed. Her vision about it had to mean something. Hope tiptoed into her, quiet and hesitant, but definitely there.

She stood and faced the cave. No strange lights flashed, but a warmth swept through her, like the tide rising. A sense of wholeness brought peace to her heart for the first time in years, since the first time she bonded to her queen. She didn't trust the feeling, but it kept coming and coming, warring with her suspicion, welcoming her to the cave. Something they needed was in there.

A flash of excitement sizzled through Sierra. "What if the fairies are in there? A bunch of queens would have a lot of magic. It would explain the flowers and the green grass."

She gestured at the impossible sight of a lily blooming in winter, the circle of green surrounded by winter.

Nell frowned. "I feel really... strange... about this cave."

She probably felt worse than strange about it but wouldn't admit it.

Corbin had no such problem sharing. "I tried to go in, but it felt like a nightmare. I don't know why." He hung his head.

Micah smiled and stood next to Sierra, gesturing her forward into the cave.

"Don't," Nell said, voice strangled. "We don't know enough to go in there."

The entrance beckoned. There might as well have been a string inside Sierra being pulled toward the cave. She took a step forward.

Nell suddenly blocked the way.

"Move," Sierra said with a low growl. Her sister's life was in the balance. She wasn't stopping now.

"Sierra, wait. The faun could be part of a trap." Nell

pointed at Micah. "After you started yammering about caves and snow and lilies and spring within winter, you passed out, and he brought us *straight* here, carrying you the whole way. He knew this cave and where it was. What's his agenda?"

Sierra scowled. "He lives here. Wouldn't you recognize this strange place when it was described? Lilies shouldn't be in bloom in the snow. Why is the grass so green around the cave like that, except for magic?"

"It could be dangerous," Nell insisted.

Of course Nell felt that way. She feared magic. And this time, she could even be right, but a compulsion grabbed Sierra, much like the way she had to follow her queen when she first called. Music filled her head, swelling, crashing into her soul.

"I don't have a choice," she replied. "I'm sorry, Nell. I really have to go." Sierra stepped around, striding to the cave through the snow, terrified and hopeful all at once.

Weaponry clattered behind her, and then she was flanked by Corbin and Nell. Nell had drawn her sword, gripping the hilt so tightly her knuckles whitened. Corbin had drawn his little herb knife.

Sierra's throat tightened at their show of support. She offered Corbin a smile, hoping he knew how much she loved him. She nodded at Nell, a mark of respect. Micah stood right behind Sierra, a solid presence. She reached her hand behind her back. His hand brushed hers, and she steeled herself.

They entered the cave.

Darkness dropped like a curtain as they inched past the entrance. Sierra shivered, wrapping her coat tighter. She didn't bother drawing her bow. The scent of metal and mold made her nose twitch.

At first there was nothing but the faint sound of water dripping. They kept walking until the opening dwindled to half its former size. The ceiling arched up into the darkness, and their eyes were slow to adjust.

"What's that up there?" Nell asked.

Sierra could barely see the tiny forms hanging along the ceiling, row after row of them. She had enough time to think, *bats*, before screams filled the cave.

A cold swoosh of air flattened her hair against her head. Instinctively, she ducked her chin and dropped to the ground. A familiar scent flowed around her: cinnamon honey, so strong she was drowning in it. Not bats.

Gasping, she scrambled to her feet, a huge mistake. Wings battered her, descending from every direction. She covered her face with her hands and swatted at the fairies. The squeals and shrieks pierced her ears, and sharp fingernails scraped down her arms, leaving bleeding welts. A fairy swarm—and judging by the size, these were all queens. They could kill them all if they decided to sting.

"Run!" Sierra cried.

Screams and shouts filled the air. She headed toward the cave entrance but stumbled over a lump at her feet. She fell hard, shoulder ramming into the rocky cave floor.

The thing she'd tripped over held a sword that reflected what little light reached this far past the entrance. It was Nell, on her hands and knees, head down, arms braced over the back of her neck, sword sticking up at an odd angle. If Sierra had fallen wrong, Nell would have sliced her in half.

Nell was screaming, over and over, with every heaving breath she drew. Fairies covered her like a blanket, swarming. There were too many of them for her to swat away. Where one was thrown off, another latched on. *No!* Not Nell! Blood welled up on her arms.

Panicked, Sierra reached out to help her, but a fairy hit Sierra hard in the face, knocking her back to the ground. Fairy queens might be only the size of butterflies, but no bug ever had that kind of strength. Blood swelled in her mouth and she swallowed. She tasted salt on the back of her tongue, just like the moment when she was bleeding on the ground in front of Jack. The queens might not want to be caught, but she had to get one to Jack. She had to save her sister.

Sierra clamored to her feet, some vague idea of charging the swarm in her mind. But before she could take a single step, a piercing pain stabbed her in her neck. Her hand flew to her keeper mark. A queen gripped her there, stinger impaling her mark. The queen's wings beat frantically, impossible to snatch. Before Sierra could take a single step, she collapsed.

Liquid fire coursed through her body, a pain like she had never felt. She couldn't hear Nell's screams anymore. Sierra was screaming herself.

Lights flashed behind her eyes again, and she felt a rumbling that twisted her stomach even through the blistering heat that seared her blood. She was stung, blinded, paralyzed in a cave full of ravaging fairy queens. The pain, the pain was beyond belief; her mind was dark. Shrieks were glass in her ears.

She convulsed on the ground, her limbs shaking involuntarily, her body jerking. With each movement, a shock of pain ricocheted through her skin, down to her bones. Surely they would snap in half from the pressure. Heat flamed along her nerves, so hot she felt like she was melting.

Sierra had always heard a sting was deadly. She almost hoped it was true because all she wanted now was relief from this agony. The ground shook more, and dust sprinkled over her face. Even in her pain, she moaned in fear at the thought of another quake. An image of the cave collapsing made her try to jump to her feet, but she couldn't move.

Something tugged on Sierra's sleeve, and she screamed, eyes wide, but she couldn't see who had her.

What happened to her fairy? What about her friends? They came in here for her. Nell was attacked. What about Corbin? Micah? Were they dead?

The unbearable heat faded a little, but she began to fade with it. She didn't know how much time had passed.

Queen, she thought, drowsy. *Did you find me? Queen... we've got to save Phoebe...* Sierra needed to explain why they had come here, but her lips wouldn't move, no matter how hard she tried.

Fury at her horrible failure pushed back the darkness long enough for her to notice when the ground began moving beneath her, pinching and ripping at her back. Someone dragged her roughly over the rocky trail until sunlight burst above her, visible even through the dark curtains that had slid over her eyes. Desperation bloomed as she thought, *If I die, what will happen to Phoebe?*

Sierra couldn't move, but she refused to sleep, not yet. Ocean waves of exhaustion crashed over her as the pain receded further. She felt thin, like a shadow on the sand at sunset. Maybe a quick nap would help. A tiny one, that's all.

A voice echoed in her head.

Sierra.

It wasn't so much a sound as a word in her mind. The hairs on her arms stood up.

Sierra, Sierra, the voice called again.

And she understood who was speaking. Sierra opened her eyes, and there on her chest sat Queen, legs crossed, utterly composed.

Hungry... the thought floated into Sierra's mind. Queen had not moved her lips, nor had Sierra, yet she knew somehow her fairy was hungry. Queen missed her mushrooms. Sierra still couldn't move, but her eyes widened. This had never happened before, but it felt so right.

The mushrooms she'd saved for luring a fairy queen were in her bag in the lower left pocket, wrapped in a white cloth. She had refused to touch them even when they were hungry. No sooner had she thought this than Queen flew over to the bag. She dug in the backpack, her wings a blur of gold and red, and tugged out the mushrooms. How did she know?

Moans came from the cave. She jerked upright and the world roiled around her. Waves of blackness danced at the edge of her vision, but she blinked them back. She needed to go to her friends. But her legs were frozen as she stared at her fairy, busily eating. Would she leave if Sierra checked on her friends?

Need you, too... the thought slowly drifted to her. And then an image floated in front of Sierra's eyes, the way the cave superimposed over her sight yesterday. This time, Queen and Sierra were on the ground, clearly dead.

Need each other... the words whispered through her

mind. They were connected in a new way, a way far more permanent than Sierra ever thought possible. Did that image mean if one of them died, the other one would, too?

Yes, yes...

Sierra stared at the queen, who returned the gaze solemnly without blinking. Was Queen really talking to her somehow?

Together, forever...

Sierra's fairy mark no longer burned. She tentatively touched it. It was raised now, a tangible tattoo she could trace with her fingers. The delicate wings were lifted like an intricate piece of jewelry on her skin. When her fingers glided over it, she sensed Queen more than ever.

Despite Sierra's long-time horror of being a keeper and the shock of this sudden change, love for Queen rose like a tide, growing larger with every breath, filling her heart. It was like an invisible door had been opened, and nothing stood between them now. Queen was a part of Sierra in a way she didn't understand. Sierra loved and needed her, even while she still feared and resented a forced destiny of service to her.

A low voice said, "She's bound you together now, in the Old Way."

Sierra didn't recognize this voice, deep and melodious. Her heart sped up—who was this? His voice sounded too perfect to be real.

She turned around to find the source. Micah stood

behind her—on legs that were no longer hairy. Or deer-shaped. Human legs completed a now very human looking Micah, who wore only a piece of cloth from Sierra's supplies, tied like a kilt around his waist that reached almost to his knees. Sierra goggled. Almost as astonishing and disconcerting, Micah was no longer scrawny and sick-looking. His chest was bronzed and strong, muscles curving smoothly. One shock after another had Sierra blinking her eyes.

She glanced around, but no one else was with them to confirm if she was hallucinating.

"They have generously healed me in the Old Way, too," he explained, as if he had always spoken clearly. "I knew this spot when you described it. The queens came to drink deeply of the old magic, which has been terribly depleted across this land. This is the birthplace, the heart, an ancient well of magic that runs deep beneath the earth."

He waited a moment for Sierra to respond, but when she kept staring without saying a word, he continued, "It is why the plants always grow here. I could not access the magic before. It was far too buried, but a fairy queen's gift is to draw it forth into the world and share with other magical creatures. Their magic does not affect me as it does humans. The fairy sting you received carried a large amount of magic and would be deadly to most humans. I am surprised, though thankful, that you reacted so differently."

Sierra felt like she had been kicked in the chest, or perhaps more appropriately, shot with an arrow.

"Wait—you-you-you're human now?" she managed to stammer.

He laughed. "No, not human. Still a faun, but the fairies have returned to me the ability to shift to all three of my forms. Human seemed most appropriate in this situation."

All three of his…

Before she could ask anything about this most unexpected state of affairs, a loud scream echoed in the cave. The scream was long and hoarse. *Corbin*!

Sierra scrambled up, but her knees gave out. Micah offered his hand, and she hesitated only for a second. He pulled her to her feet, and they stumbled into the cave again. Her knees kept collapsing, and finally, he simply scooped her up in a stunning display of grace.

She flushed, confused by the way he held her so carefully like she was a prized treasure. Affection surged through her, but there was no time to examine her feelings right now. She was just glad he'd survived. The question was, had Corbin and Nell?

Queen? Sierra thought to herself, and a flutter brushed her cheek. Queen landed on her shoulder, as she used to, and instead of sullen resentment, Sierra felt relief. Queen would probably keep the others off her. Trust and comfort radiated from the fairy, softening

Sierra's heart. Queen had never responded that way before.

The queens had returned to the cave ceiling after the swarm. When they flew toward Sierra from their cave perches, Sierra's queen zipped up and flashed back and forth in front of them in a dizzying display. No queen tried to push past the flying barrier. Queen's furious flight sent a steady, gentle breeze into Sierra's face that cooled the sweat across her skin. Her fairy, the one who had actually stung her and was always so ready to pinch or bite, was defending her. The enormity of the change was almost too much to take in.

"Nell!" Corbin was crying. "Nell!"

Sierra and Micah moved deeper into the cave, and the shadowy forms in front of them resolved into recognizable shapes. Corbin leaned over the still body of Nell, whose arms were thrown wide, hand empty of her sword. Her hair spread across the ground like spilled paint, ghostly white in the darkness. Corbin held one limp hand and rocked back and forth as he knelt beside her. Tears dripped from his cheeks, gaze fastened to her face.

Micah gently set Sierra down and stood silently behind her. The force of Corbin's grief demanded respect. She crawled to them and reached toward his shoulder to offer comfort.

"Don't touch me!" he cried.

Tears stung Sierra's eyes. Tiny streams of blood

crisscrossed almost every exposed surface of Nell's skin, dripping onto the cave floor. Tiny bite marks, tiny scratches... Nell had suffered while Sierra was dragged out of the worst of it. Her eyes flicked to Micah before returning to Nell. There was a sting mark on the side of her neck. The puncture was deep red, startling against the paleness of her skin. Even more startling, it was pulsing. Literally, her skin was jumping in time to a pulse.

Sierra shouted, "She's alive!"

Corbin moaned, "No, she's not breathing. She's gone."

Sierra pushed Corbin out of the way. Leaning forward, she pressed her lips to Nell's. They were cold and dry, but Sierra cupped her hand around Nell's jaw and pinched her nose. Sierra had seen Jack's enforcers do that when they got too rough with someone. Most healers believed that forcing life into someone was a desecration of a soul's journey, but she didn't care. Nell's journey wasn't over yet.

Sierra became Nell's breath, blowing in and watching her chest rise. The air pushed back out when Sierra lifted her face for a moment.

Corbin started to object. "It's too late," he sobbed. "Leave her in peace!"

He grabbed Sierra's shoulders, but she pushed him back. The rocky edges of pebbles pressed into her knees, but she ignored them, leaning back in. She took a deep breath. The smell of honey filled her. She blew again into Nell's mouth. Three times. Four. Sierra began to fear it wasn't going to work, but then Nell gasped, a long inhalation that paused and then whooshed the air out. Nell drew the next breath on her own, eyes closed, body still. But she was breathing.

Corbin heaved a sob of relief and gathered her in his arms.

"Thank you, Sierra," he whispered as he carried Nell out of the cave. Sierra and Micah followed. A sense of triumph filled her. She felt powerful, unstoppable. She had her queen. They had all survived. Nell would live. Well, at least Sierra hoped so.

Corbin laid Nell on a bedroll outside, and they all knelt beside her in the snow on the far edge of the clearing, even though it meant leaving the green grass. Queen had gone back to her mushrooms without further thoughts intruding into Sierra's.

Sierra held Nell's right hand while Corbin held her left. Slowly, warmth seeped back to her fingers and blood returned to her cheeks, like a statue coming to life. Her eyes flashed open. The pale, icy blue was ringed by a blue deeper than the ocean. Sierra had never had a chance to notice before. Nell opened her mouth. Everyone smiled at her, encouragingly. Then she began to scream.

CHAPTER TWENTY

The fairy stings were still at work. Sierra's ears practically bled from the force of Nell's shrieks.

Corbin's eyes were wild, hands clenched. "What's happening?" he shouted.

Nell writhed, moaned, and convulsed. Flecks of blood flew from the cuts and bites all over her, staining the snow around them.

"Is this what I did, after I was stung?" Sierra asked.

Micah replied, "Much like this, yes."

Corbin nearly fell over when he heard Micah speak and then did a double-take when he saw Micah's new appearance. Explanations had to wait, though. Corbin and Sierra threw themselves over Nell's upper body to keep her from beating her head against the rocks. Micah struggled to contain her flailing legs.

Corbin hollered through yells that continued to shatter the air. "You survived something like this?"

"That's what I'm told." Sierra grunted when Nell kneed her in the gut.

"Maybe if we can hang on—" an elbow caught Corbin in the throat.

"She'll get over it?" Sierra finished for him.

"Yeah."

Optimistic Corbin. Sierra only hoped Nell wasn't dying a slow death now instead of a fast death in the cave.

Not death... not death... Queen flew at attention next to Nell's head now. Another fairy joined. It was Corbin's queen. He was too busy to notice, but joy swelled Sierra's heart. He'd be so thrilled once he saw. If Nell was okay. A third queen joined them, unknown to them, deep russet and gold, one who would blend in beautifully in the woods. Another and another fairy flew to the scene, until there was a ring around them, fifty fairy queens or more. If they attacked again…

Micah grasped her shoulder and said, "Step back."

"What?" she replied. "Are you crazy?"

"The fairies are here."

"Yeah, the things that nearly killed us are here. That's good because why?"

A sense of sadness, of hurt, fluttered under her heart. Sierra felt… wounded. She shook her head. She didn't understand these emotions. They couldn't be coming from her. Queen perched near Nell's head, gazing at Sierra with sparkling eyes. She'd hurt Queen's feelings. *Queen* was the one who was sad.

Sierra's cheeks flushed, and she looked away for a long moment before turning back to meet those otherworldly eyes.

"I'm sorry," Sierra said to her queen.

Queen had changed, and so had Sierra. Her actions had to change, too. Queen deserved better than how she'd been treated before. Sierra now wanted to make her fairy happy, as strange as that was.

She stepped toward the edge of the circle, but Corbin grabbed her hand, fingernails digging painfully into her skin.

"What are you doing?" he exclaimed, eyeing their nonhuman audience.

"Trust your queen. She's here, too," Sierra replied, trying to do the same, and shook off his hand. She stepped past the fairies to stand next to Micah, who gazed at her with something that looked like approval. At least someone appreciated what she was trying to do.

Corbin snapped his head around, and then froze when he saw his fairy, Grace. Her wings were the yellow of daffodils, lined with gold. Blistering joy melted with confusion and hurt on his face.

"Why is this happening?" he whispered.

It wasn't his fairy who answered. It was Nell. But the voice coming from Nell's body was the voice of a grown woman, a deep, rich tone an octave lower than her usual. A strange accent lilted the words, as well, an accent Sierra had never heard. Nell's eyes remained shut even as her pale lips opened.

"Because we must tell others through you. The little fairies did not die because the queens left. The queens left because the little ones perished. Great grief accompanied their journey here, and many queens barely survived. Even their best efforts could not draw forth enough magic from their land to sustain their hatches. Without magic, you are all in danger. You must give our message, you who have ears to hear. Stop plundering nectar! Allow the earth to heal, with keepers protecting and guiding their fairies as beloved friends. This you must do to save them, yourselves, and the world."

With a deep sigh, Nell seemed to settle deeper into the ground, and the fairies all lifted to the sky with a flurry of wings that made Sierra duck.

Queen sent a feeling of mournful regret, and whispered to Sierra's mind *Will be back...* She flew away with the others, but Sierra trusted those words without thinking, even though she wasn't sure she'd really heard them. Now that the initial moment of shock had passed, she was beginning to wonder. Visions were one thing. Words clearly heard inside her head were quite another. Maybe she'd lost her mind. And if she wasn't insane, she wasn't sure she could deal with the implications of this communication.

Strong arms wrapped around her shoulders, surrounding her with warmth. Sierra lifted her hand and touched Micah's arm, uncertain about his motives but thankful for the safety she felt with him.

Micah looked to the sky to follow the queen fairies' flight back to the cave. When he looked down at Sierra and smiled, she was robbed of speech. He stepped back and bowed a small, courtly bow. It should have seemed ridiculous, given he wore only a makeshift kilt, but it was completely the opposite. Sierra could practically hear lutes playing in the background. Her scalp prickled with the sudden memory of his words, "Their magic does not affect me as it does humans."

Humans.

Who was Micah, really? What did it mean to be other than human, even when he looked like one right now? What had he seen in his life here in the mountains? Where was his family? Sierra blushed with mortification at giving him a name, like a pet. Giving a name to something that reminded her of sad Sam was one thing. But this blindingly beautiful magical being was nothing anyone could try to tame or own. His brown eyes glowed with health now, and he stood proud and tall.

He turned, and Sierra jumped when she realized the bloody bandage was gone, as well, and not a scar marred his smooth skin. She craned her neck to make sure, and he smiled down over his shoulder as she peered at his back, disbelief stamped across her face.

"It is magic in the truest sense of the word, Sierra. Magic can heal those of us able to receive it properly. And now that I am fully healed, I can take the form of a deer, a faun, or a human, as fauns did of old. Before, I only had enough energy to take the form of a deer or a faun. I am, in my most basic essence, a faun, but that is a creature with the traits of two animals together. How else is that possible but for incredible magic?"

"Oh! So I did shoot a deer, only that was you? I didn't somehow miss noticing the human half after all?" At least she could feel less stupid now.

"That is correct. I would have told you sooner, but obviously, could not. I sensed something nearby involved with magic, but what it was, I could not tell. To escape, I transformed to an ordinary animal few magical creatures would notice, but you were too quick."

"I'm really so sorry—" she began again, but he placed one finger against her lips. Words died in her throat.

"There is no reason to feel badly. You hunted for food, for survival. You are not a cruel person. Furthermore, you brought me here, where I was healed. You've been touched by that same magic now, too. Perhaps even before." He pointed to the scrape on her arm. "Is that from your fairies?"

Sierra nodded. "They bite and scratch me all the time."

She flushed, thinking about why they did.

He looked satisfied. "This explains a great deal. They are made of magic, coated with nectar filled with even more magic. Every time they bit or scratched you, they left magic in you, building ever higher. And that same magic called you here."

Queen sent a feeling of affirmation to Sierra, whose mind whirled. She felt she might need to sit down.

"Let's be clear. You're asking me to believe I could visualize the cave and survive Queen's sting because I infuriated my fairies too often over the years? Isn't that a little too ironic?"

He shrugged, unconcerned with her pronouncement. "Magic is what it is."

"That's ridiculous."

Micah's smile was slow but was the kind that invited a grin in return. "I believe you've had the potential to receive messages from your queen from your first bond, but it took a great deal of magic to free the gift. Your queens shared tremendous knowledge with me through their magic. The world was too drained for that gift of communication to develop on its own the way it would have many years ago. You were born for this, Sierra. The fairies might have meant their attacks for harm, but perhaps the earth itself meant them for good, preparing you for this moment in time."

Sierra was stunned but coherent enough to wish the earth had chosen some other method.

"But wait," she argued. "In the cave, Corbin was scratched and bit. If he was seeing or hearing anything weird, he'd tell me. And Nell is still alive when she definitely shouldn't be. So what makes me different?"

Her jaw jutted out as she prepared for a fight, but his next words scattered her arguments. "I can sense the magic in you. One fairy swarm cannot compare. Nell must have keeper blood somewhere in her family to have survived, though I do not know how she will fare when she awakens. As for Corbin, it is possible that soon he will develop the same gifts you have now. However, there is another consideration.

"You have the blood of ancient fairy keepers running through your veins from both sides of your family. Perhaps no one else has the same gifting you do. When I was growing up, before things got so... difficult... my parents and I kept a close watch on the keepers and hunters who came to these mountains. None of those humans came close to your level of power, not even the keepers. I believe you can bear more of the fairies' magic without damage."

She shook her head slowly. "I don't believe you. I've been damaged plenty of times."

"But not killed. Not even seriously wounded, even after a direct sting to your neck, to your keeper's mark, in fact, which has changed since I first saw it. Your natural gift gives off a particular scent, you know, and this scent has grown much stronger since the swarm." He took a step closer.

Sierra took a step back. "A scent? No one's ever told me I smell funny."

She was tempted to sniff herself to check—it had been a rough trip--but pride held her still.

His laugh rolled out like an ocean wave. "No, Sierra. It's a delightful fragrance that would undoubtedly let your queen know of your potential ability. I doubt humans can even sense it. It's not the scent of a magical creature, but it's similar. As soon as you got close enough, I recognized you right away as a human with one foot firmly in the world of magic. The strength of your scent suggests abilities far higher than a fairy keeper, so I was shocked when your mark was revealed. When your fairy stung you, she raised you to a new level of bonding, one that changed everything for her—and you."

Sierra wondered for a moment if this scent was anything like the rosemary and rain sweetness she had smelled on Sam and now Micah.

He caressed her new, improved mark, and it wasn't only the usual warmth that surged through her. A feeling of safety swelled inside, too, like she was at home, a real home. She felt like she'd known him forever. She wanted to lean into him, but, instead, she stumbled back.

This had to be the magic at work. It was so strange to

be this fascinated by him, so drawn to him. Maybe the magic in her recognized another creature of magic. She stepped backward again and forced her hands to stay at her sides instead of lacing her fingers through his like she wanted. She didn't know Micah, not really. She had thought he needed help, but if anything ever did *not* need her help, it was him.

In fact, nothing was stopping them from moving as quickly as possible back home. Sierra had her queen. They had to get back for Phoebe. With Nell so ill, their return journey would take longer than expected. The thought of leaving Micah made Sierra feel empty, but panic grabbed her by the throat when she counted up the days they'd been gone and realized they had only ten days left to get back to Jack.

Nell was calm now, still asleep, holding tightly to Corbin's hand. Their obvious love drew barely a faint pang from Sierra. Corbin and Sierra might still be close after this journey, since she and Nell had come to an understanding. Assuming Nell lived.

Sierra stepped away to give them privacy, and to escape Micah's knowing gaze. She leaned on a white boulder that had cracked along one side, perhaps from the quake. Micah followed, and her stomach clenched. Now they were practically alone. She didn't know what to do.

"What?" she hissed over her shoulder at him.

He stepped beside her and looked down, seeming

taller than before. "I will not forget you saved me. She would have left me behind to die, wounded in winter, less than an animal. I owe you my life."

Sierra's throat tightened. "If I hadn't shot you, your life wouldn't have needed saving. I'd say we're even. Where is your family? You don't seem much older than us; surely you have someone we could find for you?"

It was the responsible thing to offer, though it pained her to think of saying goodbye.

"That is not the way of it. You have shown me honor. I must show the same. I am fifteen winters but have lived alone for five years, since my parents died."

"I'm sorry. That sounds very hard."

He replied, "In many ways, the same lack of magic stole their lives as it stole my voice and my health. There are precious few fauns left in these mountains, and none of them have spoken in years. There is nothing to prevent me from honoring my debt to you."

A strange disappointment touched her, followed by a flare of annoyance. Was a desire to return a favor the only reason why he sought out her company?

"Look. I appreciate the sentiment, but we've got to get going. We're even. Promise."

Her eyes stung a little, but she stared at the mountain ridge below them with a stoicism Jack would have admired. She jumped when Micah glided his hands around her shoulders.

"Sierra," he said her name like a promise.

He gently turned her to face him, and she was helpless. She looked into his eyes, and again she saw herself reflected. Her hair flowed around her shoulders, pulled loose from its braid during her screaming fits. She flushed to think of him seeing her like that. But in his eyes now, Sierra admitted to herself that she looked almost... lovely. But he didn't ask her to be soft and feminine. He respected her the way she was, even though she did things she wasn't proud of. He seemed to see all the way inside her to the cold, rough places, in a way that not even Corbin ever had.

"What should we call you now?"

"I like the name you have chosen. In all honesty, with the years that have passed since I could speak, I haven't thought of my old name in many moons. Micah will do fine."

He smiled at her and she smiled back, hesitantly, secretly thrilled he wanted to keep the name she gave him.

"Why is that?" she asked. "I mean, why could you not speak? Does that have anything to do with changing into a deer?"

He shrugged. "I have long been able to transform to a deer, as it is a useful disguise at times and a fast way to travel. But I can only remain in that shape for short periods of time. A deer is a simple creature. Magical creatures take on the reality of the shape they wear. Were I to remain a deer for long, my consciousness would fade to that of a deer. I would disappear, leaving only the wild animal. Not something I'd wish to have happen, I assure you."

Sierra shuddered. "But wait—why were you already a faun when I found you after... after I shot you? Why didn't I see a deer instead?"

"Ah. Illness and wounding disrupts our ability to work magic. I cannot hold any shape but my original if I am seriously ill or wounded."

She frowned. "You'd think magic could work, no matter what, or what's the point?"

"Magic has its own laws to follow. You know this."

She did?

Micah continued, "As far as why I couldn't speak even as a faun, I know that a world without sufficient magic will damage magical creatures first. My parents told me, though, of fauns in older times who often walked as human men and women, who even decided to remain in the body of a human and let the magic fade from them. They eventually became human, because they felt it was better to live a full life without magic as a human than a magical but short life as the hunted."

"They just... became human? Non-magical? You won't accidentally get stuck as a human, will you?"

"No, humans and fauns are much more alike than faun and deer. I suspect I could live the entire time between full moons as a human without danger. Then

I'd only need to refresh my magic by reverting to my original shape for a time."

"That's... amazing."

"Indeed, it is, just as it is amazing that you can now hear your queen the way the keepers of old did."

Sierra froze at his casual confirmation of her fears. If he spoke the truth, then Queen owned Sierra now more than ever. Maybe insanity would be better.

"I don't know what you mean," Sierra said.

He stared at her like she was a pupil who had missed the point of a lesson. "If you insist. But you should know that my father passed down all the stories of Aluvia's history to me before he passed. You cannot hide certain truths from me."

To have Queen permanently invading Sierra's thoughts and emotions for the rest of her life? Even with the new love flowing between her and her fairy, she wasn't ready to discuss the change.

"Thank you for pulling me out of the cave." Sierra changed the topic. "You saved my life in there. Don't you think we're even?"

He shook his head. "You made a choice to stay with me, at the risk of great loss. What I did took no risk. Fairies cannot harm me. You led me here, which allowed my full healing. I need to offer a worthy sacrifice for you."

She poked him in the shoulder. "Stop saying stuff like that! I don't need any sacrifice from you!"

"But you have sacrificed for others here," he protested.

He was clearly crazy. Too bad. Those eyes and that scent... and that voice... and those kind, wise words... Well, if he weren't crazy, he'd be someone she could actually enjoy spending time with. If she were honest, he was even a secret candidate for that maybe-someday kiss, so she guessed it was better to find out early on that he was missing a few arrows from the quiver. It wasn't like she could really be with him, anyway. Her heart lurched. If Jack stole from the fairies, what might he take from the first faun to be seen in years? The thought made her shudder.

"Whatever. Everything I've done, I've done for myself. I love my sister and can't live without her, get it? So I'm going to save her, which means bringing Queen back to Jack and—"

"Didn't you hear what Nell said?" Corbin interrupted.

Sierra stiffened, wondering how long he'd been standing behind them. "It doesn't matter—"

"She *said* we couldn't keep taking their nectar like we do. Bad things will happen. As in, it'll destroy the world. You can't bring the queens back to Jack."

Sierra didn't care if the entire country fell into the ocean, as long as Phoebe was safe. Corbin glared at Sierra, daring her to argue.

Micah, though, eyed her with speculation. "Perhaps

we can wait to discuss the situation once we reach your sister?"

"We? What do you mean, 'we'?" Sierra blurted out.

Micah glided toward her, maneuvering through the tangled rocks on his human legs as gracefully as if he were dancing.

"Is it not obvious? I must accompany you back to your home, to fulfill my honor's requirements."

CHAPTER TWENTY-ONE

A faun—no matter his chosen shape—escorting her back to Jack? Completely impossible. They couldn't risk a slip-up, and he couldn't stay human forever. A walking faun would cause riots. Jack would want to lock Micah in a cave and charge admission. Villagers might be too willing to grab a sword and flaming torch. She tried to make Micah understand the problem with his plan.

In return, Micah calmly listed all the reasons he needed to come with them. They'd need help carrying Nell. He knew the quickest paths down the mountain. He knew which berries and foods were safe to eat. Since Sierra was obviously not a reliable hunter—to put it mildly—and Nell was unconscious, they'd need his knowledge to survive.

Once Micah presented his arguments, Corbin agreed

right away. He would have agreed to anything to get Nell to a healer faster. Sierra took a little more persuading, but Micah was coming to help, like it or not. She hated that she really did like him staying with them. A lot.

Sierra wasn't ready for someone else to care about. Loving people opened the door for pain if—*when*—something bad happened. Love was a risk, and risks were dangerous. She tried to minimize risks at all times.

Phoebe was going to *looove* this one. In fact, she would love everything about Micah.

After a quick discussion, the group decided to wait and leave in the morning, hoping Nell would be awake by then. Night was already falling. None of them wanted to go back in the cave, so they set up a little camp between the boulders that offered protection from the wind.

Sierra crawled into her bedroll and imagined running to her sister, hugging her, triumphantly showing Jack the fairy queens... but then, the daydream ground to a halt. Sierra couldn't get past the image of giving Jack the fairies, essentially sending them back into slavery. If she gave them away, could she get them back later?

Corbin's accusations echoed in her mind as the wind howled above the rocks. She lay on one side, then tossed to the other. It didn't matter—she had to get Phoebe back. The fairies' dilemma would have to wait. It wasn't like Sierra was taking them all to Jack. All she needed was one. *Queen.*

Her heart squeezed hard, but she forced deep breaths, focusing on Phoebe's sweet face. Rest seemed impossible, but eventually sleep overwhelmed her spinning mind.

They awoke to the cold. Sometime in the night, Queen and Grace had returned to them and snuggled in their respective bedrolls. Corbin's smile when he saw his fairy was brighter than the sun. Sierra breathed a sigh of relief at the sight of her own tiny queen, golden and beautiful as always.

Morning... Queen whispered. The word was accompanied by a cheery feeling of welcome.

Sierra tried not to show a response in front of the others, but mentally replied, *To you as well.*

Warm happiness flowed from Queen to Sierra. The strength of the emotion pushed back the chill of the morning. Okay, maybe this kind of communication wouldn't be so bad after all. Maybe she'd ask the others about it when they were on the road, but she felt strangely shy about discussing it.

A light snow had fallen during the night, covering over the red that stained the ground around Nell. Their journey home thus began on an optimistic note. Even more hopeful was the cloud of fairies flying above them, dipping and swirling like playful butterflies. Gone were the angry, dangerous fairies from before. They now seemed sated and pleased. Sierra didn't know why they were with them, and Queen didn't seem interested in sharing, if she knew. It was just as well that Nell hadn't gained consciousness yet. Sierra doubted Nell would find the sight of the fairies so uplifting.

Corbin's queen sat on his shoulder with a smile, though his mark hadn't changed as Sierra's had. Gazing at them, a sudden thought left Sierra thunderstruck. She wanted to groan. She couldn't tell anyone she might be hearing Queen speak, at least not for now! Corbin was sad enough that he didn't experience the visions and taste of nectar that guided them to the cave. If he knew Queen was actually *talking* to her, sharing emotions, and his queen Grace wasn't... well. It would crush him, even if Queen had to bite, scratch, and sting her way into Sierra's heart. Maybe that was the only way Queen could get in, she admitted. Still, she didn't mind waiting to share.

Nell's neck and hands were covered in scratches, and some bites had even torn through her shirt and jacket. Still, her breath was slow and steady and her cheeks were pink in the cold morning air. Corbin and Micah carried her. Sierra brought Nell's knives and bows and arrows, and Corbin wore the sword. Sierra hoped he didn't fall on it.

They half-slid down the steep paths, sending gravel skittering down the trail. The snow thinned out to mere patches here and there as they returned to the denser forest. Sierra breathed a little easier now. The trees offered cover if they had to hide.

Micah had been very quiet. She wondered what he was thinking about, if he was mad at her for not wanting him to come with them. The last thing she had intended was to hurt his feelings. She sighed.

"So... I've heard there are griffins here," Sierra said to him, in an awkward attempt at conversation.

He nodded. Corbin's breath puffed from carrying Nell, but Micah looked as if he'd been reclining on a bed somewhere. He seemed completely comfortable hiking with bare feet and legs.

"Yes, and also nagas, manticores, trolls, and dragons, along with other creatures."

"Dragons?" Sierra stumbled.

Corbin did, too, and Nell nearly hit the ground.

Micah waited while they both regained their footing and then continued, "Yes, though they are no longer as they were."

Sierra narrowed her eyes at him. "Are you being vague on purpose?"

"They are quite rare now. I haven't seen one since I was a child," he offered.

She swore his eyes twinkled. They walked in silence before Sierra asked another question.

"How long were you... like that? Unable to talk?"

Discomfort nipped at her, but she had wondered this since he first spoke.

He lifted his haunted gaze to hers. "It was eight winters of silence for me, though I had grown weak and ill as a very young faun." He shook his head. "I have forgotten many things, I think, but I am grateful to be healed from the loss of magic."

"It sounds really horrible."

"It was. I believe..." Here he paused, but then his voice gained in strength. "I believe many creatures are still suffering as I was. And I am sorry to say that keepers who hoard the nectar of their hatches contributed to this dilemma, in addition to those who came to these mountains to take the wild fairies captive."

For a moment, Sierra almost couldn't hear what he was trying to say. His voice was so musical, so lulling with such carefully chosen words. Then what he said came clear, and she recoiled as if he had struck her.

"I didn't do this to you! I mean, I shot you, but I didn't starve you."

Corbin also protested, "I've loved my hatch from the beginning! Not all keepers abuse their charges."

The phrase, *Unlike Sierra,* hovered unvoiced. He didn't look at her as he spoke, but his statement hurt, so sharp it left numbness behind.

"Not all keepers, no, I imagine not. But don't humans

take nectar from the fairies for many reasons, some even seen as noble?"

Corbin fell silent. Sierra didn't answer, either. Too many things were flashing through her mind, first and foremost, Flight. But beyond that, medicines made from nectar were used throughout the continent as well.

The pang of guilt shifted to anger. "What was I supposed to do? Let Jack beat me to death? Kill Phoebe? You don't understand." Her fairy flew down and brushed her cheek, sensing her distress, breathing peace into her.

Micah's dark eyes were steady. "As I said, you are loyal. And the fairies are drawn to you—both of you"—his gaze moved to include Corbin—"because you were born able to share a special bond with them. They desire your companionship, not just your protection. They are such social creatures."

He waved at Sierra's queen, who was fluttering above her head, doing silly dive bombs now and then. It was the kind of behavior that used to irritate Sierra but now seemed as charming as a toddler wanting to play chase. Queen meant no harm. She only wanted to cheer Sierra up. In fact, Queen loved her, through and through. Sierra felt it, steady as a heartbeat.

Queen sent love to her wordlessly, and it was delicious, like being offered cake. The depth of that love was almost tangible, a gift that could be held onto like a life-line. Queen had fought Sierra to stop the loss of the hatch's nectar but had chosen her out of love in the first place. Wild fairies had chosen to be with humans from the beginning of humanity's existence for this same reason.

This rich love hummed in the back of Sierra's mind all the time now, impossible to ignore. She was coming to accept their new relationship, though it meant changing her entire view of fairies. But she still quietly resented the theft of her choice. Her whole life changed again. Queen didn't ask. She had just bonded them, like the first time, only stronger. But that still didn't make taking her nectar okay.

Honesty was painful but necessary. "Corbin's right. I stole from her and let Jack use her magic for evil. I stole from them for him, taking too much, and they kept making more. If that makes me a horrible person, so be it. I'd do it again. I'm sorry, but I've got to protect my sister."

Queen became agitated, motions becoming faster and erratic. Her thoughts were a jumble, and Sierra couldn't decide if Queen was upset about Phoebe's possible fate or that Sierra valued her sister over the fairies.

Sierra tried to send a thought to her queen. The fumbling attempt felt odd and embarrassing, like eating a meal with her feet. *I'm sorry, Queen.* And truly, she was. She didn't sense anything in return, so she guessed she failed to communicate. Not surprising.

Sierra picked up her pace to build distance between

her and the faun and Corbin. She decided she'd start referring to Micah as such in her head: *The faun*. It didn't matter that he looked human—he was still a magical creature. He wasn't Micah. He was only a barely-known faun who happened to look like a young god and act like a hero.

CHAPTER TWENTY-TWO

When they stopped for lunch, *the faun* went foraging and returned with light pink berries. They tasted like the spun sugar Sierra used to get once a year when the fair travelled down the coast. He also had used Sierra's fairy nets to carry back piles of dark green leaves, which didn't look edible but tasted delicious after cooking, balanced by the sweet berries.

Sierra handed out the last of the bread. They needed strength to keep going. The cold sapped everyone's energy, though she imagined the boys were kept warm by carrying Nell's tall frame. They had icy water in their canteens, and Corbin dripped a few drops into Nell's mouth. He mashed some of the berries and spread some along the inside of her lips. She licked the fruit and swallowed, all on her own. Corbin gave a hoot and offered her more. Her eyes fluttered open, and Nell finally looked around.

"What in the great green forest happened to you?" she said, taking in the scabs from bites and scratches covering Sierra and Corbin. Her voice sounded scratchy and rough from all the screams, but it was definitely Nell's voice.

"You don't remember?" Corbin's voice was higher than usual.

Sierra let him take lead.

Nell slowly shook her head and raised her hand to her head. "Ooh," she moaned. "I feel like I got kicked in the head." She aimed a steely glare at Sierra. "Did you do this?"

Ah, she was back. Sierra had to smile, making Nell glower even harder.

"No, a bunch of fairies did that all on their own."

Nell's brow furrowed. She examined her hands, frowning at the visible scratches and bites.

"Was there... a cave?" Her voice dropped, as hesitant as it had ever been.

Corbin scooted closer and pillowed Nell's head on his legs. Interestingly, Sierra wasn't bothered at all.

"Yes, there was," he answered.

When Nell's gaze found *the faun*, she sputtered, "Whoa! What happened to *him*?"

Sierra knew exactly what she meant, but didn't even know how she could explain and still ignore him. She accidentally met his eyes and felt a blush burn her cheeks. He smiled and raised his eyebrow at her reaction, clearly amused. *Ugh.*

Fortunately, Nell saw the queen sitting on Sierra's shoulder and was immediately distracted. "It's a fairy! You did it!"

She sounded shocked but genuinely pleased. Warmth that had nothing to do with the weak sunlight filtering through the pines filled Sierra's heart.

"Yep, so we're on our way home. Think you can walk?"

Corbin glanced at Sierra. She figured he wanted to know if they should tell Nell what she said, how she said it. Sierra gave a slight shake of her head. One thing at a time.

Nell gasped and shrank back when she saw the small army of fairies making lazy loops around them.

"I remember them!" she whispered. She froze, eyes wide.

Corbin held her hands, and they all stared at the fairy entourage. Sierra doubted all the queens would leave the woods, but for now, they were an amazing sight. They seemed like well-fed children who had even gotten a fat slice of pie after a feast. Queen radiated satisfaction, too, full to the brim with magic once more.

Nell relaxed once it became clear they weren't swarming. These were all queens, after all, without hatches. The incident at the cave aside, usually the tiny workers did most of the swarming if they were provoked, sometimes for the most ridiculous reasons. Not too bright, the little things.

That was part of why when a queen was ready to raise young, she usually bonded to a keeper who helped care for the little fairies. Until then, though, queen fairies traveled the world, or they used to. Not many queens strayed from their hatches in recent years. Maybe that change was part of the problem.

They took things slowly the rest of the day. Nell could walk with the help of Corbin, which left Micah walking too near to Sierra for comfort. She couldn't forget what he said, about keepers causing harm to all magical creatures. Had she really been hurting Queen so terribly? Or other innocent creatures like Old Sam? It was like finding out she had been starving Phoebe without knowing it.

When the sun dipped below the trees, they made an early stop for the night. Nell was winded, though she wouldn't admit it, and Corbin was, too. Sierra was exhausted, in some deep place without words.

Nell and Corbin built a fire, a crackling warmth that sent up sparks from the added dried pine needles. The scent reminded Sierra strongly of home, and she wrapped herself in her blanket, not even interested in dinner. Queen nestled in Sierra's hair. Corbin's fairy was nearby, but the rest were off somewhere else. If Sierra concentrated, she could sense something that seemed like, *Happy, happy, warm... tired...* coming from Queen. Soon the fairy fell asleep, her soft breath whispering against Sierra's neck.

Inexplicably, Sierra felt safe. Her shoulders relaxed after being tight all day. At least the packs weren't heavy anymore, since they were out of food.

The voices of the others were a soft murmur, but she didn't pay much attention.

"Only one week..." floated through the dusk. A girl's voice. Nell.

"—have to go faster, tomorrow—"

Ignore, ignore, ignore. Sierra burrowed deeper in her blankets. Eventually, sleep claimed her.

A loud trumpet and a flash of red light disrupted Sierra's sleep. She sat up, blinking her eyes, trying to make sense of what was happening. The ground wasn't moving. No quakes. But a plume of fire curled through the trees next to her, setting the dry branches aflame.

She shouted, stumbling out of the bedroll, but the others were already awake and responding. Nell had her sword out, not even trembling in the face of the encroaching fire. The heat flowed to them in waves, the crackling becoming a roar. The smell of burnt wood singed their noses.

Queen clasped tight to Sierra's shoulder. *Run! Run!*

Run! One's panic was indistinguishable from the other's. Sierra thankfully didn't see any other fairies.

Another wave of flames showed them what they faced, illuminating a creature of ancient tales against the pitch black of the night. The impossible loomed in the flickering light, but there was no mistaking this creature: a dragon stood before them.

The beast resembled a lizard but was bigger than two full-grown bears, covered in red and orange scales that reflected the light of the flames. A long tongue snaked out as it wove its head back and forth on its long neck, as if to hypnotize them. Leathery wings hung down its back and a long tail flicked behind it. Sierra's breath shuddered out, her lungs wheezing. Then the dragon roared, rattling her bones and kicking her heart into a frenzy.

Sweat drenched her despite the cold. Her hands moved to her bow, too slowly, as if she were moving through molasses. She was going to be too late.

The dragon took a deep breath, chest expanding. Even as Sierra realized the danger in that moment, the beast's unreal beauty captivated her. She dropped her hands to her side, nearly paralyzed by the sight. Never had she seen such graceful beauty disguised as death. There was a power in its form, balanced completely by its elegance, brilliant coloring, and flowing movement. Her eyes stung, and not from fear, sadness or wood smoke. The creature was simply that incredible. If she was going to die, then she was glad she'd die seeing this.

Soft singing floated through the crackling fire, and the dragon froze. No flames came as it waited. Everyone stopped. Sierra's heart pounded so loudly it seemed like a drum for the single voice. The low, rich song flowed through their camp, but she couldn't peel her eyes away from the dragon to see where the sound was coming from. The haunting melody was so other-worldly, Sierra wanted to cry from a yearning she didn't understand.

Micah—in her panic, Sierra completely forgot to refer to him as *"the faun"* in her mind—stepped next to the creature, eyes half-closed as he lifted his voice. He sang of a new home, a home of magic and healing. He reached out his arms, and the creature tilted its head to one side and lowered its neck so Micah could stroke the scaly nose. When he finished, he told the beast, "Now, go, young dragon, and do not return. There is a cave near the top of the mountain, overflowing with fairy magic. Go there to find what you seek."

The dragon—*young* dragon?!—tilted back its head and gave a shriek that made Sierra clamp her jaw tight to keep from screaming as well. Then the creature flapped its wings, filling the night with the scent of musty caves mixed with exotic spices. It took off straight into the air, ripping branches from the trees as if they were matchsticks.

The silence after the dragon left was deafening,

except for the roar of the fire growing larger, blistering the night air. Sierra stared at Micah as though she had never seen him before. He sent a killer dragon away with a song. He convinced this huge beast to curl up in a cave through the suggestions hidden in his beautiful music. What could he convince others of?

The dragon might have left, but the fire was still a real danger. Everyone grabbed their things, slung their bedrolls haphazardly on their backs, then ran. Queen hissed from being jostled but stayed hanging on Sierra's shoulder. The run was a nightmare, full of tree roots grabbing their ankles and rocks cracking them in the shins. Branches whipped across their faces as they raced away from the towering flames. Queen burrowed into Sierra's hair, pressing against her raised fairy mark.

As they fled, Micah came alongside Sierra. Grabbing her hand, he said, "Run with me."

He took off at a pace so fast she was almost flying, her feet barely skimming over the ground. He flowed over and around obstacles she wouldn't normally even see. With his hand touching hers, she ran with more grace than she ever had. They were like two halves of a whole, moving completely in sync.

Magic. It had to be. No matter how incredible it felt, whatever was happening wasn't natural—it was more magic she didn't understand, didn't ask for. Frightened by the way she was swept up in Micah's power, Sierra yanked her hand away, stumbling in shock.

"What's happening?" she asked, still running. She hit a rock so hard she knew she'd be bruised, but she kept going.

"We've shared magic, Sierra. In the cave, the same fairies shared their magic with you and with me, so we are connected. Can you not feel it?" His hand reached out to her beseechingly as he kept pace with her.

Yes, she could sense their connection, but it scared her, and that was the honest truth. The experience was too intense. She also didn't want to burn to death, though. Grabbing his hand, she promised herself they'd talk about this in detail later.

They picked up the pace, Corbin and Nell just ahead. Micah's feet flashed faster and Sierra followed, somehow knowing all the right places to step. The two eased past Corbin and Nell. Micah guided them the fastest way down that wouldn't cause injury or get anyone killed, Corbin and Nell close behind.

When the scent of smoke began to fade, Sierra dared a look back over her shoulder and saw the orange flickering in the distance. The fire headed away from them. They'd gotten lucky. Or had a good guide. No matter that hurtful thing he'd said about keepers, the three humans of their little group, at least, would have died without him tonight. When Micah finally let go, she felt somehow reduced, like she was missing something important. Were all magical creatures so amazing?

Micah's chest heaved, making this the first time Sierra had seen him winded. It didn't detract from his stupid perfection at all.

She frowned. Queen flittered about anxiously, her wings a blurry rainbow. She thought of the merfolk with their smooth scales and seaweed hair like lace. And Sam, who, despite his skinny bones, glowed luminously white on Midsummer's Night. How was it that humanity had come to rule over these magic beings of such intense beauty?

Humans had their own strengths, she guessed, but they seemed awfully weak comparatively. Just look at the three of them, trembling and exhausted from their escape. The sun had begun to rise, so they lost only an hour of sleep, but they all could have slept all day and still not had the rest they needed.

As soon as they stopped, though, Nell pressed for answers, speaking for all of them. "Was that what I think it was?"

Micah replied, "It was a young dragon, yes, but please know it is rare for any creature in these woods to attack. My father said the dragons had mostly returned to hibernation, without enough magic to sustain such large beasts. Many years ago, when they were larger and fiercer, yes. But now, no."

"Larger? *Fiercer?*" Corbin voiced the same thought Sierra had. "Any fiercer and it would have roasted us!"

Micah chuckled, and his laughter ran over Sierra like

rain. Corbin shifted on the rock, and she wondered if he noticed Micah's laughter seemed almost physically present, too. Or was it only her, having shared magic with him?

"The magic of your fairy queens drew the young dragon, I think. I have seen many creatures in this forest that would make humans fear them, but none are as deadly as humanity itself. Humans, ever fearful, have hunted many magical creatures into near extinction. After all, part of why fairies began bonding to humans was to gain protection from other humans who would use them, enslave them, or kill them." His voice lost all humor as he finished his statement.

Sierra couldn't get the image of the dragon out of her mind. Her home seemed so tame in comparison. The only familiar magical creatures she'd seen on this journey were the fairies.

The fairies in question had found the group again and darted around the camp as if playing a child's game of chase.

Nell climbed to her feet, her face slowly draining of expression. Her pupils seemed to expand until they eclipsed the blue of her eyes, leaving them as black as night.

The same rich voice they'd heard once before rolled out from her mouth, a majestic alto. The voice simply took over like a puppeteer using a marionette.

"Humanity can be murderous. Like scavengers

stealing the bricks from a bridge, causing it to collapse, so do humans steal the life-force of our world in large ways and small. Every magic-born creature enslaved is one more hole in our foundation. Soon, if these tragedies are not stopped, the foundation will collapse. Begin with the fairies."

CHAPTER TWENTY-THREE

All the hairs on Sierra's body stood on end as Nell-who-was-not-Nell spoke. Corbin's eyes widened, his mouth moving without sound coming out.

When Nell finished her last ominous statement, she started to collapse, but Corbin caught her in time to lay her gently on the ground.

"Fascinating," Micah murmured.

"That's what you call it?" Sierra replied.

Nell's eyes snapped open, pale blue again, and she gasped, "What happened?"

It took a fair amount of time to calm her. She was ready to pound fists into the nearest tree to make this thing leave her alone, but no one knew what *it* was, much less how to make it shut up.

"Besides," Sierra said, "it seems like this voice is trying to help us. It's sending a message, right?" She pointed at Corbin. "What do *you* think she meant at the end?"

"And by 'she' let's be clear that it's *not me*," Nell snarled, then muttered more about "invisible spirits" and "complete madness."

Corbin spared her a sympathetic glance, but his eyes mostly stayed focused far into the distance as he often did when thinking hard. Sierra loved that he could set aside weird prophecies, dragon attacks, and fairy mysteries in order to think about a specific problem with every fiber of his being.

He finally answered, each word coming slowly. "I think that keepers were meant to protect fairies from the very thing we ended up doing to them ourselves. Kind of ironic, isn't it? Between the alchemists and the healers, we haven't done a very good job of keeping the fairies from getting abused—not even me."

Sierra winced at the mention of alchemists. Silence fell upon them except for the creaking of the ancient trees swaying in the wind. The sound bled loneliness into the cold dawn air.

Micah broke the awkward stillness. "I do not know about this prophecy, but my parents said magic had been dwindling their entire lives. I can tell you the world has changed even since I have been alive. There is less magic, yes, but the world feels... ill. I cannot think of the proper words for it."

Sierra thought to ask her queen through their new connection. *What did she mean by "Start with the fairies?"*

Free... Free... Free... the longing in Queen's emotions made Sierra sway, made her eyes prickle.

"I think," Sierra spoke reluctantly, still unwilling to share the source of her information, but knowing the message itself had to be shared. "I think Corbin's right. It means we're supposed to let the fairies be free. Still be with them, still help them, but stop taking any nectar, and stop thinking of them as basic creatures to use for our own advantage."

"But I never did," Corbin said, voice soft.

Sierra's cheeks burned because he was right. Micah was right, too. The message might as well be directed right at her. Sure, Jack made her take more nectar than she'd like, but she never really cared very much, did she? No, she cared about the beatings, about her lack of choice, about how Flight dominated their lives. She always hated the elixir, but not because of what it did to the fairies or the magical world. She hadn't even known that was a problem.

No, she hated what it did to people she knew, friends from the docks. She saw them grow emaciated and brittle, dreaming away their days without eating until they starved to death with a smile on their face. She hated being any part of that. But she never really thought Queen could understand enough to hate it, too. To maybe hate her keeper for using her that way.

Shame swelled in Sierra. Turning away from everyone, she strode to the edge of camp, only a few trees deep, for some privacy. She sent out a tendril of thought to Queen, sort of a sense of questioning, "???" and the fairy came. Queen glimmered in the pink morning light. The sun had risen above the trees sometime during Nell's unexpected performance, and Sierra hadn't even noticed.

Without a hatch, the fairy glowed less than usual. Queen missed her little fairies. She wanted to have a home again. Sierra knew this because she sensed it. They were becoming more and more entwined, and for once, instead of scaring Sierra, it made her feel she'd been ungrateful for their connection all this time.

She lifted her hand, and Queen landed in Sierra's cupped palm. She lifted Queen close and whispered, because she needed to say this out loud, "I'm so sorry, Queen. I—"

The words got stuck on her tongue. The *I love you* Sierra wanted to say wouldn't slip past her teeth. Old habits died hard.

"I want you to be happy, too," she said.

Queen caressed her wings against Sierra's cheeks and smiled, the fairy's little golden face charmingly beautiful. She didn't reply in words, not even in Sierra's mind. Words were unnecessary. Queen's forgiveness was there in her smile. Maybe the word 'keeper' was the wrong word to use. Sierra wasn't keeping anything; she was guarding the fairies, perhaps? She wasn't sure, but certainly if the word 'keeper' was used, it had to go both ways. Her fairy queen was Sierra's keeper, too. They were each other's keeper.

Micah approached, eyes somber. "I did not mean to hurt your feelings with what I said earlier. I understand you had little choice in your life until now. You are a strong, worthy human, deserving of your queen. It's what you do from here on out that will matter the most."

Sierra nodded, humbled by the grace he offered. "Thank you. I shouldn't have kept taking all that nectar for Jack. I knew it upset the fairies, but I didn't care. I should've found a way to change things a long time ago, but I didn't realize how much I was hurting them. I couldn't really focus on much else besides getting through each day. But I want to help fix things now. I want to do right by Queen."

"And so you shall."

He squeezed her hand for a moment before returning to the others. Contentment wiped away some of her shame and sadness. Micah and Queen both forgave her. Maybe one day she could forgive herself.

The four travelers took the morning to rest and plan their return strategy. Until now, Sierra hadn't permitted herself to consider what would happen after reaching this point. Careful planning was necessary, but time was running out. With her newfound affection for Queen, Sierra felt even more reluctant to state this out loud, but her love for her sister hadn't changed. "Look, this sounds harsh, but I have to get my sister."

No one looked surprised.

"We're only a week or so out. Let's go, act like I'm going to set up a new hatch and give all the nectar to Jack—"

Queen fluttered, and Sierra waved her down.

"No, no, it'd be pretend, see? We *pretend* we're going to do what he wants, but then we'll take Phoebe and run with Queen."

"Where to? Where can't Jack find you?" Corbin asked, kicking a tree trunk.

So her optimistic friend had finally realized this would not be easy. "I don't know. We'll figure that part out as we go. The important part is to get Phoebe safe."

Nell looked like she wanted to argue, but then she bit her lip and fell silent. Sierra raised her eyebrow. Nell hushing herself was about as unexpected as her prophecy earlier. Sierra wondered if Nell had even asked herself what she'd do when they got back.

The day went quickly once they got moving, with very little conversation, all lost in their own thoughts. That night, Corbin built up a fire twice the size as usual, as if the light would keep back their fears of what was to come. When they voted to take turns keeping watch, Micah said he'd take the first shift.

Relief filled Sierra, surprising her. She didn't know when she handed him her trust. So few had it. And here was Micah, not even human, with unknown powers. Trust probably began after the cave but crystallized for sure after he apologized for hurting her feelings. The fact that he could steer away a small dragon didn't hurt, either.

She looked around the clearing and realized her inner circle of people she'd fight and die for had grown. It used to be only Phoebe and grew to include Corbin during their childhood. That was it. Now, though, Sierra thought Nell might have wriggled her way in. Their time after the quake forced Sierra to admit not everything was so black and white.

She'd fight for Queenie, too. Sierra's journey to find her fairy was for her sister, but the journey to come after they saved Phoebe, that was for Queenie...

And when did I start calling her Queenie? Sierra wondered.

The fairy's giggle floated through Sierra's mind like silk and made her smile despite herself. Queenie apparently liked the new nickname. And Micah?

Sierra forced herself to meet his eyes, acknowledging to herself, if to no one else, she had feelings for him. A lot of them.

There was true friendship for sure, but there was the

potential for more, though she wasn't really ready to think on *those* feelings yet. Simply being near him made her wish they had all the time in the world in these woods.

But time was not their friend. They had seven days before Phoebe would be sent away to Bentwood. Micah didn't have a chance against that kind of urgency.

CHAPTER TWENTY-FOUR

The next morning, they packed up and set off. According to Micah, they'd reach the end of the mountains in the next couple of days. He knew the shortest way down.

Corbin walked near Sierra, eyes darting to her now and then. She waited for him to gather his courage. Sure enough, after a lunch of cold greens and berries, he paced beside her. They walked a long time in silence before he finally spoke.

"I think if we're going to set the fairies free, we have to start at home. With Jack and his people, because they know us already. We need to get our port to stop using nectar altogether. And they need to let us take our fairies to roam the forest for a while, you know, to sort of replenish the land with magic." He licked his lips as Sierra stared at him.

"You've gone mad," she said, which was the nicest thing she could think of.

"No, listen! If Nell were to share some of what she's told us—"

Nell rolled her eyes. "If you think I'm going to get up in front of the men I work for and tell them they've got to stop making Flight, you really have lost your mind."

Corbin dragged his hands through his hair. "Not in *front* of Jack—in front of the village elders. If we can get *our* port and villages to let us treat the fairies properly, maybe word will spread to the other keepers. All these queens keep following us. Maybe the keepers will come looking for their queens, and then we can teach them. If all the keepers band together and refuse to be manipulated by the dark alchemists and healers, then what can they do?"

His eyes shined with hope. Sierra could tell he'd spent all morning plotting this coup. Sweet, naive Corbin.

"What can they do?" Sierra didn't even try to sound calm. "They can torture us. They can torture people we love." She sliced her hand through the air like a guillotine. "They'd take Phoebe for sure! Do you want to see your parents hanging in chains, whipped, because you put yourself on a throne and dictated to all the elders how to treat fairies? They think of them like field mice or worse: a bunch of ants. Who cares if ants have rights? Not the elders. They're too busy taking bubble baths in tubs made of silver."

She'd never seen such wealth herself, but Jack described it to her once. They had often paid him to do their dirty work, especially when he was younger. Nell was rising in the crews through being an enforcer, but Sierra's father had worked his way up performing even rougher duties, the kind involving a knife in the dark.

"But someone has to stand up to them!" Corbin cried.

The girls shared a look. Then Nell stared at the ground.

"Sierra's right, Corbin." Nell's voice was soft for once, even gentle. "I know Jack. If we try to get him to stop his business, even if we swayed the elders, he'd kill us."

Corbin tried once more. "But he needs Sierra. He wouldn't risk killing his source of nectar!"

"He could kill Phoebe, or Bentwood could. And would," Sierra pointed out flatly.

Nell added, "And there are other keepers he can find, keepers who might not care about our message once they get their queens back."

Sierra sighed. "We can't do anything until I have Phoebe safe. Then, Corbin, maybe we can try something, okay? But wait."

We run... A thought intruded into Sierra's mind, and she saw an image of them meandering through the forest, through the mountains, into lands she'd never even heard of. The ghostly image floated superimposed over her vision, and she blinked rapidly as it faded.

All at once, tears pressed against her eyes. Even if they escaped with Phoebe and Queen successfully, Nell's message suggested the world itself would suffer catastrophically unless their entire society changed. Impossible.

So Sierra did what she did best. She locked the problem away in a corner of her mind to deal with later. They discussed possible strategies after dinner. After much debate, they arrived at a fairly simple plan. Sierra would show Jack her queen. He would tell Bentwood that Phoebe wasn't coming until next year, giving them breathing space from that threat.

Sierra would set up a hatch for Queenie as a decoy while they gathered supplies and money. Then she'd take Phoebe and run away as quickly as they could, bringing Queen with them. Corbin and Nell would stay behind and act normal for several months, hopefully keeping Grace and the rest of the queens secret. With all the other queens away from their keepers, Jack wouldn't be able to abuse any of them, and Nell would pass on anything she heard from Jack's crew. It was the best any of them could come up with. Queenie even seemed to understand and agree.

If Corbin elected to talk to the elders at Port Ostara after that point, that was his business. Sierra would even come back and help, if she could find a safe place for her sister. It was the closest to a compromise they could reach.

The next morning, Sierra found a spare moment alone with Nell and asked, "What will you do if you start to, you know, talk?"

Sierra raised her eyebrows high when she said "talk" so there was no doubt what she meant.

"Throw myself against a wall?" Nell grimaced.

Sierra snorted. The sound was unexpected in the quiet morning air, and she clapped her hand over her mouth. The boys up ahead looked back quizzically, but she waved at them to keep walking. Again, the decision to not laugh seemed to require she start giggling like a seven year old. Nell started to chuckle as well, and soon they were howling with laughter, a more pleasant stress-relief than crying.

After they wiped their tears, Sierra returned to the subject. "No, seriously, won't Jack kill you for saying those kinds of things in front of his crew? I mean, are you able to *hear* yourself?"

Nell sighed. "Not at first, but this last time was sort of like being pushed underwater by something. The words were muffled, and it was like something stood between me and my body." She shrugged. "It's a creepy feeling, but when it leaves, I'm peaceful. I don't know how to explain it."

As they watched Queenie flit and fly in front of them, Sierra smiled. "No need to explain."

"Honestly, I'm not sure I'll end up staying an enforcer," Nell said in a quick whisper, eyes darting to Corbin. "Corbin said his parents could train me as a healer, maybe. I'm thinking something more peaceful might suit... us... better."

She flushed a pretty pink, and Sierra was happy for them. No jealousy soured the moment at all, for which she was thankful.

"I think that's great, Nell. My father, well, he's not a great boss, and you deserve better."

They exchanged tentative smiles. Perhaps instead of losing Corbin as she had feared, Sierra would gain a new close friend.

The miles passed quickly now that they were so close to their goal. Each step brought Sierra closer to her little sister. She could now allow herself to think about Phoebe again, to wonder how she was. It didn't hurt to think of her anymore, because it was all going to be okay.

If Sierra closed her eyes, she could picture Phoebe perfectly: the doe-brown eyes, the carrot-red hair, always with the cowlick on the right side of her brow. She was small for her age, like a little wren dipped in red paint. Her voice captivated everyone, but especially Old Sam, who crooned in joy when she sang like a little bird with her clear soprano. She was altogether too lovely and beautiful to be any part of Jack's schemes.

Sierra eyed her fairy, hoping Queenie wouldn't attack Jack when she first saw him. She seemed to have received a lot of information about him and vibrated with anger whenever Sierra so much as thought his name. If Queenie killed Jack, his men could kill Phoebe in retaliation before anyone could escape with her. Then again, if *all* the queens would swarm again, Sierra could urge them to attack as a last ditch effort to escape if worst came to worst. The thought made her laugh, the image of Jack running for the hills with a bunch of fairies pinching the seat of his pants. Maybe they'd even sting him and save her the trouble of dealing with him. She savored the image like a tasty leg of lamb and kept on walking, toward home.

CHAPTER TWENTY-FIVE

On their last night in the mountains, heaviness weighed on Sierra's heart. She lay on her bedroll, trying to determine the cause of her sadness. She'd be home in about a week. After nearly a month, that was nothing. She should be exultant! Then she saw Micah standing guard again, leaning against a tree to her right, and her confusion coalesced, like placing her finger on the exact spot of a bruise. They were leaving the Skyclad Mountains the next day. They'd be leaving his home.

He touched the tree next to him like a mother might touch her child. Sierra only had faint memories of her mother, but she'd like to think her mother looked at her with the same tenderness Micah gave to the forest when he thought no one was watching.

At least she thought he didn't know she was watching, but then he said, "Good evening, Sierra."

Ignoring him seemed rude, but so did interrupting what seemed to be a private moment.

"I'm—I'm sorry to bother you," Sierra stammered. She hesitated, then walked over to him. The others were already asleep.

Micah's white teeth flashed in the darkness. The moon glowed above the trees, casting its pale light on his handsome features. She rather wished she couldn't see him. Keeping her wits about her was easier that way.

His voice was soft when he said, "You, my lady, are never a bother."

Something fluttered in her stomach at his voice, a twist in her belly that wasn't nausea but something new and different.

Sierra gestured at the forest. "Having second thoughts?"

An owl called from the trees behind her, and she startled. He took a step closer, as if to soothe her, but his nearness had the opposite effect.

He listened to the owl as it hooted again, and he shook his head. "I know what I've decided is best."

"I don't." The words came out twisted, wrong, and she clenched her fists at the surprised hurt that flashed across his handsome face before he composed himself. She tried again. "I mean... it's wrong taking you from your home," she added, clumsily.

"My home has been a sad place for me since I lost my parents and my voice. Do not fear for me. Leaving will be a good experience, a new adventure." His voice was as deep and rich as the velvet night sky—and as soft. "Besides," he continued, "I would like to see your home."

"My home?" she squeaked.

He took yet another step closer, and it was all she could do not to retreat. She kept her back straight, but looking into his eyes made her pulse thunder. She did not think about him being a faun at all. Instead, she saw warm brown eyes shining in the moonlight, gazing down on her with what seemed to be... affection? Longing? She couldn't tell.

He touched her forehead. "I can all but see the wheels turning, Fairy Keeper. Where is your charge right now, anyway?"

A thought was enough now to get a response from Queenie. *Dream time, sleepy...*

Sierra smiled, a little bit of a goofy, lopsided grin at the fairy's happy tone. "She's about to fall asleep."

He leaned forward. "And how did you know? You denied hearing her before. I can see her from here, but your eyes are not so sharp."

Ice trickled down her back. "It was a logical guess, Micah. She was lying down when I came over here."

"Why do you deny what is so obvious? You can never own your full powers until you do."

Why wouldn't he leave her alone about it? By all the

stars, she didn't ask to have some kind of mental and emotional connection with her fairy. Corbin might hate her for this. She'd caught him gazing at her new keeper mark several times already. She ran her fingertips across the raised edges of her mark, tracing the scrolling lines beneath her fingers.

Micah nodded as he watched her. "Yes, that mark. I've never seen anything like it, nor heard of anything such as that from my parents. You're special, Sierra, more powerful than even the first keeper who bonded to a queen."

He captured her gaze with his eyes and wasn't letting go. "Your mark is not the only reason you are special, either."

He reached out, there in the moonlight, and caressed her cheek. Barely breathing, Sierra leaned into his hand just enough to leave her unbalanced in every way possible.

He whispered, "I'm coming with you. Perhaps I am not ready to say goodbye to... my new friends."

She thought his lips curled into a smile, but the darkness hid his face too much to know for sure.

"Okay," was all she managed to say. Brilliant. Just brilliant. She stumbled back to her bedroll, unable to tear her eyes away from him. Even when she lay down and forced herself to close her eyes, she still saw him glowing in the moonlight, like something right out of a bard's tale.

As they left the dense trees the next morning, it was clear spring was on its way at last. Buds of wildflowers peeked through the brown sea of the plains. The field buzzed with the rasping sounds of familiar grey leafhoppers and strange, low-flying insects. The grasses tickled her legs through the many tears of her pants.

Micah now wore pants, too. All the humans had decreed the knee-length kilt too strange for town. Pants and a homespun shirt, borrowed from Corbin, would hopefully help Micah blend in better. He wondered aloud several times how men could stand such coverings on their legs—far too restrictive—but otherwise didn't complain. Sierra noted the shirt effectively hid the muscled torso but didn't detract from his stupid handsomeness.

Spring might be on its way, but winter hadn't completely released its grip. Frost greeted them each morning, and they creaked their way out of their bedrolls. Sometimes the queens flew with them, making joyful squeals and giggles. Other times, they roamed far, and only Sierra and Corbin's queens remained with their little rag-tag group of four.

Each day, Sierra's excitement grew to be back near home. She might not love much about it, but Phoebe was waiting.

CHAPTER TWENTY-SIX

The day Sierra could finally smell the ocean, triumph surged through her. She couldn't believe they'd done it. Queenie zoomed by, and Sierra was so relieved she wanted to shout, so she did. Raising her fists to the blue sky, she let out a holler that made her friends laugh. She'd managed to mostly push aside the heavy price for Phoebe's freedom that Queen would pay if they couldn't manage to escape Jack after all. But the possibility sat on the edge of Sierra's thoughts, like a scab she couldn't stop picking at.

She asked Queenie to tell the other queens to stay away from humans for now. It was the only way to keep their existence secret. The fairies would stay in the nearby forests, away from the ports. Even Corbin's fairy Grace patted his cheek and then flew off with the group. Only Queenie remained, hidden in Sierra's hair.

The four of them didn't even stop by Keeper Hannon's house in the press for time, though Corbin swore he'd return right away once Phoebe was safe. The old keeper deserved to know his queen might be one of those who had returned. Instead, the group hiked all the way into Port Beltane. Their first night back in an inn was a luxury after so many nights on the hard ground.

Unlike the last time they stayed there, Sierra didn't even mind sharing a room with Nell. They had warm water for washing out their many wounds, finally. The innkeeper looked alarmed by their ragged appearance but was too afraid of Jack's reputation to refuse them a room. People around here who didn't treat Jack's representatives well... didn't do well themselves. Sierra tried to explain to the innkeeper that she had no reason to fear, but the poor woman wouldn't listen.

And all their scratches and wounds kept people from staring at Micah. Well, stopped the men. The young ladies seemed to do nothing but stare at him. He might have hidden his magical nature, but he couldn't hide his gorgeousness. Sierra glared at every girl who flirted with him and was pleased when he politely rebuffed each one.

The whole last day of their journey, Sierra was flying. Port Mabon came and went with hardly a notice. *Phoebe!* Sierra would see her little sister so soon. Phoebe would be thrilled to see Queenie, too, and to meet Micah and to see Corbin. Sierra's friendship with Nell would be shocking, but Phoebe was always quick to kindness. Sierra knew they'd get along fine.

When the group finally crossed into Tuathail and hiked over the small rise to Jack's land, Sierra's heart stuttered with a combination of excitement and fear. The house looked smaller than when she left, though she supposed it was the same. A few more earthquakes must have rocked its foundation, because the far corner of the house now slanted at a precarious angle.

She paused for a moment, her mind's eye full of soaring mountains, ragged cliffs, wide open meadows. This building looked too frail and small to be the prison she always believed it to be.

Then her father stepped out of the door. Sierra could have sworn she shrank two feet, back to the child who feared him so. He looked thinner than she remembered, but his walk remained powerful. His cold eyes made her shoulders tighten, and his snake-like gracefulness still sent shivers of fear down her back. She shook her head. He didn't have a hold on them anymore. They would be free.

Sierra beamed, a smile that made Jack blink, and she ran the rest of the way down the path, with Queenie now flying at her shoulder.

"We did it!" Sierra called, struggling to keep her surging triumphant feelings hidden. All she wanted was to see Pheobe. His plans to send her away in a year didn't matter at all now. Sierra would have Phoebe far from him long before he could send her to Bentwood.

Jack glanced at the queen as he approached Sierra. Queenie's wings shimmered in the golden light, and Jack offered Sierra a quick, tight smile when he stopped right in front of her.

"I'm sure you'll be able to get the new hatch set up today," he said.

Today? This wasn't the response Sierra expected, but she supposed he was anxious to start making money.

"Is Phoebe inside?" she asked, wondering why Phoebe hadn't run out to greet her. Sierra craned her neck to peer around her father. *"Phoebes?"*

Micah, Nell, and Corbin were still several paces back. Sierra's father caught Nell's eye and waved her forward. She glanced at Corbin but immediately followed Jack's orders. Sierra pressed her lips together but couldn't even blame her. Jack was a hard man to cross.

"Sir?" Nell asked, ready, shoulders straight and tall.

"You're two days late," he said.

Nell's brow furrowed, and it looked like she was counting to herself.

No. It couldn't be. Sierra counted the days herself. Between her passing out and Nell's near-coma state, missing time would have been easy. Maybe they'd all been unconscious after the fairy attack longer than they had known. They might really be too late. Coldness filled her stomach. Her throat was closing up. "What are you saying, Jack?"

"Your sister is already gone. The deal is done, Sierra. Elder Bentwood collected her and took her to Port Iona two days ago. She should be arriving there right about now, in fact."

His eyes were thunderous, as if he somehow blamed her for the early loss of his youngest child. Fury flamed inside Sierra, and she took a step toward him, her hands fisted and raised.

"Really?" was all he said, voice soft, but his hand slid to his hip. Before she could blink, the silver flash of a knife was at her throat. "Never threaten me, daughter. Ever."

Then he lowered the knife and stepped back. Nell shifted her feet.

"I realize the news about Phoebe comes as a shock and you are not in your right mind. Go now to your hatch, and we'll not speak of this again."

He clearly thought he was being magnanimous. Showing her mercy.

This time when the rage and grief flowed, she let it surge through her like an unbroken, wild horse. Her hand snapped out without her conscious thought. The back of her hand connected to his face with a resounding crack, exactly as he had done to her too many times to count. It was extremely satisfying.

Nell froze. Sierra barely noticed Micah or Corbin

coming up behind her. Her blood thrummed with the deep desire for revenge.

"You'll regret this. I'll see to it," Sierra promised.

He gave one shout of laughter, but it wasn't funny at all. It was chilling. He wiped away a trickle of blood dripping from his split lip. She hoped it stung.

"You can try. But Sierra, if you fight me, you'll die, and even now I don't want that."

She shook her head and backed away. "I'm going to get her. You stay away from her."

He narrowed his eyes. "I gave my word. She belongs to Bentwood."

Sierra understood the situation. She did. He'd kill her before letting Phoebe leave Bentwood. "Well, I gave my word I'd save her."

Jack sighed, and her brain screamed to run, but she couldn't move. She was rooted to the ground, aware he was about to throw that knife or stab her, anything to keep her from disrupting his plans. His word had to stand or it wasn't good for anything.

But before he could send the knife flashing through the air, Nell drew her bow. Jack and Sierra both sucked in identical breaths. Nell's arrow was nocked, ready and aimed—right at Jack.

His lips twisted as he lowered his weapon and raised his hands slowly beside his head. "I'm surprised she won you over, Nell. I figured you for more loyalty. And our Sierra can be quite irritating."

Nell's blue eyes were wide, but otherwise not one inch of fear showed. Sierra was proud, like a mother watching a child taking its first steps.

"You're not lying, sir," Nell said. "But I'm sorry. I can't let you do that."

"You going to kill me?"

"No, sir. I wouldn't do that." But she didn't lower her bow.

What would Nell do with her little sisters now? Surely any other way of leaving Jack's business would be preferable to pulling a weapon on him. He might have released her from his crew without a fuss if she had asked just right—but not after this.

So much for their careful plan. They all started backing away from Jack. Sierra's queen made several piercing high-pitched yelps and then streaked off across the field without an explanation.

"Don't do something you will all regret," Jack said, his hands still next to his head, Nell's bow still drawn.

Her breath was coming fast now, maybe the start of another fit or possibly just a nervous breakdown. She'd ruined her future in one short moment. Jack wouldn't forgive this. Plus, trying to learn a new skill like healing took time, and now she didn't have any.

As soon as they were out Jack's sight, Sierra told Nell, "Go get your family. Bring what they need, and all your coins, too."

Relief and gratitude rushed over her face. She took

off at a run that made Sierra's fastest speed look impossibly slow.

Corbin's dark eyes were full of surprise and thankfulness. "You're willing to take her whole family with us?"

Sierra understood his response. It wasn't something she would have done before this trip. "She saved my life, Corbin. You know what Jack does to those who betray him. My father's not hurting her sisters or her mother. Ever."

Micah leaned close and whispered in her ear, "Honor. This is what I mean."

Threatening her own father was pretty much the opposite of honor to her. But when Micah leaned back and met her eyes, their connection made her feel stronger.

"Hang on, Phoebe," Sierra whispered. "I'm coming for you."

CHAPTER TWENTY-SEVEN

Traveling as a group of four had been hard. Traveling with four plus Nell's mother and three sisters was even harder. Wailing children, scraped knees, hungry people. The commotion wore on Sierra. The fairies, though, provided constant entertainment for the little girls, who oohed and ahhed over every wing and every twitter.

Thankfully, Port Iona was only two days away, even traveling slowly. They kept off the main roads and watched carefully for any signs of pursuit. When they were about half a day's journey from Port Ionoa, they found the smallest hostel available in a remote village off the road. Corbin bargained with the innkeeper, using all his charm, and managed to arrange for Nell's family to stay there in secret for several weeks for a good price.

Nell hugged her sisters for a long time before she let them go.

"We'll come back for them as soon as it's over," Sierra promised her as Nell looked over her shoulder one last time before the village disappeared over the rocky hillside.

Once they arrived on the outskirts of the port near dusk, finding out Phoebe's location took no effort at all. No one there knew Nell was foresworn, and she pretended she was checking up on her boss's daughter, asking some of the runners. But getting Phoebe out would be a different matter. Port Iona was a peninsula that stuck out like a sore thumb into the ocean. Bentwood's center of operations was on the tip, without any docks. The peninsula was full of his people—a fortress.

Sierra stood on a rock, gazing in frustration out at the ocean. The familiar scent of salt and sea reminded her of home. No magic mountains to climb now. They'd kicked around a dozen ideas or more about how to rescue Phoebe, but all the plans had more holes than a fairy net. No boats were allowed to approach the peninsula, not that they had one anyway. Guards waited along the single road entrance to the mainland—they'd never sneak Phoebe past them even if they could get Sierra in unrecognized.

Corbin stepped up beside her and tugged on her braid. "We'll get there. Somehow."

"It's too bad we can't swim that far. They'd never expect us to get to Phoebe from any other way than across that narrow road with the iron gate."

Corbin nearly slipped off the algae as he spun from the rock and shouted, "Sierra! You're a genius!"

Before she could ask what he was talking about, Corbin turned to Micah. "Can you talk to any creature made of magic?"

Micah stared at Corbin like he'd spoken gibberish.

Corbin waved his hands, trying to get his point across. "Like with the dragon? Lots of magical creatures have the ability to speak cross-species."

Micah shrugged. "Before I lost my voice, I could communicate with all the different animals that dwelled in my mountains. Whether or not my ability extends to other creatures, I do not know."

"Merfolk," Corbin announced.

They all stared at him, uncomprehending.

He growled in frustration and pointed at the water. "*Merfolk!*"

Then Sierra understood what his plan had to be, and hope rose like a fountain. "*Oh!*"

"Exactly," said Corbin.

Queenie did a backflip, her excitement thrumming through Sierra.

Nell cleared her throat, stating wryly, "Anyone going to explain to the rest of us? It sounds good, but I don't get it."

Corbin put an arm around her shoulders as he explained to everyone, "Bentwood uses merfolk to carry their deep sea nets and drag the ocean floor for clams and oysters. The thing is, I've heard he keeps some of them pinned up as hostages to keep the other merfolk in line. I wouldn't put it past him."

Micah's eyes flashed dangerously. "Merfolk are a kind and helpful people. Who would do something like this?"

"Supposedly, their work started off as part of a barter system, so the merfolk could get certain foods, iron tools, and medicines and would pay with service. Something changed over time, though, and Bentwood's been working the merfolk like slaves since, well... since I can remember."

Sierra hid a smile at Corbin's use of what she privately called his "lecture voice." He loved to teach and share.

He continued, his voice rising with excitement, "But the merfolk could carry us to the other side of the peninsula, right up to the shore of his fortress, without us ever being seen!"

Nell chewed on her lip. "We'd still have to get to Phoebe once we landed, but yeah, it'd be a clever trick, assuming you could convince the merfolk to help us and not drown us."

"You want me to ask for their help, knowing we

cannot do anything to set them free?" Micah looked stricken.

Nell snarled. "Who says we can't?"

Sierra expected Corbin to be uncomfortable with the idea of fighting, but he held his little herb knife, his face deadly serious. As always, he could read her mind.

"Bentwood's got Phoebe. He's got merfolk kept hostage. He's a dark alchemist who abuses his people. Yes, Sierra, I can fight."

A swell of love sprang up in Sierra for her friends who would do what was right no matter what. But fighting their way into the city would be suicide with just the four of them. She couldn't let them throw their lives away. There had to be a better way.

Suddenly, her little fantasy about Jack and a fairy swarm was more than an idle, impossible daydream. It was something that could save them all. But no one would like it. To put it mildly.

Nell's source told them Phoebe was down in the cellar of the main operations building. They called it the new trainee center, where they broke people and ensured no one would dare refuse an order. Phoebe had been there for two days. Sierra didn't have time to mess around.

"Here's another idea," Sierra offered, trying to sound casual. "Once we get on the peninsula, if Queen can draw the other fairies here, what if they swarm the operations building? Bentwood's people would be too busy rolling around on the ground to stop us while we run in and grab Phoebe."

Now everyone really did look horrified. It was one thing to think about fighting Bentwood, but asking innocent fairies to possibly attack a bunch of his people seemed too unclean for anyone else to consider.

As expected, Corbin, with his unbreakable moral code, objected. "How can you even think of doing that? If they were given a choice, I bet most of the people there would choose to help us, but they can't. They don't all deserve to die, which is what would happen, you know. Even fairy keepers can die from a sting. I've never heard of a non-fairy-keeper surviving a sting, until Nell."

Sierra agreed but didn't have the luxury of caring. Micah was the only one who didn't look shocked. His face was completely neutral. She didn't know what that meant, but she was thankful someone wasn't looking at her like *she* was a dark alchemist. She could all but hear sand hissing through an hourglass, though.

Sierra turned to Queen. "Is that something you can do? Can you rally the other queens to swarm?"

Queen flashed in the air, agitated. *Don't want to...* the words were sharp in Sierra's mind. Queenie squealed a little in distress. *I knew you'd live. They probably won't.*

"I know, but that's the point, Queenie. We may have to hurt a lot of people to get Phoebe out safe, and it's not our fault they've chosen to work for that man."

They are with the bad man? Man who kills merfolk and takes our nectar?

Sierra stared intently into Queen's brilliant golden eyes, so large for her tiny face. Sierra felt she could lean forward and fall right into them. "Yes, that's what I mean."

Heat laced through her from Queen's rage, an anger that set the little fairy's wings vibrating. The strength of the feeling tinged Sierra's vision with red, forcing her to breathe deeply to keep from staggering. This sharing-emotions business required a lot of getting used to.

We will do what we must.

It wasn't so much a thought as a feeling. As it turned out, it was a feeling Sierra could get completely behind.

She smiled at Queenie, aware it was a cold smile, but it wasn't directed at her fairy. Sierra was imagining hordes of screaming Port Iona men running for their lives, sparing her friends, while she got her sister. Queenie, sharing those images, sent a feeling of fierce satisfaction, proving they were entirely united in their burning desire for justice.

"Uh—what's going on?" Nell broke into their conversation.

Only then did Sierra realize she had fallen to her knees, Queenie still standing on her palms. Queenie was glowing brighter than she had since the worker fairies died, but she wasn't golden. She shined with a sullen red hue she'd never shown before, and Sierra's neck simmered with heat.

Corbin choked out, "Your mark—it's glowing."

She couldn't see it, but she sensed it.

Nell planted herself right in front of Sierra. "Care to share? You've been holding back, Fairy... Keeper."

Sierra blinked and Queenie disengaged, flittering off into the fading blue sky. Sierra gazed after her queen until she disappeared in the distance.

CHAPTER TWENTY-EIGHT

Explanations didn't come easy for Sierra. By the time she stammered her way through the confusing story of how things had changed with Queenie, she wished she had Jack's ability to twist words to her own benefit. Obviously, that trait skipped her.

"What do you mean, she *talks* to you?" Corbin yelped.

Sierra hung her head and gritted her teeth. They didn't have time for this. She didn't need the guilt. And for all the money in the world, she wouldn't want to hurt Corbin this way.

"It's not exactly like words, though sometimes I hear words, yeah, okay? I'm sharing my brain with a tiny magical creature who has always acted like she wished I were dead. Micah says you might develop this same thing, so don't judge."

Sierra glared at Corbin, heat suffusing her cheeks from shame and embarrassment. She should have told him before now. She could have been more gentle in private. They always shared everything. She wasn't sure if she was sorry he didn't have this connection with his fairy, or jealous. But it was a handy ability to have right now.

The fairies could be a weapon and would even the odds of saving Phoebe, even if no one else wanted to use them that way.

Sierra glanced at Micah, who said nothing. She couldn't hold his gaze. Even knowing he might hate her if she asked the queens to swarm, she'd do it to save her sister.

Corbin pushed past his shock to plead for more time. "Look, give me one day—*one day*—to go before the elders at the port and explain our situation. They don't all work for Bentwood. You sneak in with the merfolk for Phoebe. Meanwhile, we'll provide a distraction *and* hopefully get to save the fairies. Then we can try to help the merfolk later."

Nell's snort was audible in the fading darkness, but he continued as if he didn't hear.

Sierra asked Nell, "Is he insane?"

She replied, "I'd rather not answer that."

Corbin huffed. "I'm just saying, maybe we can still work this out peacefully."

His palms were spread wide, asking Sierra to

reconsider. His fairy had rejoined them—it was clear she loved him from the way she cuddled against him, but his mark hadn't changed, and he surely hadn't seen any bizarre glowing colors lately. Lucky him.

"Fine. You and Nell go in together, through the main road," Sierra decided. "Try to get the elders to hear you. Micah and I will see if we can get these merfolk to sneak us in to get Phoebe. We'll meet you in the port's main square after the hearing. Send your fairy to find us if we're not there. But if they refuse you or don't believe you, which I don't see why they would, then I'm going to do whatever it takes."

Corbin's face lit up. He stopped listening as soon as she said he could try his plan to protect the fairies and the world. Nell frowned as she looked off into the dark waters of the ocean. Then she sharpened all her knives and gave Sierra and Micah two of her biggest.

That night, sleep hid just out of Sierra's grasp for a long while. She tried not to think about Phoebe, what might be happening to her, so close and so far all at the same time. Exhaustion eventually took her from her worries.

She awoke before the sun completely rose above the sea. It didn't take them long to get ready, but before they went their separate ways, Sierra had to speak to Corbin.

"Are we... okay?" she asked as they hugged goodbye, standing a little way off from Nell and Micah.

Corbin tilted his head and smiled that sweet smile of

his. Of course he knew exactly what she meant without her having to explain.

"It's not your fault, little sister. I'm really glad for you. You finally seem content with Queen. About time!" He nudged her shoulder.

"Well, I hope you and Nell take care. I think she's liked you for a long time, Corbin," Sierra admitted. "She really cares for you, so I hope you two are happy."

"I am! But you'll always be my best friend, Sierra." He tugged her braid, making her smile. "I'm glad you two have finally been getting along, though, you know?"

She did. It looked like she would get to keep her closest friend after all.

She didn't want to let him go on without her. He was walking into danger, but he was an eager puppy, aglow with all the optimism she'd had beaten out of her years ago. Sierra wished he had less of it, but if he wasn't so hopeful, he wouldn't be Corbin. She hugged him, resigned to this truth.

Nell clasped his hand. Sierra worried less with Nell at his side. She was no fool and knew the odds. But saying goodbye to her put a strange catch in Sierra's throat, too. As Nell and Corbin walked off down the main path, their shadows merged for an instant. Sierra had to smile at the symbolism.

"You care for him, yes?" Micah's velvety voice made her startle.

She raised her eyebrows. She thought it had been clear how she felt. "He's been a brother to me."

"But perhaps more than a brother?" Micah asked. For once, he wasn't meeting her eyes.

Sierra blinked, pulse picking up at this unexpected line of questioning. "Uh, no. Not Corbin and me. Not that way."

She blushed. Had Micah guessed she'd tried really hard not to think of *him* that way?

In case she'd been too obvious and embarrassed herself, she casually added, "I'm not looking to court yet anyway. It's not the right time for me."

There. Now he wouldn't think she'd been pining after him and his big brown eyes. Which she definitely hadn't been. Certainly not. And she really couldn't afford to focus on anything as frivolous as courtship right now, so she was telling the truth, if not all of it.

Micah looked at Sierra for a long moment, making her skin prickle. "Maybe someday, then," he said.

He spoke so softly she almost wondered if she heard him correctly, but then he turned to face the sea, obviously done speaking.

She didn't know what that meant. Did he think she'd care for Corbin one day as more than a friend? She didn't have time to find out or explain to Micah how wrong he was. Her mind was already turning toward their next task, as it always did. Phoebe needed help.

Sierra hunkered down on one of the slick rocks

jutting out of the sea. The surf broke a mile out from shore, and the waters nearby were fairly shallow compared to the deep ocean, but she'd seen plenty of merfolk in similar eddies and coves before. Today, though, the water seemed empty.

"We need to call one of them," Sierra said. "Any ideas?"

She wasn't sure where Queenie was. Sierra thought of her, focused on her and got a faint response, a sort of questioning, *"What?"* But Queenie wouldn't be of much use in this situation, Sierra decided, and let their connection fade into the background.

Micah stared thoughtfully at the glass-green water, then squatted next to Sierra, dipped one hand in, and hummed slightly. He closed his eyes and stilled, sitting like a statue. He stayed in that position long after Sierra had to move to shake her legs out.

He stood without warning, eyes flashing open. "One comes."

Sierra strained to see any merfolk, but she didn't catch so much as a glimpse before one was suddenly there. Young and pale as an opal, he had gills slicing a dark line down each side of his throat. His age was hard to determine, but he appeared to be around the same age as Phoebe, perhaps a year or two older. Without the customary tattooing on his arms and torso worn by adult merfolk, this was clearly a child merman, often called a seawee. His dark green hair spread across his shoulders like kelp cascading down his back. His eyes were green as well, with a thin ring of black around the edge of each iris.

He didn't speak but gestured to the water.

Micah said, "He can talk under the surface but not above. He understands we need passage to the fortress. The adult merfolk could not come, but this seawee was intrigued. I suspect he is adventurous, so we might convince him to help."

Sierra stared at Micah, realizing she'd need to go under the green water to hear the seawee's response. The *cold* green water. In her *clothes*, because she sure wasn't taking them off in front of the little merman and Micah.

The ripe smell of dead fish and rotting seaweed along the rocky coast wrinkled her nose, but she took off her coat and then laid it by the rocks. She decided to only lower her face under, even though her bottom would stick up in the air in a far from flattering fashion. She dipped her hand in the water and yipped at the frigid temperature.

The seawee made a strange chortle through his gills. He patted the water impatiently, gesturing with a welcoming smile. He wasn't all that different from them, at least the part above surface, even with dark green hair. The bottom half of his body was a long, green fishtail. The scales glittered in the sun shining through the shallow water. Yet his appearance seemed natural in the ocean like this.

She took a deep breath. Leaning forward, she plunged her face in the water. The icy temperature forced several bubbles of air out of her mouth. Water leaked in through her tightened lips, tasting of salt. She kept her eyelids squinched shut, hating the way sea water always stung, but when cold, wet hands reached up and grabbed her biceps, her eyes snapped open.

The seawee's hair turned light green under the water and streamed out around his head like a halo. His eyes were piercing, completely black now, deep, shadowed pools in that pale, pale face. She struggled, but it was too late.

"Don't worry. It's better this way," the seawee said, clearly in her ear, a ringing undertone to his voice. Then he pulled the rest of her in the water and swam rapidly toward the bottom.

CHAPTER TWENTY-NINE

The seawee pulled Sierra down, down, down, turning the sun above into a pale, watery disc. She thrashed in his muscular arms as the powerful strokes of his tail sent them zooming straight to the sandy bottom of the ocean cove.

"You'll be fine, m'lady. Take a breath and see," he said.

Likely story. Her lungs burned, but Sierra continued to struggle. He held her there, bubbles trickling through her mouth in panic as she gazed upward. She spotted Micah, face horrified, peering into the shallows. His head was turning this way and that, trying to spot her.

He was remarkably easy for her to see despite the water between them. He jumped in with a sudden splash. Clearly swimming wasn't a common faun activity because he began to sink while throwing his limbs around ineffectively. But even as he sank lower, he continued looking for her. Sierra tried to yell, losing more precious breath. He turned to see her, and he tried kicking her direction, spinning slowly in the water. He'd never reach her before she ran out of air.

"Trust me. Breathe," the seawee told Sierra.

She looked over her shoulder at him, eyes wild and furious.

"No, truly, I swear to you, if you are with me and I so choose it, you can breathe underwater. You are with a creature of magic who has vouched for you, so we will share with you this secret that few humans ever learn." The words were clear, not garbled or gurgly like they should have been.

She didn't believe him, but it didn't matter. She'd either die from lack of oxygen or from drowning. Her body refused to give up without a fight, and even though she tried to stop, she couldn't prevent her lungs from trying to take a breath. They simply had to expand.

The cold water swirled into her chest cavity. With that horrible chill, she expected to die. Her only thought now was that Phoebe would never be rescued, and Sierra felt so heavy she didn't even need the seawee to hold her on the ocean floor. She waited for her lungs to reject the water, waited for the burning coughing and choking that should have come but hadn't. Micah was still thrashing and sinking, but Sierra floated gently.

When the seawee sensed her quietness, he pulled them over to Micah. One touch of the seawee's hand

and Micah stopped fighting. Some magical communication, Sierra could only guess.

Her vision remained strangely clear under the water, perhaps a part of the seawee's magic or maybe because of the plentiful sunlight that reached this depth. A fish darted by like a bird might above, its yellow and red scales flashing in the sun. Kelp and seaweed dotted the ocean floor, along with the garbage of the humans from the city. The beauty was still there, though obviously stained. Sierra met the child merman's eyes, suddenly ashamed to be human. She wished she had forced Corbin and Nell to stay with them. Corbin would have loved to experience this, but all Sierra wanted was to get out of here and reach Phoebe.

"Welcome to our world beneath the waves, human and faun. My name is Tristan. You need help, I understand, to reach your sister?"

Sierra nodded and explained their situation, even though it felt strange to place their hope in the hands of a child only slightly older than Phoebe. But he was the one who came to the call. Tristan the seawee listened carefully, saying nothing until Sierra finished.

"You ask us to take a tremendous risk. My mother and father would not agree, I'm sure. Should the human Bentwood learn of our role in delivering you to your sister, his prize, he might hurt our captured loved ones as punishment."

That was true. She couldn't argue.

"What do you offer us in exchange for this great risk?" Tristan's eyes were like a night sky devoid of stars, black against the emerald water.

What could she offer him? She was one girl, only a fairy keeper.

"If she destroys this man's stronghold, wouldn't that set your people free?" Micah asked, completely nonplussed to be having a conversation on the ocean floor. His shirt billowed out from his chest, and his dark hair waved in the currents.

The seawee appeared to give this some thought. "It would free our people who live in this area, which is better than freeing none. I cannot argue your point. The eldest mermen have long talked of a rebellion, but they fear the loss of the others. I doubt they will ever take action," the seawee said, rolling his eyes. "If your intention is to overthrow this bottom-feeder who abuses our people, then I'll deliver you with all speed to the fortress, no matter what my father might say. Things cannot go on as they are. It is my future at risk, too."

There it was. The bottom line: their world was broken. It was drying out, cracking, imploding. Aluvia was big, but not that big. Things couldn't go on as they had been. Something had to change. And a quiet escape wasn't likely.

She drew herself up as straight as she could, given that she was floating. "I expect I will have to call on the fairy queens to attack the people of this port to save my sister. So, yes."

Tristan nodded with satisfaction. Any magical creature understood the likely results of that scenario.

They sped through the water so fast that a steady stream of bubbles rushed across Sierra's skin. The young merman held her and Micah's hands and pulled them along in his wake as if they weighed nothing. She supposed down here, in a way, they didn't.

The journey was surreal, cloaked in silence except for the soft swish of water swirling past them. She could almost swear the seawee's skin itself seemed to glow with its own dim light, illuminating their eerie passage.

Sierra was thankful, so thankful, for Micah's presence. He believed in her, which was even more important than ever now that her mission had unexpectedly gotten bigger. It was a burden, but one he seemed willing to share with her.

In a matter of minutes, they reached the edge of the fortress, the peak that jutted out the farthest into the sea. Crumbling, algae-covered rocks anchored a fence lining the entire peninsula. But this far under the water there were holes where the rock had crumbled away from the stress of a thousand earthquakes.

"Up that hole, there." Tristan pointed to a dark, narrow channel.

Sierra's skin crawled to look at it.

"If you swim up the hole, you will surface in a small

eddy inside the fence where Bentwood's men try to grow tiny clams for easy harvest. The clams never seem to flourish—because we keep taking them at night and letting them grow wild in the ocean." He laughed, a sparkling sound that demanded a smile in return. "They leave the area empty of guards quite often, since there is no strategic attack point they know about on this side of the peninsula. It's the best I have to offer. I will come by later to see if you need help, but I cannot make any promises."

His offer was more than they had dared hope. Micah and Sierra exchanged a triumphant glance. They had a secret way into Bentwood's fortress, a way he and his guards knew nothing about. Corbin and Nell would reach the port's main square soon, but Sierra had no way to let them know that she and Micah were in place.

Queenie! Sierra ran her fingers along her keeper mark and hoped the fairy heard. They would need her soon. They had a lot of work to do today.

CHAPTER THIRTY

The courtyard was empty except for the tiny ocean pool from which Sierra and Micah arrived. Sunlight burned bright against eyes already used to the darker water. The very lack of people around the area made her instantly nervous.

Micah touched her back and whispered, "This is far too open."

It was true.

Two stone columns stood to their right, leading into an open-air breezeway. Walls lined the path like towering giants along either side. Sierra had traveled this walkway before with her father. The cobblestoned lane wound around and around until it reached the square in the center of the port where all public meetings were held. There wasn't a straight path in this city. The roads all spiraled and turned in on themselves in crazy, convoluted ways, much like the mind of the man who designed it.

Port Iona had been a tiny dock falling into disrepair before Bentwood took over and built it up. It still held a few sacred altars from the ancient druids and a library where, supposedly, scholars from around Aluvia had come to study. Bentwood didn't care anything about faiths and knowledge of long-gone people, though. Too bad he had no soul.

According to Nell's sources, Phoebe would be down in the lowest level of the main operation building, which meant turning left instead of right. Sierra expected to see guards along each fork in the path, but she didn't. Their absence made the space between her shoulder blades scream with tension. Knowing Bentwood, surely he had guards on duty everywhere on the peninsula. If the guards weren't here, where were they... and why?

"Do you think Corbin's gotten his petition heard in the square?" Sierra whispered. "Maybe the guards have been sent to maintain order while the elders held court?"

The bizarre idea of someone petitioning for justice here would be like a free carnival to Bentwood's people. They had probably shown up in droves. Someone was probably selling toasted nuts and cider along the side, too.

Micah was silent for a moment. "I fear it will be less of a hearing and more of an execution."

His choice of words made her stumble on the rough cobbled path.

She spun to face him, the blood draining from her face. "You really think they'll kill him? I thought maybe they'd laugh at him and send him away. Maybe send him to the dungeons for a fortnight, at the worst."

Micah shook his head. "I have thought upon what you've said and what the seawee said. His story of the merfolk's plight strengthened my fears. The man you've described is ruthless. If I wanted to stop any and all questions about my authority, I would do something drastic, wouldn't you?"

Panic shot through her. Micah made too much sense. Horrible, perfect sense. She should have known how Bentwood would respond. She'd watched Jack deal with him for years.

She hadn't even believed the elders would listen to Corbin, but figured it'd at least be a good distraction while she snuck in. The ground should open up and swallow her whole. Dear, sweet Corbin. She may have thought it was a waste of time before, but Micah crystallized the situation. Corbin *couldn't* speak before the elders. And Nell! She would go down with him. Not even her fighting skills would be enough to prevent their capture.

"We've got to stop them!" The words exploded out of Sierra. Maybe it was already too late. No. It couldn't be. Her resolved hardened. Bentwood was going to do something drastic? *She* was going to do something drastic.

With a burst of adrenaline, she slapped her hand over her mark and, for once, truly rejoiced in the heat that seared through her. She called to Queenie without hesitation. The fairy wasn't there yet, but she was nearby. Sierra made her decision: no matter if it was right or wrong, she wouldn't risk her sister—or her friends.

Bring the queens, she told her fairy. *All of them.* Sierra could always change her mind at the last moment, but she needed them there, just in case. *Bring them, Queenie!* The queen's agreement hummed through her mark, then Micah's hand touched her shoulder.

"I will go to him, as you cannot," he said.

The words didn't make sense.

He explained, "Your Corbin. I will go seek him and the warrior woman for you. You must get your sister."

"He's not my Corbin," was all she could think to say. It wasn't enough. She wanted Micah to understand no one else had ever drawn her heart. They stared at each other for a long moment, a thousand days in a heartbeat, her mind full of Micah's deep chocolate brown eyes. She found herself wishing for the impossible. But she knew better than to believe in true love. He only wanted to fulfill his life-debt. This risk was a big one—it would do.

"If you do this for me, you will be free of any debt you owe." Sierra wanted to be clear.

"Do you wish me gone, then?" His voice was wistful, sad.

Her heart lurched. She wanted to yell *I want you to stay, you idiot!* But the words wouldn't come out of her mouth. Fear was too strong, the fear long ago instilled in her by her father's hands. Don't love and you couldn't be hurt. Only, it turned out, trying *not* to love hurt horribly.

She didn't have time for this conversation. She couldn't. Her sister was being tortured, Corbin might be dying, and she didn't know if anything had happened to Nell.

Sierra managed to say, "No, I don't want you to go away forever, but I need you to go now. Get them, please."

He nodded and then started to turn but paused, picked up her hand, still damp from the sea, and kissed it ever so gently on the back like gentlemen of old. His lips were as soft as rose petals. His eyes held hers, sending sparks dancing through her veins, until he turned to run down the lane. She didn't even think to ask how she'd find him. Some kind of hero she was turning out to be.

She had no real choice but to go forward and trust her friends to do their jobs. If she didn't find Phoebe, everyone had wasted their lives for nothing. She carefully placed one foot in front of the other, pressing so close to the wall that it kept catching her wet sleeve. The salty wind blew hard, funneled by the walls on either side, chilling her. She shivered. Hopefully, she wouldn't start sneezing or coughing.

Low murmurs drifted on the wind from around the next corner, and she paused. Two guards, she decided, at the door of the basement "training rooms." Usually by this point in the proceedings, the trainees were so broken it didn't take many guards to keep them in. And where would they go? Unless they knew how to call a merman, they were fresh out of luck, on the far side of the peninsula, right next to the sea.

Sierra took a moment to assess her odds. She might not be an enforcer, but as the daughter of a dark alchemist, she had seen her fair share of violence and could fight dirty if she had to. Sending one more call to her fairy queen in hopes she would arrive soon, Sierra picked up a pebble from the ground and tossed it down the path. Then she touched the handle of her knife, the one Nell gave her. Being Nell's, it was as long as Sierra's forearm and sharper than broken glass. She'd only use it in case of emergency, though. Phoebe would be horrified to know even men like these had died during her rescue.

The hushed voices stopped, and Sierra prepared herself. One of them walked near the corner. She hoped he didn't peek first, or it would all be over. She was sneaky and fast, but she wasn't two hundred pounds. Hurriedly, she tossed a second pebble farther down the path, making him think his prey was escaping. It worked.

The guard picked up his lumbering pace, and Sierra pressed herself against the side of the wall as he barreled around the corner. She gave him two seconds to keep running, and then she ran up behind him and jumped. Hooking her right arm around his neck, she pulled back hard and quick, clasping her opposite shoulder. Quickly, she bent her left arm up and over the back of his neck, pushing his head down to keep the pressure on his throat. Cutting the air off from his windpipe with a chokehold was a slow way to knock someone out, but it was fairly silent. With the adrenaline rushing through her, Sierra was strong enough to hold on tight.

He slid forward against the wall, thankfully not crashing to the ground, and clawed at her arms as he tried and failed to give his friend a warning. Sierra kept her head tucked down behind his so he couldn't get to her eyes. When he finally passed out, she took out the knife and gave him a good rap on the head to make sure he stayed out long enough. She needed to get ready for the second guard.

But before she reached her previous position, the other guard came around the corner, saying, "Hey, Tom, you get lost or something?"

He stopped short at the sight of his unconscious friend and Sierra standing there with a knife. The fact that there was no blood on it seemed to be a fact missed by him.

"Murderer!" he cried, while pulling out his sword.

Even a knife as long as her forearm wasn't going to be a match for a broadsword and body armor. Sierra dodged and jumped as he slashed at her. He was clumsier than he should have been, sword missing by a hands-width. Must have been drinking or dosing himself with some elixir, maybe even Flight. Ironic. Good thing, too, or he would have stabbed her right away. She was fast, but he was still a professional mercenary, even if not in top form. Sierra dodged past his lumbering steps in a way that would have made Jack proud. The angry man turned again and ran at her like a crazed bull.

Backed into a corner, Sierra used his momentum to slice across the man's forehead and push past him. Blood gushed over his eyes and he bellowed, unable to see. If he didn't shut up, he'd draw reinforcements and she'd never get Phoebe out of there.

Queenie, Sierra screamed in her mind, and her fairy queen was there, a golden light, next to the man.

"Stop him," Sierra shouted.

Without a second's hesitation, Queenie aimed her delicate little stinger and stabbed it once right in his fleshy neck. The result was immediate.

The guard froze. One hand reached up to clamp the side of his neck, much like the way his partner had tried to grab his throat to breathe. There was no blood here. Just fairy magic, a toxin in its pure state for most humans, racing through his veins, speeding forward with every beat of his too-rapid heart.

Sierra held her breath, stumbling two steps back, looking around to see if anyone had heard, but the path remained clear. The guard fell to the ground, twitching like a man having a seizure. She wondered if he'd start prophesying, too, but the answer to that question was apparently no, because blue suffused his face, and soon his chest stopped moving. This was a bad way to die, but she couldn't regret their choice, hers and Queenie's.

Sierra held her hand to her fairy queen and thought at her, *Thank you, thank you.*

Queenie flew over and kissed her cheek. Sierra's answering smile quickly faded as she stared at the dead man and then past him to the door where her sister waited.

Time to rescue Phoebe.

CHAPTER THIRTY-ONE

The door to the "trainees" was blocked from the outside. Sierra tried to lift the heavy wooden board preventing anyone from escaping and realized it was chained into place. A heavy iron lock clasped through the center of the thick links. Of course. She shook her head at her own foolishness.

Finding the keys on the dead guard was easy enough, but her hands shook as she walked back to the door. Killing a man—using Queenie as a weapon—had left Sierra with a sick feeling she hadn't expected. She didn't want to think about what would happen to a crowd of people like that. Hopefully she wouldn't have to make that decision. She twisted the key into the lock, lifted it from the door, and took a deep breath.

Would Phoebe still be in here? What if they'd moved her? What if... what if it was too late and she was dead or sent to be a runner somewhere else? Sierra pushed all the bad thoughts from her mind. One step at a time.

Setting aside the board, she pushed the door open, wincing at the loud creak. Light fell across five pale faces inside, not just the one Sierra expected. Bentwood had been busy. The people squinted against the light, throwing their arms up over their eyes. Only one did not move, a small figure sitting against the far wall. Phoebe.

Her hair was matted and darker than the last time Sierra saw her, as if her lightness had been stolen. Then Phoebe looked up, and something flickered in her expression. Confusion, hope, and fear raced across her face one after another. Sierra wanted to run to her, but her feet were glued to the stone floor. What if Phoebe was too hurt to move? Sierra hadn't allowed the thought to cross her mind until now.

The other prisoners staggered up and pushed past her into the light, roughly shoving her shoulder, but she kept her eyes fastened on her sister. The distant splashing behind her suggested some were jumping into the freezing water, but she couldn't spare them any energy.

"Phoebe, it's me. Little Bug, are you okay?" Two trembling steps turned into a quick run that brought her to her sister's side.

She touched Phoebe's arms as if the softest contact

might crush her. Sierra could barely hear over the roar of her heart beating. Her little sister, her sweet Phoebe.

"Sierra?" Phoebe's voice sounded rusty like an unoiled hinge, and she began to cry. Huge tears poured down her cheeks, and she wrapped too-thin arms around Sierra's neck and held her tighter than a lifeline.

Staggered by the embrace, Sierra smelled sweat and mustiness, but also the special scent that was all her little sister. She crushed Phoebe in a hug of her own, flooded with relief, knees weak.

"Can you walk?" Sierra wiped away tears of her own.

Phoebe's right knee was grossly swollen, but she managed to limp slowly. They stepped out into the light, and she took a wavering breath, as if tasting the sunlight for the first time in months. Maybe Phoebe had only arrived in Port Iona two days ago, but even a day in a dungeon was too long for Sierra's girl to be there.

Phoebe stopped short at the sight of the obviously dead guard. The death, unwanted though it was, was uglier with her seeing it, too.

"I'm sorry." Sierra wasn't ashamed, but she regretted hurting her sister's tender heart even more.

Phoebe asked, tone flat, "Did you kill him?"

Sierra nodded. Asking Queenie to sting him was the same as stabbing him herself.

"Good," Phoebe replied.

Sierra's jaw dropped. She gazed down at the top of

her sister's head and wondered what kind of damage had happened that she couldn't see.

There was no time to ask, not now.

Sierra allowed herself to gaze into Queenie's eyes and said, "Find the others, please."

Queenie bobbed for a minute and then zipped off with only the speed a queen fairy could have.

Phoebe stared and said, "That's different."

Sierra sighed as she led her back through the winding passages to the little opening to the water. Phoebe didn't know the half of it.

The seawee was gone, of course. Sierra slapped at the water, hoping maybe he was waiting for them beneath the surface.

Phoebe sank to the ground next to Sierra. "We're never going to get out of here."

Sierra stopped her fruitless search for the little merman and grabbed her sister's shoulders. "I *will* get you out of here. You're going to be fine. Just *fine!*"

They had to be. She kneeled and pulled Phoebe close. She was always thin, but now her shoulder bones pressed against her shirt in sharp relief.

Warmth dripped against Sierra's neck, and she realized Phoebe was crying again. Sierra made a silent pledge: Bentwood would *never* get near them again.

Phoebe shook her head, as if trying to rid herself of some horrible memory.

"I want to go home," she said, voice tiny and pathetic.

Some of her tears splashed into the icy water beside them, spreading tiny ripples across the water.

Sierra wanted to sit patiently, but her back felt exposed. Corbin must be making his speech in the square right now, which was the only explanation for why no one had noticed Sierra's intrusion yet.

"Come on, Phoebes," Sierra said. "I'm sorry, sweetie, but we've got to go. We have to find Corbin and Nell."

Phoebe's red-rimmed eyes flashed up to Sierra as she reared back. "Corbin's here? And *Nell?*"

Sierra breathed a sigh of relief. Here was her Phoebe, thinking and reacting.

"Long story. But yes. So let's go." Their chances of making it undiscovered all the way through the winding tunnels to the courtyard were nil, but desperation drove her beyond logic. As they stood, a wet hand gripped Sierra's ankle. She squawked at the icy grip but realized it was Tristan the seawee.

He waved them forward with quick, sharp gestures.

"Do you trust me?" Sierra asked Phoebe.

She looked confused and replied, "Of course."

"Good." Sierra pushed Phoebe into the water.

CHAPTER THIRTY-TWO

Sierra dove into the water. The shock of the cold stole her breath, but her panic only stirred a little. Her sister was in Tristan's arms, cheeks puffed with held air.

"It's okay, milady. You are safe here. I heard your call."

That was strange. He was looking right at Phoebe, but she hadn't called him. Hmm. Well, he must have heard her say she wanted to go home. Whatever. Sierra would take it.

She swam over to them. "He allows us to breathe, Phoebe."

Breathing underwater was pretty wonderful, an unexpected miracle in a time of trouble. Sierra did a backflip for her sister's amusement, and it worked. Phoebe laughed and lost half her air. The little merman held her tightly still. Phoebe eventually squeezed her eyes shut and took a breath. Her eyes opened wide when nothing bad happened.

Sierra wished she could give her more time to adjust, but there wasn't any left. Sierra wrapped her arms around them both and said, "We've got to get to the main entrance."

"Is stealth an issue?" asked Tristan.

"Not anymore. I think they're distracted by our friends."

He nodded, then they were off like a shot. Phoebe's eyes opened wide as they flew through the currents, making the darting fish around them look slow. Sierra gave Phoebe a fast run-down on why Corbin and Nell were in danger. Even a skeleton of an explanation contained plenty of news.

They reached the shore of the peninsula within minutes. Sierra stumbled out of the water, soaked once again, teeth chattering, but realized her sister had stopped.

Phoebe still stood knee-deep in the water. She and Tristan were staring at each other with a strange intensity, gazes locked, saying nothing. Phoebe slowly lifted a hand to say farewell, and the seawee saluted her and then disappeared into the depths.

"What was that?" Sierra asked, pulling on Phoebe's arm to make her move.

"I have no idea," she mused, speaking as if waking

from a dream. "But it's like knowing something important I can't quite remember."

Sierra would worry later about what one of the merfolk might want with her sister. There was no time to figure out what the mysterious salute meant, or even how he had known they were waiting. Their feet smacked the ground as they took off running, Phoebe leaning heavily on Sierra.

The guards to the peninsula entrance were absent. That did not bode well. Beyond that, the paths were all but vacant. Only homeless people who lived along the alleys meandered down the cobbled pathways. The shops were closed. They put on another burst of speed, as fast as Phoebe could stand with her knee, and Sierra only hoped they were not too late.

Unlike the streets leading to it, the main square was full to bursting. Every person in the peninsula had to be there. The two girls entered at the back, far from the upraised platform that occupied the center of the space. Four heavy chairs sat prominently on the stage in a row, where the elders of the port sat. Bentwood was up there, a small smile playing on his lips as Corbin finished his speech. The girls were too far to hear, but Corbin was so earnest with his flourishing hand gestures, it bruised Sierra's already pounding heart. Nell stood to one side of him without her weapons.

The hair rose on the back of Sierra's neck. They were defenseless up there. No one could speak to the port's elders while armed. Sierra clutched her knife tighter. In this crowd, it could easily get knocked out of her hand, and she feared she was going to need it.

"Bentwood *must not* see you, Phoebe, do you understand? He considers you his property now. You've got to stay hidden. He could kill you for leaving, and Jack wouldn't stop him."

Phoebe nodded, eyes dilated wide in fear. Sierra took off her wool cloak, wet as it was, and put it over her sister, pulling the hood up to cover her red hair. Sierra found a discreet spot in the doorway of a closed shop on the back corner of the square.

"I'll come back here. If it all goes bad, turn and run. Go to Corbin's parents."

Phoebe shook her head desperately.

Sierra gently held Phoebe's chin to force their eyes to meet. "I won't have you back in his hands. It would kill me. You run if you have to, do you understand?"

Tears filled Phoebe's eyes, but this time she nodded.

Sierra wished Micah was there to stand guard. She wanted Phoebe safe. She felt a pang of worry for him, too. Where was he? She wished she knew.

Leaving Phoebe alone to go to Corbin and Nell was like being torn in half. Too much love for too many people destroyed you. But it was too late now. Sierra couldn't leave them up there to be killed.

She squeezed her way through the crowd. Each time a group of people noticed her trying to get by, they recoiled at the sight of her soaked clothing, giving her a bit more space to move. Even the poorest wore their best cloaks when the elders held a meeting in the port square.

Pushing and shoving to get through the gathered mob, Sierra wished she had the comforting touch of Phoebe's hand. But she was better off where she stood. Far safer. The smell of tobacco, body odor, and roasted corn filled the air, making Sierra's stomach turn.

Bentwood stood in front of the crowd. "They declare we need to set the fairies free. To live without Flight, to do without our most profitable elixir. What say you, my people?"

"Noo!" The crowd's roar shook Sierra's body. The growl beneath the roar told her she'd somehow better get Corbin and Nell out of here soon.

"They say *magic* will save us. Let me show you what magic brings us."

Two burly men climbed onto the stage, dragging Micah between their arms. Blood dripped from his mouth, and he stumbled as they yanked him along. Micah's hands were chained, and his ankles were hobbled. His legs looked strange, like they bent differently than a human's… and hooves were just barely visible below the hem of his pants.

Sierra's mouth went dry, and a strange roaring filled her ears. Her knees barely held her up. He'd changed back into a faun. How terribly had they hurt him that he lost his hold on his magic? And what more would they do?

What had she done to him, bringing him here?

Queenie? Sierra thought, desperate to save Micah. *Queen, are the other queens ready?*

It looked like they were going to need them.

They forced Micah next to Bentwood. Corbin's mouth hung open, and Nell's cheeks were as pale as her hair. Sierra's feet were frozen to the ground.

The men each took out a knife, and shock ran through Sierra like a lightning bolt.

Words whispered past her lips, almost like a prayer. "Not him! Not him!"

Her eyes burned as she stared at Micah's hunched figure. It was the very thing she had feared. She told him not to come, didn't she? And he'd come with her anyway.

They slapped him across the face.

"No! Stop!" The words exploded from her but were lost in the noise of the crowd.

They shook him and laughed at him. Sierra shouted louder, "Leave him alone! *Please!*"

Tears rolled from her eyes. *Please!* She was ready to beg for his life. He didn't even know how much he meant to her. She had never let him see.

She shoved past people, uncaring about their startled cries. She cursed her small size. She'd never reach the stage in time.

"*Queen!*" she cried, but the fairy still wasn't there.

One of the men brandished his knife, and the crowd leaned forward in anticipation of a show. Sierra wanted to vomit.

But instead of the man slashing Micah's throat, he sliced down the legs of Micah's pants over and over. Bits of fabric flew off the stage, floating in the wind. Then the man stood back, leaving Micah alone center stage. He had nowhere to go. Micah was completely exposed for what he was, his furry faun's legs clearly visible among the ragged strips of pants. The crowd gasped.

"It's an abomination!" someone cried, and people started shouting.

Micah's head hung down.

A new burst of energy slammed through Sierra. She pushed and weaved through the crowd again, eyes fixed on him. Corbin backed up to Nell, and Sierra could tell they were having a quick, hushed conference. Nell looked out over the crowd, sky blue eyes widening when she spotted Sierra making her way toward them. Nell's gaze flickered to Bentwood before she shook her head at Sierra, the message clear: *Don't do anything stupid.* Sierra shook hers back and pressed forward. She swore she could see Nell sigh from here.

"That's right. They want to bring an army of these mismatched creatures to take over our world! They'll make you all slaves!" Bentwood's big, booming voice carried to the end of the courtyard.

Fury was stamped on Nell and Corbin's face, but Sierra knew their rage would do no good. Suddenly, though, Nell's head tilted back in a familiar way. *Oh no,* Sierra groaned. *Not now.*

Nell grabbed at her throat frantically, but her message wouldn't be stopped. So much for keeping her new talent a secret from the alchemists.

"Why do you listen to a man known to lie and cheat? A man who steals your children and sells you only elixirs that enslave you?" Her new deep, gravelly voice soared over the crowd now quieted in shock.

Dread filled Sierra, but she kept moving forward.

Nell continued, "Have you not felt the groaning of the earth as the very land shakes in death? Where have all the fairies gone? Have you not wondered? The queens left in despair, you fools, and their little ones died from lack of magic. You have stolen from them for too long. The whole earth suffers. You are all tied together and must work together to save Aluvia for your children and your children's children!"

A heavy hush flowed across the crowd. Her eyes were black as night now, startling in her pale, pale face, and people cried out as they saw her. Radiance shined from her, shocking even Sierra. Corbin's eyes were nearly popping out of his head, but to his credit he watched the crowd carefully. If Nell passed out after this one, they'd all be in trouble.

Looks of fear and suspicion faded and turned to

shame as Nell raised her voice louder. "Look at this lone, frightened creature of magic! Yes, magic! But where is his threat? Is he the one with the knife in his hand?"

Sierra's knife was cold in her hand. She was getting closer.

"Where is this army this man says is coming? Besides the one of his that keeps you pinned here in this square?"

Mutterings filled the crowd, people hesitantly nodding.

Bentwood glared, jerking his head at the two men by Micah. While the man with the knife guarded Micah, the other hustled toward Nell, clearly intending to shut her up. With a shout, Corbin blocked him, the two of them grappling.

Go, Corbin! Hang on a bit longer! Sierra edged even closer.

Nell cried out, "Why do you not fight back, people of Port Iona, and take back what is yours?"

Sierra silently begged Micah to meet her gaze, but he continued staring at the ground. She tensed her muscles, preparing to jump onto the platform as soon as she reached the edge. She was almost there when she saw a face that made her knees too weak to move.

Her father stepped onto the stage.

CHAPTER THIRTY-THREE

*S*ierra's heart took off, racing faster than a merman's tail. Nell remained in the grip of the prophecy. Micah was still in chains, and Corbin was wrestling the man away from Nell. In a matter of seconds, Bentwood would no doubt call up reinforcements. Sierra's rubbery legs would have to hold her. An icy wind slapped her in the face, giving her courage. She pushed aside the last two people in her way as Jack swung up his bow and arrow, then shot Micah in the chest.

Sierra had no breath left to scream. He crumpled on the stage, her father's feathered arrow buried in his chest. When Micah groaned in pain, obviously still alive, Sierra gasped. Thanks to the unexpected wind blasting through the courtyard, her father had missed Micah's heart, but he was already drawing another arrow.

"No! Stop it!" Sierra vaulted up in front of Micah, rattling the wooden floorboards, uncaring about the cries of the people in the crowd.

The elders stood, uncertain of what to do. This was a colleague's daughter, after all. They'd let him handle her.

Jack lowered his bow slightly and smiled. "Are you sure he's worth it? You know he's already dead, even if I didn't hit his heart. A unicorn arrow means even a miss is a bull's-eye."

Despair acted as a weighted chain around Sierra's neck. With an intensity matched only by her rage, she reached her mind to her fairy.

Queen! she called with all her soul. *Bring the queens! Bring them all now!*

At least Phoebe was safe no matter what happened. As long as she followed Sierra's directions, her life would be spared, even though it would cost so much.

Sierra looked Jack right in the eye. "He's worth everything. And you're nothing."

His face became immobile. That was his work face. She was only business now.

Jack redirected his aim from Micah to her. She pulled up her knife, but it was a worthless defense against her father's bow. Jack sent the arrow flying.

Sierra steeled herself for the hit, but Queen zipped in front of her.

A sharp sound like shattered glass roared through Sierra's ears. Queen fell, fluttered to the ground, light dim, wings quivering. Sharp pain stabbed Sierra, right where her heart stuttered in her chest. Her legs buckled as horror swamped her soul.

"Queenie," she whispered, kneeling beside the little fairy. The arrowhead was huge in comparison to Queen, taking up her entire midsection. Queens were incredibly strong, but Jack's weapon of choice pitted magic against magic.

Sierra yanked out the narrow, wickedly pointed tip, and thick golden fluid rushed from Queen's body. Sierra's chest tightened in response, but not only from the unexpected ripping pain at the thought of losing her fairy. A physical pain vibrated inside, jolting her stomach, squeezing her heart like a fist. She wondered if she was sharing Queen's death. And if the fairy queen was dying, was Sierra?

Waves of heat and cold flashed along Sierra's limbs, and a white explosion of light filled her eyes. She found herself lying down next to Queen. Her body seemed to have no choice. Corbin shouted, but it sounded as if he were a very far distance away. Micah lay on the ground, unmoving. She could barely make out Nell's voice, her prophetic words garbled and faded, but then silence draped across Sierra's mind.

She closed her eyes, but, instead of blackness, Sierra saw a golden sea below her, deep under the earth. She had a new way to see, a new set of eyes. The people around her were visible, though her eyes were still closed. It was as if she'd always had this type of vision.

Time slowed to a crawl. Everything around her was tinged with gray. Below the earth there remained a golden glow, but raw, red spots seeped through like lava boiling up in a golden river. She wanted to reach her hands into the golden river and take a deep drink. She understood somehow the energy of that river would revive her. In fact, her head was filled with knowledge, so much information she gasped as a torrent of arcane understanding flew through her mind. Through it all, she sensed Queen's presence, her thoughts in the background as Sierra experienced what Queen knew. They were sharing at a level deeper than Sierra ever imagined. The door that opened between them that day at the cave was blown off its hinges.

And the golden river below? That was the magic holding their world together. Sierra felt she'd always known this. But the river was poisoned. The decay reached out, making her bones ache. She didn't want to move, couldn't imagine how she would ever move again.

"An unexpected bonus," Jack said, prodding Sierra with one booted toe. When she didn't move, he returned to the other end of the stage.

Queen, Sierra called. *Don't leave me. Don't leave me.*

Queen had saved her. Queen had given up her own life for Sierra. In all the years they'd been tied together,

Sierra had never known how much Queen loved her. Sierra's fairy queen loved her the way she loved Phoebe.

Queen loved Sierra like they were a part of each other. What was she saying? Sierra *was* a part of her.

And Queen was a part of the earth, part of the magic of their world.

Which meant so was Sierra.

She concentrated against the increasing hum in her ears and saw Queen's link to the earth. It was like a golden ribbon tying her to the stream below, but it was fraying. It billowed in a breeze that came off the golden river but didn't move Sierra's hair or caress her skin, made as it was of magic, not air. Sierra couldn't see it before, but she did now. Whatever had happened with Queen, they were knit together now beyond conscious thought.

Focusing on the golden flow of magic below, Sierra reached out with imaginary hands and strained toward it, knowing Queenie needed it. So Sierra dipped mental hands into the warm, sparkling waters and pulled, willing it to raise a new ribbon to her, siphoning off energy. A tiny waterspout formed, and Sierra pulled harder until the magic danced up from the stream and connected to her heart. The joining shocked her breathless; a jolt of pure energy poured into her.

She was fire. She was wind. She was earth. Her skin was too tight to hold her.

The earth pulsed now. Sierra sensed the entire depth

and breadth of the land. She was utterly grounded, and was suddenly as ancient as the rocks that had stood against the pounding waves for eons.

She swirled the magic inside, the heat sparking along her spine. A thin line of shining energy connected her and her fairy. Sierra sent the energy crashing down the little ribbon to Queenie. She wouldn't die, not if Sierra could help it. Not after she finally realized how much she needed her fairy queen. How much Sierra loved her.

Sierra had little control of this new, strange power, and a tidal wave swamped Queenie, washing away the ragged hole in her body. The flow of time returned with a snap. The fairy spun into the sky with a shock that reached to Sierra's toes. Queenie shrieked, but the shriek turned to a tiny shout of triumph as her wings beat smoothly and her body was whole again. But the energy was too much for one fairy to hold. The power was like an electrical storm. They needed to be grounded, or the power would eat them alive.

Queenie flew to Micah and touched him. His head bowed back as she flooded him with magic. The power flash-burned the arrow to dust and started to heal him at a blindingly fast pace. Sending him so much magic drained the shocking overload on Queen's system, on *their* system, enough so Sierra could see the regular, plain earth around her, too. It was a sad, sad place, but with so much potential. She saw how Aluvia was meant to be. Even now, the ground glowed ever so slightly. Micah glowed bright. Queenie was incandescent.

With regret, Sierra slowly relinquished her new ribbon to the golden glow below. She couldn't function properly with that double vision layered on top of everything. It amazed her that magical creatures must walk around with that kind of sight.

Then the ground started to tremble.

CHAPTER THIRTY-FOUR

Queen flung herself at Sierra and burrowed into her hair. Sierra's age-old terror erupted as the ground did. The shivering and groaning of the earth nearly flung them to the ground. People in the crowd screamed. They ran into each other in their attempts to get away, but they were piled in this space like fairies in an overcrowded hatch. Cracks crawled up the buildings nearby.

Keep Phoebe safe! Sierra begged Queen, who zoomed into the air with a cry, zipping across the top of the crowd.

Micah's arm landed across Sierra's waist, pulling her close to him, holding her tightly even when they both fell from the stage as it shimmied and bounced.

Sierra curled up into a ball as her body slammed into the ground. Micah grunted as he rolled them to soften the impact. For that moment that lasted an eternity, Sierra was certain she was about to be swallowed up into the center of the earth.

But then a voice whispered inside her mind, one she had never heard before. It said, *But now you've seen inside the center of the earth... and it's beautiful.*

The voice offered comfort, and, for once in her life, she took what help was offered. Thankful Micah was with her, she squeezed her eyes tight and tried to stay calm. If only she could know Phoebe was fine, that'd be easier to do.

Yes, yes... sister's safe, Queen whispered, sending an image of a dusty but alert Phoebe crouched in the far corner of the square. Relief flooded Sierra, even though the earthquake continued. She could get through this now.

When the shaking stopped, Sierra and Micah heaved deep sighs, stood, and looked around. Bentwood had fallen, buried beneath a pile of rocks. It was pretty clear he wouldn't be bothering Phoebe ever again. Sierra wasn't exultant, though. She was glad Phoebe was safe from him, but Sierra's earlier need for violence disappeared during her final bonding to Queenie.

Jack had fallen, too, near her, ten feet away from the stage, but he was already pushing his way to his feet. Corbin and Nell were still on the platform, which remained standing strong. Nell's eyes still shined as black as the night.

With the red dust making a haze in the air, she spoke again, "So speaks the earth that has been too drained! So cry out the rocks from which you have stolen! This is the reason for the quakes that have grown in number! People of Aluvia, if you continue to misuse the fairies and steal their nectar and their magic, your ports will soon tumble into the sea! This is the truth! You are all held in the palm of the earth in a great net made of magic. The fairies are meant to keep the net spread wide as they fly through the wild places of Aluvia. They must spread their nectar wherever they go, sharing with other magical creatures! But you steal their nectar before they can collect enough for themselves. Even the fairy keepers aren't enough to keep them healthy. The little fairies have died—and you are at fault! You are stealing from the land and from yourselves!"

Men and women were nodding, crying in their panic about the quake. Such events had become too frequent to ignore. Nell made sense to them. They crowded around her now, not to attack her but to hear more. Nell was winning them over.

Jack drew his bow again. No wind stirred to deflect that deadly arrow now. And this time, he aimed right at Nell.

There was no time to stop him. Sierra couldn't move faster than a speeding arrow. But Nell alone had the ability through her prophecies to convince the people to change their ways. Sierra could only think of one thing to do, even if it condemned her and possibly Micah right along with her father.

Phoebe is safe, Phoebe is safe, Sierra reminded herself. Using her new understanding, she reached far down into the earth at their feet to the glowing river. Pulling hard, she yanked up as much of the energy as she could, sending it into Queen, into Micah, into the air, anything to drain the magic below to a dangerous new level. Sierra hoped she was right about what would happen next.

The tremor was immediate, forcing Jack to lower his bow while he regained his footing. The people around her shrieked and ran again, pushing and trampling each other in their haste to get out before the next big quake hit. Because it was coming. Coming right at her. Red angry energy reached up from below like molten lava. She took a deep breath and hoped Nell was far enough away to escape the worst of it. If Sierra didn't do this, though, Nell was dead for sure. Sierra's heart broke at the thought of possibly hurting Micah, but he would agree with her, she knew.

She thought to her fairy, *Queen, I love you. I'll always love you. Thank you for saving me.*

Queenie sent a burst of pure love from her place at Phoebe's side.

Sierra whispered to Micah, "I'm sorry. I wish I could've had more time with you."

With a deep breath, she yanked one more time on

the cord she had created between her and the magic underneath her feet.

Come and get me, she thought.

And then the earthquake hit them like a hurricane. The sky went dark as the ground exploded in one swift motion, ripped into pieces because Sierra had taken too much magical energy from the earth's depleted supply.

The ground underneath Jack didn't crumble so much as simply disintegrate in a giant billow of dust. Jack screamed as he fell, landing heavily on an up-thrust sliver of stone at the bottom of the gaping jaws of the earth. The rock pierced his chest as easily as his arrow had pierced Micah's. Blood flowed, a pool of red seeping round Jack's still body as the quake continued. His chest didn't move. Sierra hadn't thought she'd feel anything but relief when he died, but there was an odd grief at the sight anyway. Losing a father was not an easy task, even a terrible father like Jack.

Sierra clung to the rocks at her feet, trying to hang onto the bucking ground. She even began to think they might make it. But then a giant hole opened at her feet. Before she could back away, a crack widened between her and Micah. He gripped Sierra's hand tightly, and then the world tilted.

The ground she had been standing on broke away from the rest of the earth and began falling toward the hole at a steep angle, taking her with it. Sierra shrieked, clawing at the rocks. Micah lost his grip on her for a long moment, long enough for her to slide near the edge of the small cliff that had been created when the gap opened. He grabbed her by the arms.

"I won't let you go," he promised through clenched teeth.

Nell stood high above them, still prophesying through the chaos and destruction. People were collapsing to their knees around her, acknowledging her power as a priestess of some kind, like the druids who disappeared over a hundred years ago. Even the elders listened to her, faces full of fear and awe.

A sigh released inside of Sierra, taking with it her fear. She had done her job. Only one job remained.

"Take care of Phoebe," she told Micah.

"I won't let you go," he insisted.

The piece of earth Sierra clung to slid farther toward the hole. Micah's arms formed her only bridge to stable land.

"Fight, you stubborn girl!"

But she was done fighting. She couldn't fight anymore.

Sierra smiled, trying to memorize his face as she gazed at him this last time. "Take care of her for me."

Tears spilled from his beautiful brown eyes, tears for Sierra. Why had she never believed he really cared for her? She'd wasted so much time with all her fears.

Feeling almost in a dream, she let go of one arm, and pulled his face low enough to kiss. One peaceful, first kiss framed by terror. His lips were as soft as she always imagined. Then she pushed him away from the edge and sent a wordless goodbye to Queenie.

The ground crumbled beneath Sierra, and she fell. She wasn't even scared. She closed her eyes as the wind rushed upward through her hair.

So this is what the moment before death is like, she thought, right before she landed.

CHAPTER THIRTY-FIVE

Strangely, the ground wasn't hard. In fact, it was much softer than Sierra would have imagined. And was it rising?

Sierra's eyes popped open. Golden glowing light surrounded her. Startled, she flailed, but then Queenie sent her a mental picture of what was happening. Sierra was on a bed of floating fairies. They had all finally come to Queen's calling.

Instead of swarming to kill, they gathered to save. To save Sierra, which was the same as saving Queenie. Sierra relaxed into the soft warmth and smell, the cinnamon sweetness of her calling. As the fairies lifted her from the pit, it had never felt truer or more wonderful.

She was a fairy keeper. And she loved her fairy. Sierra told Queenie so with every heartbeat as they rose.

They shared a link so close that words were unnecessary.

Micah greeted Sierra as her toes touched the ground. He pulled her to him, and, for once, she didn't resist. He crushed her in a hug so tight she could barely breathe, but she didn't care. She pressed her face into his chest and wrapped her arms around his back. He held her with such tenderness, she felt like she was still floating on a bed of fairies. Their golden glow surrounded them as the fairies buzzed in excitement.

Sierra pulled back enough to touch Micah's chest where the arrow had pierced him. The palest golden scar lined his chest, but he was otherwise healed. She leaned her cheek against that scar, so thankful Queenie shared her magic. She saved him. Him *and* Sierra.

A throat cleared nearby. Sierra pulled away reflexively, pushing Micah behind her, eyes searching for the source of the sound in the great mill of people around them.

Phoebe said, "And this is…?"

Sierra wrapped her arms around her sister, then turned to face the amazing person she had slipped into caring for, her friend and her maybe-someday dream. Because he was most definitely a dream, even if he was also magic.

"Meet Micah," Sierra said.

He bowed and kissed Phoebe's hand.

Yeah, he was definitely magic.

Phoebe rolled her eyes up at Sierra. "Is he real?"

She laughed and hugged her sister tight. "Strangely, somehow, yes."

"And Bentwood and Jack?" Phoebe asked, voice hesitant.

Sierra shook her head. "They both died in the quake. I'm sorry, Phoebe."

"Don't be. We'll be okay."

They looked at each other, spending a moment grieving the loss of their father, or rather, of what could have been if he had been a different kind of man. Their story with Jack was now a closed book that would never have a happy ending. Painful, maybe, but when it came down to it, Sierra wouldn't change anything. It had all led her to this point. She squeezed Phoebe's hand.

Phoebe squeezed back, taking a deep breath. "And now what?"

They surveyed the crowd still clinging to Nell's ringing words. Corbin remained beside her, a surprisingly staunch warrior.

Sierra had no idea.

Micah said, "Now the fairy keepers must go forth with this message across our world. The fairies must spread far and wide to balance our world again."

He clasped Sierra's other hand. Their fingers fit together perfectly.

"It will be a great adventure," he said solemnly. "It is a

journey I would be most honored to undertake with you and your friends and sister."

The world seemed suspended for a long moment until Sierra's heart was so full it could burst. He wanted to be with her. They could stay together, though what the future would hold, she wasn't really sure. For once, she was okay with that. Right at that moment, anything seemed possible.

"No more debts?" Sierra asked, just to be sure.

"No debts. This is a new beginning, yes?"

She smiled and said, "Then, let's go."

"Yes? With me?"

He looked incredulous, but Sierra was done running.

"Yes!" She laughed, the kind of joyful sound she had hardly ever made. She thought that was about to change.

Yesss!! cried Queenie, and she spiraled straight into the cloudless sky, brighter than the sun.

The End

A PREVIEW OF BOOK TWO

MER-CHARMER - CHAPTER ONE

The ocean never gave up. It just kept rolling in, no matter what else went on in the world. Phoebe Quinn liked to think she and the ocean shared that in common.

Today, Phoebe's chest still heaved from her run down to the shore. The gut-wrenching memories had slithered into her mind again, setting off the panic. When those recollections came calling, four years dissolved in a heartbeat, leaving her a terrified ten-year-old all over again.

But she wasn't ten anymore, she reminded herself, taking in a deep breath.

Phoebe perched on the edge of her favorite rock along her favorite coastline and tried to lose herself in the haunting call of the seabirds and the inevitability of the foaming waves. She knew she shouldn't have disobeyed her big sister by coming here, but Phoebe couldn't stay inside the house another minute. Besides, Sierra wouldn't be back until tomorrow. She'd never know.

The salty tang of the coastal air usually lifted Phoebe's spirits, but even the power of the ocean couldn't quell her anxiety today.

She bit her lip, fixing her gaze on the horizon. When she'd arrived back home four years ago, Phoebe hoped she could forget what she'd suffered. And at first it seemed like everything was fine. Life went on, after all.

But the horrors she'd experienced in Elder Bentwood's dungeon whispered in her mind more and more often. It didn't seem to matter that she'd only been locked up for days; those few days felt like years. The vivid memories clung like the stench of a dead thing, growing increasingly difficult to ignore. Especially lately.

The sun would set before too long, already a ball of fire painting the sea with shades of pink and red. The forest hung back from the coast here, leaving a thin ridge of sand and rocks between the shady pine trees and the shoreline. A natural jetty in the middle of the cove reached out into the deeper waters, the boulders uneven as if sent tumbling like dice from a giant's hand. Her favorite was the last in the row, where water lapped right along the edge during low tide. She loved to daydream there, nearly surrounded by water yet sheltered from the worst of the waves by the outcroppings further into the ocean. On the far side of the jetty, an inlet held a delightfully deep pool, cradled by boulders. Yet on the other side, the sandy shore was shallow, easing into the sea with a gentle, lazy slope. The cove was a cozy place, and Phoebe could use a little cozy now.

Sea foam sprayed her legs as the wind blew, and she shifted her position. Her knee twinged as she leaned on it, the same spot that ached in the cold. She ruthlessly ignored a vision welling up from the past: her leg bruised and purple, swollen like a sausage. That's not reality. This is now. She closed her eyes and focused. The silence of the cove. The wind lifting her hair from her face. But she couldn't quite resist touching her knee in affirmation. Strong, straight, supple. They hadn't broken her. At least not her body.

When she took a deep breath and craned her neck to watch a gull spiral over the coast, a glimpse of white poking out from behind a small boulder alongside the pool caught her eye. A quick smile lit her face, lifting her dark thoughts.

Nothing brought peace and joy like her merfolk friends. Even though she was fourteen now, within shouting distance of adulthood, she still loved getting little gifts from Tristan, gifts given for no other reason than him thinking about her. The fact that her best friend and his sister, Mina, were merfolk was icing on the cake. Phoebe often wondered how she could be so surrounded by magic but remain so utterly and frustratingly non-magical herself. If she had even a sliver of magic, she was sure she'd never feel afraid or alone again.

What would the gift be today? A giant sand dollar or conch shell? A smooth white stone from the depths of the ocean? She pondered the possibilities as she rose and picked her away across the slippery moss-covered rocks to whatever lay hidden behind the boulder to her left. It wasn't Tristan's usual place to leave a surprise, but, then again, he liked to keep her on her toes. She grinned with anticipation and then jumped around the boulder, hands spread, ready to grab whatever delight lay waiting.

A strange shape floated in the water, half-laying on the rocks. That wasn't a shell, no, and not a smooth stone, too many parts...

Phoebe's mind whirled as she tried to make sense of what she saw. White sticks of some kind, tangled together, with the green of seaweed.

Then everything came together in her mind with a snap. Those weren't sticks. They were polished bones.

The bones swirled in ripples that rolled between the rocks. Bits of sinew and cartilage held the skeleton together, but barely. Her scream was short but intense.

Phoebe gasped, gagged, and almost threw up. She forced a swallow and crawled closer to the edge of the pool to get a better look.

The half-submerged skull grinning grotesquely looked human in the water, but a tail fin made it impossible to doubt what kind of creature this had actually been. The merfolk remains must have gotten caught in the inlet during low tide. Tristan and Mina needed to know right away. Maybe they would know if someone was missing.

A wave crashed along the shore, and the skeleton bobbed and turned over, revealing a giant black handprint marring the back of the skull. Phoebe sucked in a deep breath at the sight, the print shocking against the bleached white of the bone. Worse, the skull itself was crushed at the tip of each fingerprint. Spider-webbed cracks branched out from each puncture as if strong claws had punched right through the bone. This hadn't been an accident. Phoebe fought the roiling nausea, trying not to fall to her knees. What could do something like this?

Maybe her friends would come if she sang. They often did, along with the youngest of the merfolk, the little seawees. Shivering, Phoebe returned to the end of the jetty and lifted her voice, focusing on the way the sound skipped across the water. She chose a haunting melody, though she generally preferred cheerful songs. Right now, a soulful dirge best suited the situation. She let herself explore the dark nooks and crannies of her fears and the horror of the moment, her gaze creeping toward the corpse over and over before she yanked her focus back to the ocean. She scanned the water for the familiar tails, then paused, chewing on her lip. Why weren't they coming?

She hadn't seen Tristan or Mina in three whole days. In the past, they visited more often, especially when they knew her sister was traveling and Phoebe would be alone. But as they grew older, work took more of their time. Merfolk took responsibility to their community very seriously.

They were probably working in the deeper waters now, in fact. She should swim out past the rocks to better try to call her friends, but the thought of sharing the same water with the dead body was too much. Besides, a few months back, she promised Sierra not to swim in the ocean anymore. At the time, such an irrational request had infuriated Phoebe. Today, that promise gave her a handy excuse.

"Tristan! Mina!" she called with her hands cupped around her mouth, leaning forward into the cove. Her friends seemed to have a special knowing when she called them by name.

The water began churning, signaling the arrival of someone, but her best friends were nowhere to be found. Tiny fins of a dozen seawees broke the surface as the little ones arrived to frolic. Mischievous grins beamed up at her from under the water as they waved, long hair floating about their heads.

She waved back, pleased to see them but alarmed at

the possibility of them finding the skeleton. The little ones had come daily when Phoebe first returned from Bentwood's dungeon, but she hadn't seen them often these days, either.

Luckily, they stayed a bit out to sea, squealing in delight when she began an upbeat tune for them. Next to the little ones, a green tail slapped the water, larger than the others. A bronze flipper broke through the surface beside it. Tristan and Mina were here. Phoebe smiled with relief, but then her grin faded. She dreaded giving them the bad news.

The space between her shoulder blades prickled. She glanced uneasily behind her. Was someone there? But then Tristan popped out of the water next to her, his dark green hair streaming over his shoulders. He waved at her and shook his head, sending his wet hair flying. Brisk droplets sprinkled Phoebe's homespun dress. He did that on purpose, no doubt. He chortled at her, but since he was out of the water he only produced a guttural coughing noise. The deep green scales covering his tail ended at his waistline. Once he became an adult in merfolk society, ink-black tattoos would decorate his torso and arms, but for now, his chest was starkly pale beneath the water.

He was thinner than in the past, his ribs outlined along his sides. His twin sister, Mina, arrived a half-second later, her black hair a shocking contrast to her pale skin gleaming like an opal, also missing the tattooed marks of adulthood. Her bronze scales ran up her body from her tail to directly under her arms. It reminded Phoebe of the fancy strapless evening gowns worn by wealthy ladies in the biggest port cities. Though Mina, too, appeared more tired than usual, they were both still beautiful. The gills of their necks were dark slashes across their pallor, but their green eyes twinkled. Phoebe hated the thought of stealing the light from their eyes.

The idea of touching the water made her skin crawl, but there was no other way for them to speak together. The cold sting lasted only a second as Phoebe lay on her belly atop the rock, leaned her head over the edge, and lowered her face below the water without hesitation, bubbles sliding over her cheeks.

Her friends' green eyes darkened to solid black as they used magic to allow her to breathe. Phoebe understood the magic they could lend to her far more than the first terrifying time Tristan held her thrashing under the water during her escape from Elder Bentwood's fortress.

"Greetings, my friends!" she said. "I'm afraid I have some terrible news. You should send the seawees away; this isn't anything they should hear."

Tristan's grin faded as he examined her face. Phoebe had a moment of discomfort as she met his gaze. He'd grown from a cute little seawee to a very cute young merman over the last four years.

Mina swam to the little seawees swirling like otters in the water. "Go on home, now. You know your parents don't like you to be gone for long! And you aren't supposed to come to shore anymore!"

This was news to Phoebe. Why not? Did it have something to do with the body? At least it explained the strange absence of seawees over the recent weeks.

The little ones looked at Phoebe, lips pouting, but obeyed, scurrying away with speed. With a small smile softening her demand, Mina shook her head at the little ones as they retreated. Her amusement slid away as she returned to her brother and Phoebe. It was odd for Phoebe to see such a somber expression on Mina instead of her usual jovial one.

"Phoebe, what's going on?" Tristan asked.

A lump sat heavy in Phoebe's stomach. "Something washed up near the shore today. Something upsetting."

The two merfolk exchanged anxious glances.

Tristan asked, "Are you okay?"

"I'm fine, but I found... a body. A merfolk's body. A skeleton, really. It washed up into the rock pool, and it clearly has a tail. I'm so sorry."

Their faces looked like she had struck them, eyes wide and faces paler than usual.

"There's more," Phoebe added, miserably.

"Worse?" Tristan asked, his voice hoarse. The reddish hue of the sunset turned his green hair a strange shade of brown, a sickly hue quite different than the usual vibrant color.

She nodded. "The death looks intentional. There are strange marks on its skull and, well, holes. Like claws punched through it, while gripping the head."

"Where?" Mina whispered, hands pressed to her cheeks.

"No, Mina, you don't need to look," Tristan said.

"Don't be a fool, brother. We're doing this together," she said, though she looked ill.

The two exchanged a knowing glance, and Phoebe felt a stab of envy. *Sierra will never treat me like an equal.*

Phoebe lifted herself from the water and gestured to the inlet, standing up to point them to the body. The twins skirted around the skeleton. Tristan hesitantly touched the arm bone with one hand and shivered. Both leaned over the skull, examining the ruined back. They exchanged another long look. *What did that mean?* They returned to Phoebe, and she dipped her head underwater again.

"This body looks old, being stripped so bare, but I admit I've never seen dark marks like that or the crushed parts of the bone," Tristan said.

"What could do such a thing?" Phoebe whispered.

"There are many predators in the deep that would leave just bones, but we know of nothing that could burn into a skull, if that's indeed what happened. It can't be anything good," Mina said.

Tristan smacked his sister on the arm.

Alarm raced through Phoebe. "So, you're in danger?"

Tristan offered a reassuring smile and shook his head. "Our village is protected. You don't need to worry for us. But the elders will need to know. This merfolk must have gone off on his or her own." His voice trailed off for a moment.

"And needs a proper ceremony to be put to rest," Mina said. They both bowed their heads, and Phoebe, feeling awkward and uncertain, followed suit. She'd been fascinated by the merfolk from the first moment she met Tristan, when he helped rescue her from Bentwood, but there was still so much she didn't understand about them.

"Come back tomorrow morning, please, and tell me what you learn," Phoebe begged. She'd never stop worrying without knowing if he—they—were safe from whatever caused the death of the poor merfolk.

"We must work from early in the morning, unfortunately. We could come at our noon break… but your sister is coming home tomorrow, is she not? She wouldn't be pleased to see you back here with us, especially with the sad remains you've found."

"I'll take care of Sierra. Don't worry."

Tristan quirked his eyebrows. "She is very fierce."

"Maybe I can be, too."

Mina laughed, and Phoebe flushed.

"Apologies, sweet friend," Mina said after Tristan gave her a scowl. She spread her hands wide. "I mean only that your nature is so kind and sweet, I find it hard to see you engaging in combat. With a heart like yours, to wound another is to wound yourself."

Feeling only slightly mollified, Phoebe said, "Sierra's got plenty to worry about already. What she doesn't know won't hurt her."

Tristan's eyes grew wide. The dark marks under them were lilac half-moons. "You surprise me, Phoebe. I thought you honored your sister."

She flushed. "I do—but you know how she overreacts."

"Much like our family," Mina said dryly.

"Are they still upset because of our friendship?" Phoebe frowned.

"It's not you," Mina replied. "They just can't forget how many generations of merfolk lived in slavery to humans. And then that poor seawee died recently in the fishing nets of humans who ignored our new treaty. Some of our people are angrier at humans more now than ever, but that has nothing to do with you. Those old barracudas wouldn't like you even if you were the most perfect person in all of Aluvia, which you are!"

"I'm sorry if our friendship has caused you grief—" Phoebe began, but Tristan cut her off.

"Please don't worry, Phoebe. We know how to

manage our families as you do. But I do think Sierra would want to know your daily habits. She loves you." He smiled, softening the slight chiding.

Well, Sierra might want to know, but this was one time she didn't need to know.

"If you meet me at noon, I'll be back before she is. Her journeys have been running longer now that some people want to use nectar again. They're already forgetting how bad things were. I'm afraid she's hiding how serious the trouble is becoming. It seems even on short trips, she's always late these days, arriving at dinnertime at least. And when she's home, she spends most of her time in the forest with her fairies, anyway."

She tried to keep the hurt from her voice, but must not have succeeded. Tristan shook his head ruefully.

He said, "You know you are her world, Phoebe. She gave up everything for you, fought for you, saved you—"

"You saved me, too."

This time, Tristan's face flushed, bringing delicate rose to his pale cheeks. "I did only what was right and just. Anyone would have."

No, they wouldn't have, Phoebe knew. She studied his familiar face, remembering the hectic underwater flight from Bentwood's, the way her gaze had locked on Tristan's when they said goodbye, as if something bound them. The same tension built between them now.

Mina cleared her throat. "We must go take care of

this sad situation, Phoebe," she said, "but we'll come back tomorrow when the sun is at its zenith."

"Promise?" Phoebe replied, looking over to include Mina.

"We would never lie to you," Tristan said, eyes serious.

Phoebe smiled at him, thankful that Tristan, at least, didn't see her as a frail tag-a-long little sister. She gazed into his eyes and felt a flutter that had become familiar over the last year. She briefly wondered if one day he might see her as more than a childhood friend. Of course, that was just a dream. They lived in different worlds, even if she was able to visit theirs now and again.

She nodded. "Thank you."

With worry shadowing their faces, the two merfolk pulled the skeletal remains along with them as they swam away. The rock pool was empty now, but Phoebe was sure she'd never forget the whiteness of bone among the seaweed, like unexpectedly jagged, sharp teeth in the mouth of an animal believed to be docile. The ocean was dangerous, she understood that. But today, she began to realize just how little she knew about those dangers.

ACKNOWLEDGMENTS

Many thanks to Snowy Wings Publishing for this second edition of FAIRY KEEPER. I'm so excited to be a part of such a wonderful group of people! Thanks also to Matthew Cox, PJ Hoover, and Clare Dugmore.

The original edition was produced Curiosity Quills Press, to whom I'll always be thankful, especially for my editor Krystal Wade, and talented cover artist Amalia Chitulescu.

This manuscript would never have been completed, though, if my friend, author Carol Pavliska, hadn't been there without fail. I'm grateful also to Lara, who gave vital feedback as a voracious reader of MG and YA works. All of my friends have been so supportive and loving!

SCBWI has been a wonderful support network, as well as the broader online writing community.

And of course, none of this would be possible without my family. To my parents, my sister, and my mother-in-law. And to my husband and my children. I love you all. Thank you for everything. How fortunate I am that my biggest fans are also my family.

This second edition would definitely not be possible without all of you who have read and left lovely reviews over the years. Thank you so much for reading and sharing my books!

ABOUT THE AUTHOR

Amy writes fantasy and light science fiction for young readers and the young at heart. She is the author of the World of Aluvia series and SHORTCUTS (CBAY Books, 2019), for grades 4 and up. She is also a former reading teacher and school librarian.

As an Army kid, she moved eight times before she was eighteen, so she feels especially fortunate to be married to her high school sweetheart. Together they're raising two daughters in San Antonio.

A perfect day for Amy involves rain pattering on the windows, popcorn, and every member of her family curled up in one cozy room reading a good book.

You can find Amy online at www.amybearce.com and at:

OTHER BOOKS BY AMY BEARCE

MER-CHARMER: World of Aluvia Book 2

Phoebe's power lies at the heart of the ocean, but the power of the ocean might just break her heart.

To save her beloved merfolk from an ancient sea beast, 14-year-old Phoebe dives into the ocean and discovers her own magic. But when the beast decides she is the tastiest prey in the ocean, she must learn to control her wayward sea magic, earned at a shocking cost, or lose the very people she loves the most.

DRAGON REDEEMER: World of Aluvia Book 3

The voice calls. A sword will answer.

To win their fight to protect their world's magic, Nell and her friends must find the fiery sword of Aluvia before their new enemy does. Nell up against the toughest foe she's ever faced—and this one has ice-breathing dragons on his side.

SHORTCUTS (CBAY BOOKS, April 2019)

When psychic powers and secrets collide, no one is safe.

Parker is a fun-loving girl with a secret supernatural gift of psychic empathy who tries to turn heartbreak to happiness when a new student arrives with a mysterious, tragic past. But her psychic power goes haywire, threatening to expose dangerous secrets… starting with her own.

MORE FROM SNOWY WINGS

Starswept by Mary Fan

A sudden encounter with an Adryil boy upends her world. Iris longs to learn about him and his faraway realm, but after the authorities arrest him for trespassing, the only evidence she has of his existence is the mysterious alien device he slipped to her. When she starts hearing his voice in her head, she wonders if her world of backstabbing artists and pressure for perfection is driving her insane. Then, she discovers that her visions of him are real—by way of telepathy—and soon finds herself lost in the kind of impossible love she depicts in her music.

But even as their bond deepens, Iris realizes that he's hiding something from her—and it's dangerous. Her quest for answers leads her past her sheltered world to a strange planet lightyears away, where she uncovers secrets about Earth's alien allies that shatter everything she knows.

Available now!

Gods and Demons, by Selenia Paz

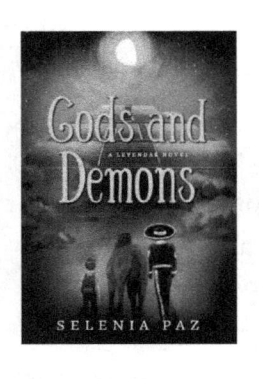

Miguel did not think he would be returning to Mexico so soon, but when El Charro appears and asks for his help in finding out who is behind the darkness that appears to be spreading, Miguel agrees. La Llorona, searching for the same truth, enlists the help of Natalia, who wants to guarantee the safety of her brother and all children like him. As they travel their separate but similar paths, the legends they come across help them to understand that there may be other forces at play—some more powerful and ancient than they could have imagined.

Available now!

Phoenix Descending (Book One of Curse of the Phoenix) by Dorothy Dreyer
Who must she become in order to survive?

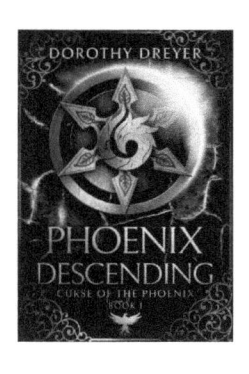

Since the outbreak of the phoenix fever in Drothidia, Tori Kagari has already lost one family member to the fatal disease. Now, with the fever threatening to wipe out her entire family, she must go against everything she believes in order to save them—even if that means making a deal with the enemy. When Tori agrees to join forces with the unscrupulous Khadulians, she must take on a false identity in order to infiltrate the queendom of Avarell and fulfill her part of the bargain, all while under the watchful eye of the unforgiving Queen's Guard. But time is running out, and every lie, theft, and abduction she is forced to carry out may not be enough to free her family or herself from death. Available now!

www.snowywingspublishing.com

www.ingramcontent.com/pod-product-compliance
Lightning Source LLC
LaVergne TN
LVHW050600171224
799298LV00001B/35